Driving Miss Crazy

Driving Miss Crazy

D.C. Diplomats Series Book 1

D.J. Van Oss

Chapter One

THE INSISTENT BEEP OF THE MICROWAVE TIMER sounded from the kitchen.

Adrian Adams checked his watch. "Whoops. There's the backup timer, kiddo. We'll have to go through the checklist again on the way to the door."

"Dad!"

"Water bottle?"

"Check."

"Sunscreen?"

"It's raining, Dad."

"It could clear up. Sunscreen?"

"Check."

"Umbrella?"

"Check."

"Boots?"

"Dad, I'm wearing them." Charlie, his seven-year-old daughter, sighed. "They're on my feet. Look at my feet, Dad. These are my boots."

Adrian looked down at her blue-eyed, elfin face staring up at him. His little girl's dark brown hair peeked out from under a bright yellow rain hat, the perfect match for her yellow Dora boots, which were, sure enough, on her feet.

"See?" For a moment, Charlie's exasperated expression reminded him so much of her mother it stole his breath.

Then he checked his watch again. "Well, let's just hope you have everything else for school."

"If I don't, it's probably in the emergency pack you put in Mrs. Tibbet's office."

Adrian thought a moment. "Right. I'm wondering if maybe we should have another emergency pack in the gym office with your inhaler in it?"

Charlie sighed again. "Why don't you just use one of the emergency packs from the car?"

"No, we have to have two in case you go on a last-minute overnight."

"You never even let me go on *one* overnight, even to Uncle Danny's."

"We're going to be late." Adrian grabbed her waterproof backpack and the lunch box he'd filled with as-healthy-as-possible stuff, and led the way out the front door. Their simple brownstone here in Cathedral Heights was a little large for just two, but it had been in the Adams family for decades and held a lot of memories. Sometimes more than he cared to think about.

"Can I ride in the front?" Charlie pleaded as she followed him down the stairs. She jumped in a puddle on the sidewalk with both feet, making a deliberate splash.

"No, you ride in the back. It's safer."

"But then I can't choose the music and you always play that old music and it drives me crazy."

"Hey, the Beatles are classic and timeless." He tossed her lunch and backpack into the opposite seat. "You'll thank me someday when you have an appreciation for real music."

Charlie climbed into her booster seat, and Adrian buckled her in, the back of his blue driver's uniform absorbing the scattered, cold drops of light spring rain.

"Miss Tutti says *Murz*art is real music and she makes us play it on the recorder and we stink."

Adrian adjusted the straps on her car seat. "Miss Tutti is a hundred years old. She wouldn't know good music if it dropped on her head like a piano."

Charlie's eyebrows arched with interest. "Can I tell her that?"

"Of course not." Adrian shut her door and slid behind the wheel of his company's Mercedes S550. "Unless she gives you a bad grade this semester," he muttered.

He started the car, checked all the mirrors twice, and pulled out into the street as the rain-sensing wipers began whumping across the windshield. As a driver for Hallmark Sedan Service, he knew pretty much every side road, one-way street, and unmarked alley in the whole Washington, DC area.

It was early spring, and the cherry blossoms were just starting to bud—the best time of year in the capital next to fall. Of course, he always thought of Karen when he thought of cherry blossoms. Every spring she would cut a few branches from the small, brave tree in their tiny front yard and place them in the vase on the front hallway table. The blossoms—her favorite—were the first thing you smelled when you came into the house. That and whatever new dish Karen had created for dinner.

Adrian smiled at another memory. He had never thought oven-fried pickles would be good, but they were.

He turned onto Easton Road, which meant Charlie's school was only two blocks away. Spring was always a little bittersweet for them both. Losing a wife was bad enough. He figured a little girl losing her mom was probably worse. But Charlie never seemed to let it get to her.

It wasn't like she never talked about it. Charlie kind of wore her heart on her sleeve. Even though it was hard for him to hear her talk about Karen so glibly sometimes, the counselors said it was better that way, so she didn't keep everything all bottled up inside. He definitely didn't want her to end up on some sour psychiatrist's couch someday, blaming life for taking her mom from her, having run off to join some cult in Montana that worshiped endangered chipmunks or something.

It had been over four years now, and Charlie seemed to be doing okay, but he wasn't going to take any chances with her. There was nothing wrong with playing it safe. If that meant no sleepovers at other houses or wearing kneepads when she rode her bike, so be it. One big heartbreak in life was enough for anyone.

He pulled into the drop-off lane of Van Allen Elementary School. He got out to get the door for Charlie while she unbuckled herself.

"Here we are, miss," he said with a fake British accent after opening her door.

"Thank you, Jeeves," she said as she hopped down, just as she always did. "I would give you a tip, but I'm only seven and I don't have a job yet. Maybe if you let me work at Aunt Beth's candy store?"

He shook his head. "You'd eat her out of business." He thought for a moment. "You know as long as I'm here—and I'm going to be here for a long time—you'll never have to worry about anything, right? I'll always take care of you."

Charlie smiled as she hoisted her backpack on her tiny shoulder. The speech was familiar. "I know, Dad. Bye."

"I'll see you to the door."

Her shoulders slumped. "You don't need to. It's right there and Mr. Coggin is there and my friends are there and you're going to embarrass me again."

Adrian stopped. "Again? Since when do I embarrass you?"

Charlie just gave him a dirty look that somehow still seemed sweet and then headed up the two steps to the door.

Adrian's phone was vibrating in his pocket. He fished it out and saw it was his work number. He answered while watching her chattering with one of her school friends as she went through the school's open double doors. Maybe he should mention tighter security to the principal?

"Hey, Kevin," Adrian said into his cell. "What's up?"

"Are you on your way in?" his co-worker asked on the other end of the line.

"Yeah, just heading over. Why?" Adrian got in the car and started it. "I'm not late yet."

"No, it's not that. I thought I'd just give you a heads up. I think Martin is going to talk to you. I just overheard some stuff, and I didn't want you to get blindsided."

"What stuff?" Adrian's brow furrowed.

"About your route and your hours. You know, the same stuff they brought up last fall."

Adrian rotated the wheel and turned back onto Easton after checking for traffic. "I'll be there in fifteen minutes."

Great. First the medical expenses and now this. The last thing he needed was more bad news.

Chapter Two

MAGGIE MACNALLY WRESTLED A PARTICULARLY LARGE BOLT of green chenille off a top shelf in the backroom of Bella Bella, the custom dress shop where she'd worked for her old college roommate for the two or so years she'd been back in DC. She struggled to balance the fabric on her shoulder as she descended a shaky stepladder.

"That emerald green looks great with your hair, girl," Jelly said from the doorway to the sales area. "I should design a dress for you."

"I don't have anywhere to wear a fancy dress," Maggie said through the pins in her teeth as she stepped off the ladder. She carried the bolt to the cutting table and brushed a cobweb out of her short black hair. "And you're already busy enough anyway."

"Speaking of which, can you come help me up front? A couple of mannequins in the window look like they're trying to hit on each other. They keep slipping."

"Sure thing." Maggie had been helping Jelly at the design studio/store in between attempts to find a steady job in the family trade of politics. Born prematurely in the States when her parents were briefly stationed in Washington, she had been raised in Ireland, where she was fed a steady diet of diplomacy by both her parents and grandparents. A moderately successful four years here at Georgetown had not only given her a diploma but a best friend and roommate in Jelly. Her family had hoped she would follow in the their footsteps, especially her grandmother, now the Ambassador of Ireland to the United States.

She had struggled to find her niche back in Ireland after college. It always seemed like the rest of her family moved naturally in the world of meetings, hand shaking, and long lunch conversations about "Corporate Risk Registers" and corrigenda to this and that. She had always found it somewhat boring, to be honest. Now, as an automatic US citizen and with the help of her influential grandmother, she was trying to take advantage of her unique situation. Unfortunately, her attempts at developing a political career in the US had also been less than stellar, as a string of failed minor jobs procured by her grandmother had proven.

She'd considered Bella Bella only a stopgap job, a way to put her hobby of sewing for fun to temporary use and repay Jelly for giving her a place to stay. She was mildly surprised to find herself a "natural" (as Jelly called her) at making Jelly's brand of sophisticated yet fun clothing.

Jelly popped her head back in the room. "Now they're doing the splits. Not the look I was going for."

Maggie dropped what she was doing and hurried to help.

Jellico Jones had owned Bella Bella for three years, a venture she started right after she completed a hard-won Professional MBA at the nearby Kogod School of Business. Short yet feisty, she had already gathered a reputation as a local designer with a casual, fun flair. Her creations graced the closets of some of the more cosmopolitan residents in Georgetown, and her *Jelly* line of handmade scarves was making inroads into some of the area's tonier boutiques. Maggie knew her friend was sinking everything she made back into the shop, and it showed—from the stylish window settings to the slightly funky interior. It was classy but also trendy, and its sunny location on Thirtieth Street brought in a fair amount of walk-in traffic. It wasn't the main drag like M Street, but Jelly planned to be there someday.

Maggie helped battle the ornery mannequins and then followed Jelly, picking her way carefully over the short railing, out of the display window, and back inside the store's main display area.

Jelly wiped her dusty hands on her pants. "Put that on the list of new things we can't afford—mannequins. These things must be holdovers from the disco era."

Maggie straightened her shirtsleeves and blew a loose strand of hair from her forehead. "I don't know how you do it. There's so much to take care of. The customers, the inventory, making the clothes."

"Don't I know it. I'm so glad you showed up here last fall. If I didn't have you to help, I'd be underwater." She thought for a moment. "Did I tell you I'm working on a deal with Chestnutt's over on Potomac? They want to feature a few of our infinity scarves."

Maggie beamed. "Jelly, that's terrific! Someday I'll be able to tell everyone back home 'I knew her when.' "

Jelly feigned surprise. "You aren't leaving me, are you, girl?"

Maggie laughed. "Of course not. I don't think so." She was thinking. "At least, not for a while."

Jelly's smile disappeared. "What do you mean? You got something new planned? Is it another store?" Her eyes grew wide. "It's not with"—she affected a snooty accent—"Elizabeth Hand at Dory & Hunk, is it?"

Maggie laughed again. "No, I don't think I could manage wearing a tutu. And what does she have her salesgirls wearing on their heads?"

"Red berets. No, excuse me." She affected the accent again. "*Raspberry* berets."

Maggie wrinkled her nose. "So shabby." She grew a little more serious. "But... I don't know..."

"What, girl?"

Maggie sighed. "I haven't had the best track record when it comes to kick-starting a career the past couple of years."

Jelly shrugged. "Takes some people a little longer to find their niche. I had to waitress at The Cloverleaf for two years while I worked my way through business school."

"That's just it. You knew what you wanted to do. I don't know what I want to get off my butt and go do at all. It just seems so easy for the rest of my family." Her parents back in Ireland were well known as movers and shakers in the Irish Parliament. Even her cousin was a political party head.

"Well, it hasn't been for lack of trying. At least, you can eliminate all the things you didn't like. Or that didn't involve a visit from the FBI."

Maggie folded a scarf. "The Commonwealth Office job? That was just a misunderstanding."

"I'll say. I don't think the Turkish embassy delivers pizza."

"I told you, someone in the office gave me the wrong number. Besides, they didn't have to be so rude. I was just trying to order lunch."

"You probably had an expired two-for-one breadsticks coupon."

"Funny."

"Let's see, then there was your campaign assistant job for that DC delegate where you misspelled her name on all the posters."

"It was just one letter. And I *told* them the right name over the phone."

Jelly shook her head sadly. "I know. Poor Elizabeth Moron. I mean, *Moran*."

Maggie sighed again. "Okay, I get the picture. And to save time, let's just skip past the internship at the UNIC where I accidentally called the Prime Minister of Algeria a chicken anus, or the Department of the Interior job where I ordered five hundred *boxes* of toilet paper instead of five hundred *rolls*."

"That would have come in handy for the pigeon poop job," Jelly said slyly.

"I'm not telling the pigeon story again. And they were doves, not pigeons."

"Please," Jelly begged. "I love the pigeon story! Tell it with the date you got after the guy from the cleaning service asked you out."

"No. And don't get me started on the *men* either."

"But your man stories are so much fun. Who was the guy that picked you up in the white van with no windows?"

Maggie covered her face with her hand. "Okay, that was Barry. He wanted me to dye my hair red and wear hats so I'd look more like his mother."

"Creepy."

"Yeah, and then I find out he's an orphan."

"Okay, that's call-the-police creepy."

"And Devin, can't forget Devin, handsome, witty successful senior bank manager Devin. The perfect gentleman. Brought me a rose from his garden on our first date."

"What a sweet gesture."

"His wife didn't seem to think so when she found out."

Jelly winced and shook her head. "Youch."

Maggie shrugged. "Oh, and last but not least, there was the really cute guy from the National Gallery who was teaching me how to oil paint. I managed to date him for a week until he got arrested for trying to sell a forged Picasso."

Jelly held up her hands. "Hey, those things could have happened to anybody."

"But that *anybody* was *me*, and I'm twenty-five—almost twenty-six," Maggie suddenly realized, "and I'm still trying to figure out what I'm supposed to be doing with my life. Not to mention having to deal with all the Barrys and Devins and whatnot."

Jelly sighed. "Well, join the club." She put her hands on her friend's shoulders. "Hey, girl, it'll all work out. Look, you're doing a great job here. You and I have a great bachelorette pad just upstairs; I got five more years and the store's paid off, two months of inventory on the way." She looked around the room, ticking off items on her fingers. "Let's see…two disco-obsessed mannequins, a front display case with cracked glass, a water leak in the ceiling from a bad pipe no one can find, a water heater that sounds like it's making love to a train wreck every time it heats up—yeah, we're screwed."

Maggie laughed. "I suppose it's how you see it. I just expected that by now I'd have at least been more of a success." She looked out the window. "Like everyone in my family."

Jelly nodded. "We've been down this road before. I know practically your whole family back home is knee-deep in politics. And your grandma is some high mucky-mucky here at the Irish Embassy, but from what you've told me, she's also an ice queen with an attitude."

"Well, sure, she may be tough, but she's done so much with her life. I mean, all of the stories I hear about her traveling. And who she meets—queens and presidents—you name it. And she always seems to know just what to do. Even when I was a little girl, she'd kind of boss my grandfather around. He played along, of course, but she was always ready to take charge." Maggie realized she now thought of her *mamó* more as Ireland's Ambassador to the US than as her grandmother. "I wish I had just a *little* of that in me. Just once."

Jelly shrugged. "It'll all come clear. Trust me." The front door dinged and a customer walked in. As the stylish young woman began browsing through the discount rack, Jelly gestured with her head. "For now, we need to get back to taking care of business."

Maggie started sorting spring dresses, her mind still trying to piece together her future.

She tried to envision herself more like her grandmother, ensconced in her stately office, making important decisions for her country, meeting foreign diplomats, going to balls. That was a life of distinction, the prestigious life her parents had wanted her to emulate ever since she could remember. She still remembered them taking her to see her *mamó* give a speech on the steps of the Irish Parliament House when she was a little girl.

But here she was, working as the only employee in a small dress shop. No future, no relationships, a string of failed attempts to make a name of her own for herself in this most political of all towns.

Her luck had to change sometime or... maybe she needed to change it herself. Maybe she should be more like Jelly, take the bull by the horns and finally make something happen for herself.

But what? Work in a dress shop? Her parents would love that.

Maggie glanced at the wall where the clock showed it was after ten. Past time for her tea and Jelly's coffee from Red Zone, the coffee place next door. She pushed her jumbled thoughts to the side. Jelly was right. They had work to do.

But she knew one thing. Something had to change, and soon.

Chapter Three

"SO, YOU'RE SAYING you're letting me go?" Adrian was standing in the office of Marty Suskind, the main dispatcher.

Marty had been head dispatcher of Prestige Driving Services for almost twenty years and had always been good to Adrian.

Now, he avoided looking Adrian in the eyes. "No, it's not like that. You know if it were my decision we'd work it out, but the company has new rules regarding hours."

"And mine don't work anymore." Adrian felt his face flush. "I've told them I need the flexibility for Charlie. They didn't have a problem with it before."

"I know, but like I said, the policies have changed. HR and all that. I'm sorry. Look, I'll keep my ears open, of course. We have connections with the other agencies around, and with your federal clearance and record, I think you'll be able to pick something up real quick. Or if you can find someone to take care of Charlie—"

"Nope." Adrian hardened his voice. "It's hard enough leaving her at school for six hours every day. The other day someone let the iguana out of his cage in her class, and it bit the custodian." He rubbed his eyes briefly. "The thing could have given him parasites or some tropical disease. I can't let anything happen to her now." He sighed. "I just can't."

"Sure, sure," Marty said sympathetically. "Just a thought."

Adrian sighed again. "I know." He stood and gathered his coat. "Thanks for looking out for me."

Marty got up and stuck out his hand. "Anything for your family. Say hi to Danny when you see him, okay?"

Adrian shook his hand. "Sure thing. I'm sure he'd like to have you over for some of Beth's chili sometime."

"*Beth's* chili?" Marty laughed. "Hey, I said I was sorry."

Adrian also managed a smile at the thought of his sister-in-law's notoriously evil chili. He paused, then pulled out his key chain, unhooked the keys to the Mercedes and put them on the desk. "Forgot about these. Let me know if something comes up, okay?"

"Of course."

Adrian pulled on his coat and headed toward the nearest Metro station. He tried not to think about the house payments and Charlie and the medical bills he was still paying off. He needed work, and quick.

He rubbed his chin. Time to make some phone calls and call in a few favors.

* * *

"Here's your coffee." Maggie set a steaming paper cup on Jelly's crowded desk where she was busy going over some receipts.

"Thanks," Jelly said, not looking up.

"Gerard says hi," Maggie said slyly.

"Does he?" Jelly said, still not looking up.

"Yes, he says, 'When is Jelly coming over again? I think I want to marry her. I have a date set and—'"

Jelly slapped Maggie's thigh with the back of her hand. "Girl, shush. You're terrible."

"Well, you haven't been over there in a while. I think he misses you."

"I'm busy. Lot's going on."

"Well, don't get too busy for fun," Maggie advised.

"I hear that." Jelly took a sip from her coffee. "Mmm. He does make good coffee." She sat back. "And that man *is* easy on the eyes."

"He definitely likes you," Maggie said, fiddling with a box of antique buttons that needed sorting. "Talks about you *all* the time."

"Well, maybe he can just talk himself over here sometime and we'll have ourselves a little conversation."

"Yes, you can talk about your future together and how many babies you want to have," Maggie teased.

"What're you, in grade school? And speaking of futures." She got up from her desk, taking her coffee with her. "I was thinking while you were next door. C'mere, girl. Sit down." She motioned to the over-stuffed red velvet chair behind the counter.

"Are you firing me?" Maggie bumped the box of buttons, spilling them.

"Don't be stupid." Jelly perched on the counter, her legs dangling over the edge. "I have a proposition for you."

"Okay…" Maggie sat, as ordered, and gave Jelly a quizzical look.

"You've been here for six months now, and I have to tell you, I've been designing for a lot longer than that, and I can see talent. Plus, you've got a way with the customers. Like that German lady that was in here two weeks ago. I didn't know you spoke German, and there you were chattering away with her."

"Oh, well, I only took one class."

"Well, it must have been enough. Got her to buy two customs."

Maggie shrugged. "Well, I do love the customers—the people. And the clothes…I just kind of make what I feel. It sort of comes to me."

Jelly nodded. "That's why I say you're a natural. Match that with some more training and you could make this a career. And that's why I want to offer you a partnership."

"A partnership? In the store?"

Jelly nodded again. "Yup. We're growing, no small thanks to you, and I think we can make it bigger, maybe even add another store some-day, or even a chain of boutiques. Who knows? But we've got to move while things are cooking, or we might miss our chance."

"We?" Maggie sat back. "But I don't know anything about running a business."

"I'm not asking you to take over, just to be partners. I've got the degree for what that's worth, and you're getting experience."

Maggie knew Jelly wouldn't be offering this if she didn't believe in her abilities, and she was flattered. But co-owner of a store? It wasn't really what she'd come to DC to do. She wasn't sure exactly how much money that would take, but she was pretty sure she didn't have it, which meant she'd have to take out a loan. Or worse, ask her parents. As if they would agree to her investing in a dress shop. Plus, it was a huge responsibility, and she'd hardly made a success of the things she'd already tried here.

"I know you've got to think about it." Jelly hopped off the desk. "And we'd have to work out the details, but I thought I'd put the bug in your ear. We'll talk about it more later this week. But Maggie," she said, locking eyes with her, "I've seen your work, girl. And all those outfits we stitched together for kicks in college? I'm pretty sure you have what it takes. You might think you're Miss Flighty and don't know which end's coming or going, but I think there's more in that head of yours than just Irish air. You didn't get through Georgetown on just your charm, you know." She walked to the door that led to the stock room. "Besides, it'd be fun."

After she disappeared into the back room, Maggie pondered the unexpected offer. Sure she had some experience with design, and she had to admit she did love it, but she wasn't sure she could pull it off. Besides, she reminded herself again, she had come here to start a different career.

The determination to make her own way, to follow the path of her successful grandmother returned. There had to be some job of some importance she could find in this famous town, something that would start to build her career and her life.

She just needed that one break.

Chapter Four

AT LEAST IT WAS A JOB, Adrian decided, as he tied on an apron in Bartlett's Candy Shop.

He began refilling a row of candy jars with bags from a cart. He couldn't help remembering when he and his younger brother, Danny, would sneak malted milk balls from Parson's dime store on the corner near their house. After yesterday's bad news, he had needed something for work, and fast. Bartlett's was an old-fashioned store that sold classic candy and homemade confections.

Danny's in-laws owned the store, and Beth, Danny's wife, worked here on the mornings their kids were at school, helping her dad out behind the counter and doing the books. It was a small but thriving business just off the Georgetown district, drawing a fair amount of tourists, especially now after a food show featured its famous white-chocolate-covered strawberries.

Adrian obviously knew it wasn't going to be a long-term job, but Beth was being generous with her offer, and he did need some money to fill in the cracks while he waited for his next opportunity.

Which he hoped would be soon. He had gotten the word out yesterday to all of his contacts in the driving service business, and he was trying to remain confident that his experience and connections would turn up something.

The door to the shop dinged lightly, and Danny walked in wearing his sharply cut police uniform. Adrian crossed the floor to meet his brother. Three years younger than Adrian, Danny was inches shorter than Adrian's six feet, with more of their French-Canadian mother's decidedly aquiline nose. He wore his Diplomatic Security Service uniform well and with authority, and had risen through the ranks fairly quickly for his age. He had dreams of becoming a US Marshal, but that would have to wait until his family was a little older.

Adrian thought briefly that this would have been him too, if he had been able to finish the program at the FLETC—the Federal Law Enforcement Training Centers. But Karen's illness had changed those plans, along with just about everything else in his life, and taking care of Charlie had become more imperative than finishing federal training.

"Officer Adams. Good to see you."

"Citizen," Danny returned with false gravity. He looked around the shop. "How are things in the candy business? Sweet?"

"Hilarious." Adrian gestured to the young, cheerful woman behind the counter on the other end of the store. "The boss is an evil taskmaster, though. Makes me actually work and stuff."

Danny nodded. "Humph. Tell me about it. This morning she made me fold the laundry." He faked a shudder, then gave a brief wave to Beth, who gave her husband a knowing smile. "Seriously, though, bro, sorry to hear about the job. I'm glad we could help out a little, but you have any leads?"

Adrian shrugged. "I have the word out, but nothing just yet. Tell Beth thanks for letting me fill in here, though."

"Of course. I mean I know it's not much, but I figure it can keep you going. You'll find something soon, I think, with your experience. No problem."

Adrian appreciated his brother's encouragement, although he knew it was going to be a challenge to find a job with the flexibility he needed.

"So," Danny continued, "Beth and I were wondering if you and Charlie wanted to come over for dinner this Saturday."

Adrian's eyes narrowed in suspicion. "Every time you ask me and Charlie over for dinner there's always some single woman there who happened to have just dropped in to get a cup of sugar or pet the guppy or whatever."

Danny held his hands open in apology. "What can I say? We're very popular with our neighbors."

"Well, then, you have a *lot* of weird neighbors who also happen to be single women. Like that last one."

"Which one? The one with the crew cut or the one with the Pekinese?"

"I was thinking of the one wearing the earrings made from her own kidney stones."

"Yeah, Carly. Classy lady. She's a *model*, you know."

"Yes, an *ear* model. Oh, and then there was the clown."

"Imogene? She wasn't a clown. She just wore a lot of makeup."

"Okay, then how do you explain the size fourteen feet?"

"I don't think you should call a girl a clown just because she has big feet."

"Then she shouldn't have worn red shoes."

"Well"—Danny smiled—"you know what they say about a woman with big feet."

"Yes, they say, 'Watch out for those huge feet.' "

Danny rubbed his chin. "Okay, then what was wrong with Olivia?"

"Olivia…was she the one with the beard or the mustache?"

"C'mon, there was no one with a beard or a mustache." Danny paused, thinking. "Well, not a beard anyway."

Adrian shook his head. "You're forgetting the one who managed the insect section of the pet store."

"That wasn't a beard, it was just a really fuzzy turtleneck sweater."

"She looked like she was being swallowed by a gorilla suit."

Danny threw up his hands. "Okay, then, I give up."

"Finally! That's what I've been waiting for. I told you, I'm not ready to go looking again."

"Well, those were all quality ladies, my friend."

"Uh huh. You were always a terrible liar."

Danny acted hurt. "Hey, I was always a *terrific* liar. Remember that time we broke the bunk beds and I told Dad it was the dog?"

"Don't change the subject."

"I'm not. The subject is life, Ady." He grew serious. "We just want you to know…you know Beth and I are there for you, right?"

"Of course, I know."

"Well, I know you're my big brother, but some of being there for you is to maybe kick your butt every once in a while. Metaphorically speaking, of course."

Adrian's tone softened. "Sure, but—"

"So consider this a friendly butt kicking," Danny continued. "I'm worried that you're, you know, not getting out there."

"Oh, I'm out there. I was out there this morning, taking Charlie to school, taking out the garbage, cleaning up the neighbor's dog poop on our lawn."

"You know what I mean."

Adrian did, and it always made him feel defensive. "Well, sometimes real life get's in the way. We don't all get to have the perfect job with the perfect wife…" He trailed off, not wanting to say something out of anger he'd regret.

"You're right," Danny said, sympathetic but firm. "But everybody has their own 'real life' to deal with. For me, it's waking up every day to go to a job I love but knowing my wife's worried that I'm maybe not coming home because some nutbag decided to shoot up an embassy. Real life is Beth taking care of three kids while trying to help run her dad's candy store because he's getting old and can't handle all of the work anymore." He put his hands on his hips. "Look, I know you lost Karen, Ady, but if you keep staying stuck where you are, you're going to crumble in on yourself."

Adrian held out his hands. "Hey, I'm trying to go forward. I'm trying to get a better job for Charlie and me. You know that."

"That's just money. I'm talking about companionship. Family. Maybe even someone to love."

"I may get to that. Sometime."

"You never did like to take risks."

Adrian felt his face grow warm. "Well, I can't really afford to take a lot of risks right now, can I?"

"Yeah, but where does that leave you? C'mon, Ady—and I'm saying this because I love you—it's time to let go of that part of Karen and live your life. She'll always be Charlie's mom, she'll always be a part of you, but it's time to start taking some steps forward. Make some friends, get out. You know we're happy to watch Charlie any time."

Adrian knew his brother loved him, but there wasn't any way he could understand what he had gone through. "I appreciate that. We'll see."

He was relieved to spot Beth catch her husband's eye and nod in the direction of the clock.

"Look, I've got to go," Danny said, "but I want you to think about this. You're my brother and I care. You know I only want what's best for you."

"That's exactly what I want for Charlie, too."

Danny sighed, but at least he dropped the argument. "Okay, so how about Saturday night? Beth's making her famous Brazilian pot roast."

"So I should bring some pizza from Bartoni's?"

"Right."

Adrian decided to throw him a bone. "Okay, but no accidental guests dropping by to get your recipe for potato salad or something."

Danny smiled and held up three fingers. "Promise. Just think about what I said. Beth thinks the same thing too, you know. Speaking of which I've got my own date for lunch." He caught his wife's eye behind the counter and winked.

After they said their goodbyes, Adrian resumed filling the front canisters, feeling a tinge of jealousy for his brother and the wife he still had around to smile at him. He watched the various couples walking by outside the shop's front window. Not all of them seemed happy, of course, but there were a few that were obviously enamored with each other, holding hands, laughing.

How could anyone expect to find that twice? And what if it didn't work out? What about Charlie? Could she take losing another person, even if it wasn't her mom?

Could *he*?

He rubbed the empty finger where he'd once worn a ring. No, it was too risky. No one should have to go through that again.

* * *

Maggie stared at her phone screen, biting her lower lip in indecision. She'd been picking it up off and on for the last ten minutes, trying to decide whether to push the phone icon next to her mother's name. It was one thirty in the afternoon in Ireland, which meant who knew what government function they might be at and she might be interrupting. She'd never asked her parents for money before, and this would definitely be a large loan. She'd have to be certain it was what she wanted. And certain she wanted to swallow some pride as well.

She put the phone down. The courage wasn't there just yet.

Jelly's offer yesterday had dogged her thoughts for the last twenty-four hours, sticking in her mind more than she had expected. She found herself playing out different scenarios in her mind—designing, creating, expanding the business. And Jelly was right: regardless of how successful they were, it would be fun. But she also knew it would disappoint her family, and maybe even herself. Was she really ready to settle for less than what she'd been raised to do all her life?

"I'd say a penny for your thoughts, but I think you'd get short-changed."

Maggie looked up to see Jelly standing in the doorway of the back room of Bella Bella.

"Hmm? Oh, hi."

"Looks like you have a lot on your mind." Jelly came over to where Maggie was seated in the stuffed red chair by the counter.

Maggie frowned. "I suppose so."

"Boss getting you down?"

"Of course not."

"Then it must be men. The FedEx guy hit on you again? Meet a new guy at the coffee shop?" Her eyes narrowed. "It's not Gerard, is it?"

Maggie managed a smile. "No, but if you don't do something soon, I might change my mind."

Her cell phone started ringing, startling her as it rattled on the counter. She gave an apologetic look to Jelly and picked it up.

"Hello," she said without bothering to look at who was calling.

"Hello, Margaret." The voice on the other end of the line was distinct, familiar, and undeniably sophisticated.

"*Mamó*," Maggie said, instantly recognizing her grandmother's voice. "How are you? How are things at the embassy?"

"That's why I called." Maggie's grandmother always got to the point, a habit probably acquired from years of negotiation as a high-ranking diplomat. "I want you to come by tomorrow morning."

"Tomorrow? I'll have to make sure Jelly can spare me."

Jelly was already nodding her head okay. "The ambassador?" she whispered.

Maggie nodded back at her. "Looks like it's no problem, Mamó. But I don't have a car." She hadn't driven in years, and certainly not here in DC.

"I'm sending a driver for you. At ten o'clock. He'll fetch you from that seamstress shop where you work."

Maggie didn't bother to correct her. "Okay, I'll give you the address."

"Unnecessary. The driver will pick you up at ten sharp. I'll see you then, Margaret."

The phone beeped and the call was ended. That was Ambassador MacCarthy, short and to the point.

Maggie realized she'd been holding her breath and blew it out.

"Something important?" Jelly queried.

Maggie bit her lower lip, as she always did when she was nervous. "I'm not sure."

Her grandmother wasn't usually one for social calls during her workday. In fact, since Maggie had been in DC, she'd visited her grandmother's house, but not once had she been summoned to the embassy.

Mamó had been instrumental in setting up some of her job attempts, but those had been pretty hands-off. Going to the embassy was a different story.

She crossed her arms in thought. What could be so important?

* * *

Adrian glanced at the clock on the candy shop's wall. He'd better get moving if he was going to pick up Charlie from school on time. He resisted the temptation to sneak a last few malted milk balls out of a nearby jar. *Work at this job too much longer and I'll gain fifty pounds.*

Hopefully, it wouldn't come to that, and something would turn up. Nothing against Beth and the shop, but he wasn't a high school kid looking for a lazy after-school job. He was already starting to feel a definite pinch in his dignity.

As if someone had heard his thoughts, the store door opened with its customary jingle and a man with a vaguely familiar face entered. "Hey, Adrian. How's it going? Good to see you."

Adrian recognized him now. He tried to suppress his excitement as he wiped his hands on his apron before shaking Jack Swanson's outstretched hand. He was the dispatcher for Capital Transport, one of the other quality driver services in the DC area.

"Hi, Jack. Going so-so, if you want the truth, but maybe things are looking up. Have you found something for me?"

"Well, it's something. Not sure if you'll like it. Your message said you were working here, so I thought I'd just stop by. My wife loves Bartlett's sea-salt chocolate caramels." He smiled. "We just got a job opening today driving for a local embassy. It's just a one-shot, but once you get your foot in the door, we could probably pick you up some more work. I don't have anyone else available right now, and I heard through the grapevine you were looking."

Adrian's phone calls were paying off. He tried not to sound too eager. "Sure, where is it?"

Jack looked down at some papers in his hand. "Let's see... standard pickup and on-call for someone on Thirtieth Street. You'd be taking them to the Irish embassy."

"Irish citizen?" It was always good to know if there were going to be any potential diplomatic immunity issues.

Jack scanned the paper again. "Says here American. So... if you want it, it's yours."

Adrian looked at the work order. Not much on it; just the address, the pickup time and the last name: MacNally. Well, he definitely needed the money. "Sure, I'll take it. This all the info?"

Jack handed him the details from the folded computer printout he had with him. "Sorry it's just the one pickup. But you can fill in with some other jobs as needed."

"Thanks, Jack. Appreciate it. A lot."

"No sweat. Glad I could help. See you around." He turned to the shop door, then stopped. "This also the place that sells those strawberries?"

"I'll get you a half dozen. On the house." Adrian knew he'd be paying for them out of his paycheck, but now he wasn't as worried. He brought a pre-packed box over to Jack, who said another thanks and went to the counter to get his caramels.

Adrian quickly took off his apron and put it behind the counter. He'd text Beth later that he had left to pick up Charlie. And that he had found a new job. Even if it was just for one day.

Pausing in the back room to get his coat, he checked the name on the work order again, then pulled out his phone and began typing the address of the new client into his contacts, along with the name: *MacNally*. Hopefully not just another opinionated old guy who'd keep asking him to turn down the air conditioning and watch out for all the potholes.

Oh well, a job was a job, right?

Chapter Five

MAGGIE PAUSED ON THE SHORT STONE STEPS outside of Bella Bella, next to the gnarled hickory tree where the squirrels liked to chase each other. She had made a point of being early for her morning pickup to the embassy, but she had overdone it by about twenty minutes.

Well, just enough time to get a cup of tea from next door while she waited. Maybe it would calm her nerves.

She smoothed her full skirt. She often wore one of her own dress designs, but today she had chosen a definitely more professional belted black shirtwaist dress she had found in the little-used part of her closet, a holdover from the series of other failed jobs she'd taken in DC. A balance between elegant yet feminine, she thought, pleased with herself.

She heard some familiar chattering and reached in her pocket. A few of the braver squirrels slowly climbed down the tree and approached her, recognizing her from the treats she had given them on other days. She'd named the one sporting a stumpy tail Mr. Hampton, after her literature teacher from boarding school. She'd always thought he looked like a squirrel because he would twitch his nose when he called on you in class.

Normally Mr. Hampton would take a peanut from her hand, but today he was being skittish, seemingly more interested in the other squirrels chasing each other around the base of the tree.

Much like her thoughts, which never seemed to be able to land anywhere for very long before skittering off to another possibility.

She was finding it hard not to think about both of the new options that had cropped up in her life yesterday. Even though Maggie wasn't even sure yet what her grandmother wanted to see her about, she knew it must be important if she was sending a driver to pick her up.

Mr. Hampton had apparently gathered enough courage to creep within a few feet of her.

"What would you do?" she asked him.

The squirrel stared at her and just twitched its nose.

"You're a great help."

* * *

The GPS intoned that Adrian had arrived at his destination on Thirtieth Street. He scanned the row of elegant shops that lined the right side of the street, now looking for the correct street number. He found it, painted in black near the door, but parking was...

There. Someone was just pulling out a few cars away from the front door. Good sign for the first day on the new job.

He pulled in, then checked the clock on his dash. He was early, as he liked to be, with still about twenty minutes until pickup time. Well, better early than not. Kind of a strange place for a pickup, though. He peered out the window, finding the store name scripted in gold letters in the front window. *Bella Bella?* An array of posed manikins stood stiffly behind the glass. Some kind of clothing store. Weird for a guy to be picked up here.

He tipped his coffee mug to his mouth, then frowned. Empty. Rolling down his window, he dumped the dregs into the street, and the rich smell of fresh coffee touched his nose. There it was, farther down the row of shops. A modern neon sign of a stylized coffee cup poked out from the brick side of the corner shop. "Red Zone Coffee."

Outside the door of the coffee shop, the curves of a young woman in a simple black dress caught his eye as she moved from behind the shadow of a tree.

Adrian watched her stoop and talk to something on the ground. A squirrel? She straightened and tossed something from her pocket onto the sidewalk and then stepped inside the coffee shop. His eyes followed her as a bevy of squirrels danced around the treats and then sped back up the nearby tree.

Hmm. He checked his watch.

Definitely. Plenty of time to grab some coffee before his pickup.

* * *

"Good morning, Gerard," Maggie sang out from just inside the heavy bright red-and-yellow door. She took a moment to breathe in the rich scent of brewing coffee, deliciously mixing with the cool cherry-blossom-scented air that had followed her inside.

"And how are the squirrels today?" asked Gerard Piscopo, the gentle-giant owner of the Red Zone. He was a former NFL football player who, despite his imposing size and craggy face, had a heart of pure gold.

"Mr. Hampton seems a little slow today. He wouldn't take his peanut."

"Sorry to hear that. Like the usual with your tea?"

Maggie stood in front of the pastry cabinet, swirling her skirt back and forth, deciding whether to get a biscotti.

Gerard came over, drying a coffee mug. "Half off for you today," he whispered.

"You say that every day, Gerard."

"And every day you get it. The chocolate with the almonds?"

She figured she still had time. "Thanks." She wandered down the counter, looking at the other pastries behind the glass, keeping an eye out the front window in case any official-looking cars pulled up.

Gerard grabbed the biscotti for her with some tongs. "I'll put it on your tab. Tea's brewing under Marilyn Monroe."

Which meant her cup was steeping in the brew station under the photo of the movie star and her beauty mole. Maggie hummed softly to herself as she rocked on her heels, listening to the sounds of the shop—the whirring cappuccino maker, the ding of the bell over the door as someone entered.

Then she remembered. "Jelly will have her usual. She'll be over in a bit."

"Certainly. One large St. Louis Blues with extra cream for Miss Jellico Jones."

Maggie looked up with arched eyebrows. "Maybe you want to bring it over to her yourself today."

"Well, I may just do that if I can get someone to watch the counter for me," he responded.

"Jelly asks about you all the time," Maggie said, looking out the front window.

"Yes, and what does she ask?"

"Oh, you know, just 'How's Gerard?' and 'Did you see Gerard?' or 'Was Gerard over—' "

"You'd be a better liar if you weren't so innocent."

She scowled. "Well, that's a fine thing to say to an old friend."

"So sorry, miss," Gerard apologized extravagantly, hands apart. He placed a tall paper cup in the brew station. "I'll have this ready for Jelly when she gets here."

"You *sure* you don't want to take it to her yourself?"

"Oh, I'm pretty busy. Pretty busy around here all the time."

"Coward," Maggie said.

Gerard turned back around. "You're one to talk, miss. Half the guys here are watching you right now."

She rolled her eyes. "Half the guys here are over sixty."

"Not the guy outside." He gestured with his head toward the broad front window.

Maggie turned her head toward the window just in time to see a tall, swarthy man in a crisp gray suit and slicked-back hair quickly turn away. He had obviously been looking at her. *Cute*, she thought.

She placed the biscotti between her teeth to carry it to the table, picked up her waiting tea, turned from the counter, and bumped full into the chest of the man behind her.

Oops. The tea sloshed out of the cup, onto his tie, and down the front of his pants.

* * *

Adrian jumped back and was just about to say "it's okay," when the boiling hot tea that had soaked through his pants met his skin. "Agh!" He began swatting at his legs, even though it did no good.

"I'm so sorry," the woman said through her biscotti-filled mouth. "I'm—here—" She quickly set down the tea and biscotti on the counter, grabbed some napkins and tried dabbing at his tie.

"It's okay," Adrian managed to get out this time, his pants beginning to cool. His red tie was a mess, stained and wet.

Her face looked pained. "I'm sorry, I didn't—why were you so close?"

"Me?" Adrian said. "I was just coming up to get some coffee when I guess you decided I needed a tea bath."

Gerard intervened. "It was probably my fault, sir. The lady meant no harm."

"Sure, of course," Adrian said, calming. "I'm sorry. Look, do you have a clean towel?"

Gerard motioned to the back. "Sure thing. Use the restroom back there by the coat rack. I'll get you a coffee on the house."

"Thanks." Then to the woman, he said, "Really, it's not a big deal."

"Well, I'm still sorry. I'm not usually such a fumbler." She bit her lower lip.

"I'm sure you're not." He smiled, having only a vague idea of what a "fumbler" meant. Her Irish accent tugged at his thoughts, but it was probably just a coincidence. Lingering on her blue eyes for a moment, he headed for the restroom, glancing at his watch.

Terrific. Picking up a new client and this girl dumps hot tea down my pants. Serves him right for following her in here like some stalker. What had he been thinking? He only hoped the restroom had a hot air drier.

He shook his head. He hoped this guy he was picking up didn't give him a bad report. So much for first impressions.

* * *

Maggie watched the man duck around the corner to the hallway, pulling off his tie. It really had been an accident. Good thing he didn't get too mad. *I hope I didn't ruin his day.*

Moving a little too quickly, she whirled around. "Gerard, can I get another—" She bumped full into the chest of another man behind her.

He stepped back, grabbing her shoulders for balance.

"Ohmygosh!" Maggie instinctively grabbed his waist to also keep from falling.

"It is nothing. It was my fault," he said in a rich French accent. "I was in your way."

Maggie couldn't believe it. If she kept bumping into men she'd never get out the door. "I'm so sorry. I wasn't looking."

"It's fine. Do not worry." He motioned to a nearby chair at a small, two-person table. "Here, why don't you sit down?"

She moved to the counter to retrieve her purse and dripping teacup.

He came to help her. "My name is—" the man started to say, just as she turned and stepped on his foot.

"I'm sorry." She looked up into his eyes, now very close.

He smiled, although maybe it was more of grimace. "Not at all. There is no harm. My name is Valéry. Were you able to save your biscotti?"

He pronounced it Val-*lay*-rie, with an emphasis on the middle syllable. Maggie wasn't sure if it was his first name or last. "Oh. Yes, it's fine." She looked down. "I think I lost a few almonds, but..."

Valéry smiled, and this time it looked real. "I was just coming in for a coffee before my next meeting. I am attached to the Embassy of France near here. So, since we're now almost friends, I'm wondering if I might join you? Unless I am interrupting something with your new friend and his tie?"

Maggie recovered her senses. "Him? Oh, I don't know him. But I do have a driver coming to pick me up in about ten minutes."

"Excellent. Just enough time for a visit." Valéry moved to a table and pulled out a chair. "Here, have a seat."

She sat, mopping up around her half-filled tea and soggy biscotti. He took the chair opposite her. She glanced down the hallway where the stranger had disappeared. There was no sign of him, but she could hear a hot-air drier blasting.

Gerard came over with a towel to clean the table. "Can I get you anything, sir? Coffee? Steel-toed boots?"

Maggie narrowed her eyes at him. "Thank you, Gerard, would you mind getting this gentleman a coffee, please?" She motioned with her eyes for him to go.

"Espresso?" he asked Valéry.

"Yes. *Un crème*, please."

"With a dash of milk, of course." Gerard returned to the counter.

Valéry turned to Maggie. "I detect a touch of accent. You are... Irish?"

"From Ireland, yes. Where the Irish are from. That's where I lived most of my life anyway. I'm not there *now*, of course. I'm here. I mean, I've been here a while. In *this* country." She smiled weakly.

"I have been there a few times," Valéry said as Gerard arrived with his espresso. "*Merci*," he said.

Maggie realized she hadn't introduced herself. "Oh. I'm sorry. My name is Maggie." She stuck out her hand, which he shook with a lingering grip that made her sit up a little straighter. "And I detect an accent as well. French or Canadian?" she asked.

"Very good. French. From France. Not *now* of course."

She laughed. "Let me see..." She cleared her throat. "*Jay sooee...hear-oh...day voo rencon-trare.*"

"*Oui,* Very good." He returned a question in French.

Maggie's brow furrowed. "Um, *pour-qua...nay san-tay-voo?*"

Valéry laughed.

"What? What did I say?" Had she made a fool of herself?

Valéry chuckled, "You said, 'Why do you smell?' "

She grimaced. "Oh, I'm so sorry. My French is atrocious."

"No, no, it's very good. I'm impressed." He took a sip of his coffee. "Where did you learn?"

Maggie smoothed her dress on her knees. "I took language classes in secondary school in Dublin. My parents wanted me to learn German, Italian and French, so I did—not very well, as it turns out."

"Actually, with a little more practice you could become quite good." He took another sip of his coffee. "I could teach you if you like."

Her heart jumped a little. "Well, yes, of course. That would be brilliant, thank you." She found herself staring at his dark brown eyes, then quickly turned to look at her tea. "Well, you must be very busy with your work at the embassy."

Valéry shrugged. "It can be very mundane work, but it has its privileges. I get to work with a lot of the European governments, attend some meetings and"—he leaned close to whisper—"I get my very own driver and car."

"That must be very useful." She glanced at her watch. Her own driver was supposed to be here in about five minutes. She didn't want to be late, but she also didn't want to be rude. Not with someone as handsome as this.

"Perhaps you would like to take a drive with me one day?" Valéry asked. "They even let me take the wheel sometimes."

She could see he was making a joke, so she laughed. "Well, sure, okay." She wondered if she was blushing, then worried that she was, then blushed because she was worried she was blushing. "Well, you must have things to do. And my driver should be here any minute." She thought she should explain. "I have a meeting at the Irish Embassy. With the ambassador. Although I admit I'm not sure exactly what for yet."

Valéry's eyebrows arched. "Well, I'm sure it must be something important. Someone with your talent and charm. I know the ambassador there well. She will be of great help."

"Thank you," she replied, although she wasn't sure how he could possibly know that. Then she smiled, slightly embarrassed. Obviously, he didn't know that the ambassador was also her grandmother. "I wish I had your confidence."

Valéry shrugged. "I have been doing these—this diplomacy work? For many years, and I can tell you will do well. There is something about you."

"Thank you," she said, returning his smile. She looked out the front window to the street. Where was that driver? She noticed a likely car, but no one was in it. Grandmother or no, she certainly didn't want to be late for an appointment.

Valéry sighed and pushed a wisp of brown hair from his forehead as he stood. "Yes, our jobs do keep us very busy. I suppose I should check in to see if the British consulate has gotten back to us about the upcoming European trade negotiations. We're trying to complete a merger between two of our textile manufacturing companies and a British—" He stopped. "But I must be boring you."

"No, no. You're not boring. I mean, government things don't…I'm *used* to boring things. What I mean is, not that you're *boring*…" She trailed off, biting her lower lip.

Valéry chuckled again. "You are a very delightful woman. I hope we can meet again." He reached into his pocket, pulled out a leather card case and offered her a very official-looking business card. "Here is my personal number for the French Embassy. If you are ready for those French lessons, just look me up."

Maggie stood up a little too suddenly, her chair scooting back and making a farting noise. "Oh, excuse me," she said, even more embarrassed. "I mean, yes, thank you. I'll be sure to check you out… I mean, look you up… sometime soon."

She swallowed and smiled, taking the card from his hand. At the same moment, he reached for her other hand, drew it to his face and kissed it in one swift motion.

"*Jusqu'à la prochaine fois?* Until next time, then?" He turned and strode out of the shop, his exotic-smelling cologne wafting back in the breeze.

Maggie stood, her hand still hanging in the air where he had kissed it. "Yes," she said, to no one in particular, then slowly sat back into her chair and looked at the card she held, embossed with a gold fleur-de-lis. "Valéry LaBonté," she whispered, and placed the card carefully in her bag.

She glanced at her watch. Good, still time. She gathered her things. "Bye, Gerard. Wish me luck."

Gerard waved. "Good luck, Maggie. See you tomorrow."

Maggie turned around for a second. "Oh, and don't forget Jelly's coffee."

"I won't."

She opened the door to the coffee shop and stepped out into the crisp, early spring air. A mysterious meeting with her grandmother at the embassy, a chance meeting with a sophisticated Frenchman—things were looking up. She thought about Valéry, his smiling eyes, his perfect hair. So full of vibrancy and confidence. He seemed like the first real chance she'd had in months of meeting a man with grace and style. And who didn't drive a white van and live with his mother.

Then she scowled. Now, where was that driver?

Chapter Six

MAGGIE WAS STARTING TO GET A LITTLE WORRIED that she wasn't going to make it to the embassy on time. She made a mental note to call this whatever-service-it-was and let them know they needed to get some responsible drivers or lose her grandmother's business.

She was walking down the street, scanning for anyone who looked like they might be a driver when the guy she'd spilled her tea on walked past her, still dabbing at his pants.

"Excuse me," she said. "Hi again…do you—I'm waiting for a driver—do you think this would be their car?" She pointed to a polished black sedan at the curb.

His eyes widened. "*You're* waiting?"

Maggie was a little annoyed at his unhelpful answer. "Yes, and he's late, and I'm just wondering if you think this would be his car. It has a driving service logo thing on the side." She pointed at the car door, which featured a silkscreened logo for Capital Transport.

His eyes narrowed. "Really…"

Maggie frowned. "Look, I'm really sorry about the tie. It *was* an accident."

Now he shook his head. "I didn't realize who you were…in there."

"Right, well, it's just that today is—" She stopped and threw up her hands. "Look, I'm sorry if I bothered you." She returned to searching up and down the sidewalk. "If he doesn't get here soon, I'll just take the thing myself," she said to no one in particular as she glanced back down the street.

"If you do, make sure you don't race the engine. BMWs have a tendency to overheat."

She turned to look at him. "What do you...?"

He held out some car keys. "Here. Can I ride in the back? I've never gotten to ride in the back before."

"You're...?"

He stuck out his hand. "Adrian Adams. I'm you're driver. And you must be *Miss* MacNally?"

Maggie laughed, then tried to catch herself, then laughed again. "I'm sorry, yes." She shook his still waiting hand. "Maggie MacNally. And I'm afraid I'd be a poor driver. Haven't driven in years." Every time she saw his stained red tie, she started laughing. She covered her face with a hand.

He waited. "Whenever you're ready?"

"Yes, of course." Maggie cleared her throat, trying to regain some composure, but continued to chuckle as she gathered her purse. "I'm sorry, it's...I'm not sure why I'm laughing. Your tie..."

He looked down at his ruined tie. "Well, at least now it matches my pants."

It wasn't really that funny, but Maggie starting laughing even harder.

Adrian glanced at his watch. "Like you said, ma'am, we need to get moving or you might be late."

"Of course," Maggie said, the laughter dying away in fits.

Adrian, her driver, moved to the car and opened the door for her.

"Wait! Mr. Hampton!" She fished the remnants of a few peanuts out of the side pocket in her dress's skirt and tossed them at the waiting squirrel, who had cautiously ventured down the sidewalk toward her.

Adrian looked at the squirrel and back at her, shaking his head slightly. He gestured at the car door. "If you're done with Mr. Frampton—"

"Hampton."

"Then we should go. He probably needs to get back to his nuts, and I promised I'd have you to the embassy by"—he looked at his watch—"ten thirty."

Maggie made a face, then wiped her hands on her dress. Adrian opened the front passenger door, reached inside for a uniform jacket on the seat and put it on. Maggie found herself staring at his chest.

"Is something wrong?" Adrian looked down as if searching for a spot on his coat or something.

Maggie caught herself. "Oh. No, I was just thinking maybe a blue tie would look better with that coat. It's just a thought." She got into the back seat, not waiting for a response.

Adrian held her still open door. "Well, I'm not sure you're getting the full effect of the red tie. You know, what with the tea stains and everything."

Maggie just smiled sweetly at him. "I just thought it would match the colors of your company's logo better. Occupational hazard, I suppose. I'm a designer." She realized that might have been the first time since she'd been back in the States that she'd referred to herself as that.

Maggie sat back in her seat and he closed the door. The interior smelled like fresh leather, class and... sophistication. She liked it. Adrian plopped into the driver's seat, started the car, and went through some kind of routine, checking mirrors and the traffic of the street.

Maggie looked out the window behind her. "It's clear behind you if that's what you're waiting for."

Adrian pursed his lips as he continued to scan the traffic. "Just trying to be safe, ma'am. We wouldn't want to run over Mr. Hampton, would we?"

He finally pulled the BMW into the road.

Maggie ignored him and looked out the side window now. "I do want to be to the embassy by ten thirty. And it's *miss*, not *ma'am*." Then she thought. "Or you can call me Maggie."

Adrian nodded. "Very well, miss. And don't worry, I'm a highly competent, fully licensed and experienced red-tie-wearing transportation expert. We'll get there on time."

Maggie suppressed a laugh in spite of herself. She sat for a minute or two, then said, "Do you usually drive foreign nationals? I mean, you haven't asked me where I'm from. People usually want to know once they hear me talk."

"Ireland, I expect, since we're going to that embassy. But eastern Ireland, more specifically Dublin area, I'd say." He piloted the car slowly into a roundabout, then out the other side.

Maggie's eyebrows lifted in surprise. "That's correct. I'm from Bray, to be more specific." She was impressed, in spite of herself. Most people usually said Australia or even Canada or something equally stupid, but she was finding that in Washington, DC, people had a little more worldly sophistication, which she liked.

He suddenly laughed. "I'm sorry, I have to say, I wasn't quite expecting you. To be a woman, I mean."

She was confused. "Because I have short hair?"

"What? No, no, I meant because there wasn't a first name on the work order."

"Oh." She looked out the window. "I hope I didn't disappoint you."

"No, of course not. You're a breath of fresh air, actually."

She suddenly felt nervous and unsure of what to say. Or should she say anything? "Do you usually pick up older women? I mean, not *pick them up* of course, but... when you're working—*driving*, I mean—"

Adrian looked amused. "Yes, miss, I suppose most of my clients are a little older."

"Do these windows roll down?"

"What?"

Maggie found the button that rolled down the windows herself, moving it up, then down, then up.

"Miss, please, can you—"

"Oh, sorry," Maggie said, realizing what she was doing. "It's just such as lovely day. Oh, look at that," she said suddenly.

Adrian touched the brakes and the car jerked slightly. "What?"

"Koolman's has ice cream sandwiches for half off on Wednesdays. Have you ever had them? I have them dip it in sprinkles—you know, those candy sprinkles? They do it for you if you ask."

She could hear Adrian sigh. "Yes, miss."

Maggie was watching the moving arrow on the GPS affixed to the dash. "Are you sure—" she began to say, then stopped.

"Miss?" he said, obviously knowing she had a question.

She looked out the back window again. "I was just wondering... I thought the embassy was on Q Street and we just passed Q Street."

"Q Street has some construction, and it's also pretty busy this time of day, so I thought it would be safer to go a different route."

She turned back toward the front. "But your GPS says it's not the shortest route."

"Sometimes the shortest route isn't the best. Trust me, we'll get there on time. Maybe even a little early." He flopped his tie up and down so she could see. "Experienced red-tie-wearing transportation expert, remember?"

She covered her smile with her hand.

"How long have you been in DC, then?" Adrian asked.

But Maggie noticed something outside of the window. "Pull over. Quick!"

"Here? I can't, there's—what's wrong?"

"There's Juicy's lemonade stand. They have the best lemonade ices. Have you ever tried them?" The car kept moving. Maggie's shoulders slumped. "Oh, you missed it."

Adrian looked in the mirror. "Look, Miss—*Maggie*, we can't just whip over any time you get a whim. There's traffic and it's not safe."

"I suppose so. But you really should try them sometime."

"Maybe," Adrian said, as they continued on their way.

Maggie realized she hadn't answered his previous question. "Two years," she said. Then, realizing he probably didn't know what she meant, she added, "You asked how long I've been here. Two years almost, anyway. But I did go to school here before then. At Georgetown."

Adrian nodded. "Good school. Well, you've probably seen the cherry blossoms then. They're just starting to bloom."

Maggie nodded as well. "I know. I love them. But I've never seen the trees around the Tidal Basin."

"Really? We make it a tradition to walk the whole way around the Tidal Basin every spring. Nothing like it."

We? He must mean his wife. She peeked around his left shoulder at his hand, checking to see if he had a ring. It was wrapped around the steering wheel, so she couldn't see.

"What time is it?" she asked, hoping he'd look at his wrist.

He glanced at the clock on the dashboard. "Ten eighteen. Plenty of time."

That didn't work. She faked a couple of sniffs. "I'm sorry, do you have any tissues?"

"Yes, they're in the pouch there in front of you. On the back of the seat."

Sure enough, there was a small bag of Kleenex peeking neatly from the mesh pocket in front of her. She took one, then blew her nose as best she could, then poked the tissue up by his shoulder. "Is there a trash bag up there?"

Adrian stared straight ahead. "There's one on the door to your left."

Maggie sighed. Okay. Last chance. "I'm sorry, which one of those two buildings on the left is the Albanian Embassy?"

He pointed with his left hand. "Those two? Neither. That's a donut shop. The Albanian embassy is up on Florida."

Bingo. No ring. She smiled, pleased with herself. Then for some reason, she heard Jelly's voice in her brain saying, *No ring? Go for it!* She shook her head.

The GPS intoned that they were back on the directed route and now only a few minutes from the embassy. Maggie bit her lower lip.

"Something wrong?"

She looked up. "Hmm? Oh—I was just thinking. The ambassador can be very particular. I'm not sure I wore the right thing. Does this dress look okay to you?"

"Your dress?" He tilted the mirror to see her better. "Your dress looks fine. It's very pretty," he added.

"Thank you," she said, and to her surprise wondered if she was blushing. She straightened a wisp of hair on her forehead.

"Did you design it?" Adrian asked. "My wife used to sew. I know how hard it is to, you know, to make your own clothes."

Used to? Probably divorced, then. "This one? No, but I have done others."

"Well, it's nice."

"Thank you." She meant it sincerely.

"You're welcome." He looked at the GPS on the dash. "Just another minute, I expect."

The compliment stuck in Maggie's mind where she found herself savoring it. It had been a long time since she'd felt appreciated, she realized. He was definitely different. Smart, sense of humor, attractive. She wondered why he wasn't still married.

"What do you do there, at the embassy?"

Maggie looked up, her thoughts interrupted. "Well, I'm not sure yet, actually. But I'm sure my gran—the ambassador will fill me in today."

Adrian nodded. "Well, I hope it goes well, Miss MacNally. We're here. I'll pull into the turnout and then get the door for you."

"Thank you." Maggie was starting to feel some importance flow through her as she looked out the window at the stately face of the building. And why not? This was her big break, what she had hoped might happen when she had left Ireland behind and come to the States, and she was sure that whatever grandmother had planned for her she would do well. She wouldn't let her down this time.

Adrian opened her door, and as she stepped out, she noticed his eyes lingering on her legs. He realized what he was doing, looked up, away, then back, and then caught her eye.

"Thank you," she said.

He cleared his throat and closed the door. "You're welcome."

She looked toward the entrance of the embassy. "I can see myself in, I think." She paused; then they both spoke at the same time.

"So...do you—"

"I'll be available—"

"Go ahead," he said.

"I was—I mean, do I just call you tomorrow if I, you know, need a ride or something?"

Adrian seemed to realize something. "Yes—I'm sorry, here." He pulled out an old business card that had his cell number on it and handed it to her. "I should have mentioned this earlier; sorry. I was just dropping you off today but was told you may need me again tomorrow. I mean a *ride* tomorrow. From then on just call this number when you need transportation, and if you're available—I mean, *I'm* available I'll pick you up."

"Thank you, sir, I will do that."

"Oh, and I wasn't told to wait today, but I'm sure some other transportation has been arranged to take you home."

She felt a brief pang of disappointment. "I'm sure." She turned and walked toward the door.

"Good luck," Adrian called after her.

She looked back as she walked. "Thanks." She found herself smiling, remembering how he had complimented her dress, thinking about how attractively silly he looked standing there with his stained tie and wet pants.

She shook her head. What am I doing? First this Valéry and now...

She set her jaw as she approached the ornate iron doors to the embassy. There was too much at stake to be thinking about *another* man right now. She grasped the worn brass knob and pulled open the heavy door. *No matter how cute he is*, she thought, her smile returning.

* * *

Adrian stood beside the still-idling BMW and watched Maggie enter the embassy door. For a moment, he let his gaze linger on her. It really was a nice dress, and she filled it out well, that was for sure. He normally didn't go for short hair, but her slightly tousled black curls seemed to perfectly match her personality, as well as her bright blue eyes. And, as his Dad used to say, she was pretty easy on the eyes...

He turned his attention to entering the just-completed drive's information into the app on his phone. A sudden waft of overpowering cologne caught his attention. Glancing to the side he saw a dark-haired man in a gray European-cut suit gliding past him as he walked to his waiting car.

It was the French guy he'd seen talking to Miss MacNally in the coffee shop.

The man seemed to not notice him. He stopped, adjusted the cufflinks on his shirt and surveyed the area as if seeing if he were being followed, then got in his car.

Adrian frowned. The skeptical law enforcement side of his Adams brain was giving off warning signals. He got into his own car. Something about the guy just didn't feel right.

Seemed like a big coincidence, him being here, but it was none of his business. He started his car, adjusted the mirror, and carefully pulled into traffic.

Chapter Seven

MAGGIE HAD ONLY BEEN to the Irish Embassy two times before, and even though it was not a huge building, it still awed her a little. Nestled along Massachusetts Avenue along with many other international embassies to the United States, it was right off Sheridan Circle Park, where her driver had pulled into a small arcing driveway beneath the Irish flag.

She knew other Embassies were located nearby. Romania just next door, Greece across the road, Kenya, Cyprus—it was exciting to think of all the different countries represented in this small area, many of which she was sure would be fascinating to visit, although traveling had never really been her thing. She knew her grandmother had been everywhere, and she loved to hear her stories of tea sets in India and eating mangoes in Cameroon. But Maggie had also experienced loneliness firsthand when her parents were off on extended trips when she was a teenager. Even on the rare occasions when she had joined them, any excitement over being in a new place was dulled by the emptiness of having no one there to share it with.

An aide already seemed to be waiting inside for her, although talking on his phone. He looked up and quickly finished his conversation.

"Miss MacNally, welcome." He came over, hand outstretched.

Maggie struggled to remember his name.

"Desmond," he said, assisting her before she had to guess. "We met once before. The ambassador is with another visitor but should be ready for you shortly." He led her to a small waiting area inside. "Would you like some tea?"

"Yes, please." She sat down on the Queen Anne chair positioned by an antique table and looked around the room. She'd been told on a previous visit that the building had once been a residence for a governor some hundred years ago, and was made out of limestone from Indiana, which she knew was an American state somewhere in the Midwest. The Republic of Ireland bought the house sometime in the late forties and it had served as the residence for each ambassador since then.

The current one was her grandmother, Marian MacCarthy, formerly of the MacAuliffe's, a very influential family in Ireland after World War II. Strong and decisive, Ambassador MacCarthy had held her post for twelve years and showed no signs of slowing down, even in her early seventies. Maggie remembered when she was a little girl accidentally entering a room at her grandmother's large Dublin house where she was giving no ground to a group of obviously angry men. Part of *Mamó's* success came from her drive, although she also had the intelligence to back it up, which made her a formidable character at a bargaining table. She had always been held up as a pinnacle of achievement in Maggie's eyes.

Maggie drank in the ornate furnishings in the drawing room—the old paintings of previous ambassadors, the delicate plaster filigree on the walls—imagining herself someday coming down the curved stairs of the living hall to meet some powerful foreign dignitary. Her thoughts ended as she saw her grandmother approaching from a far doorway, Desmond not far behind.

Maggie stood up to greet her.

"I see our driver found you at your clothing shop?" She took Maggie by her hand, guiding her to a more private area of the room. A small marble table flanked by two elegant blue chairs sat under a painting of what looked like a sailor who had just eaten some bad lemons. Desmond placed a small silver teapot on the table, along with two cups so tiny Maggie wondered if they held more than two sips.

"Thank you, Desmond. And please make sure you contact Frederick," *Mamó* instructed him.

Maggie admired her grandmother's silky accent. Refined over the years, it sounded like she was upper-crust British yet still with a touch of Irish brogue.

Mamó sat down, motioning for Maggie to sit as well. "You know I don't like to waste time, so I'll get right to it."

Maggie did know that, and she waited somewhat nervously to see what this summons from Ambassador MacCarthy was all about.

"You know I've been pleased to have you back here in the States, Margaret. It's been so long since I've had real family around. But I think it's time for us to be frank. You've been here almost a year again now if I'm not mistaken, and I don't believe any of the jobs we've worked out for you have borne much fruit. What exactly are your aspirations, dear?"

Aspirations? Maggie shifted in her chair. *I wish I knew.*

Her grandmother leaned over to pour some tea into their cups. "I've been discussing your situation with your parents for some time, and we've come to an agreement. We know how your other opportunities have turned out to be less than successful for you, so I was hoping you might consider a new proposition."

Here it comes, Maggie thought. *What do they have planned for me this time? Shipping me back to Ireland? Arranged marriage to an African prince? Scullery maid?*

Her grandmother took a sip of her tea. "I have an opening in my staff—not paid, mind you, but it could lead to something more substantial if you were to apply yourself. I would provide you with a stipend to start with to help with some of your expenses."

"A position at the embassy?" Maggie said. That was definitely a surprise. "But... I don't really have any experience."

Her grandmother brushed a speck of dust from her leg. "Neither did I when I started out, but I learned from your grandfather, who learned from his." She smiled slightly. "I'd like to think it's in our blood. You do remember some of your languages, don't you? If I recall, French, some German?"

"Yes, some, and a little Italian." University had been difficult in that regard, with her parents insisting on her learning multiple languages to ready her for a career in politics.

"Good." She set her cup down and laced her fingers together. "Now, I'm sure given enough time and my shepherding you could even grow to become quite a diplomat yourself. It's not an easy life, mind you, but it does have its perks." She made a slight wave with her hand around the room as if for example. "You would be one of my personal assistants. Desmond would show you the ropes. He's quite capable. I've already discussed this with him."

Maggie thought quickly. The offer was a little sudden, but it definitely intrigued her. After all, it *was* sort of the family business, starting with her great-grandfather, who once was the mayor of Limerick. Her grandmother could have been a little more *diplomatic* with her comments on her past jobs, but she was right. Maggie hadn't really been able to make her way on her own so far.

"I don't know, *Mamó*. I mean, it sounds good, but my track record..." She twisted her fingers together. "You've already had to bail me out at least once."

"Oh, yes," her grandmother interrupted, her face expressionless. "The issue with the doves. Old news. I'm sure it was just an unfortunate situation."

Unfortunate situation? Maggie had briefly been an intern with the United Nations Development Programme in DC, assisting with the organization of an outdoor celebration announcing a new freedom initiative. She had thought that releasing a flock of doves would be a majestic celebration of freedom, not a huge cleaning bill for the dignitaries trapped with three hundred frightened birds under a canvas tent.

"I'd like to, *Mamó*. I really would, but...do you think I can?"

Her grandmother's voice grew softer. "Let me be honest, Margaret. We're family, and I know you, and I love you, even though you may not think so." She took a sip of her tea. "I know you feel like you've never fit in with what we do—your parents and I. But I think there's more to you than meets the eye. I know you've had some setbacks, but I believe this is your chance for a fresh start, a new beginning. I think this is the right opportunity for you. And I don't believe you have too many opportunities left."

"Because of the doves?"

"Not just the doves, dear, but all of your interesting misadventures. The pony rides in your college dormitory for those underprivileged children was another one, as I recall."

Maggie winced. "It rained. We had to move the event inside."

"I am aware. I paid for the repairs."

It felt like a slap, but a wakening one. First Jelly's offer, and now this. It was scary, but maybe it *was* time for a change. A real change, not just another mediocre internship where she'd never had a chance to shine. And Jelly? Surely she'd understand.

Maggie brightened. Why not her? Why not Maggie MacNally, the girl who never seemed to get a break? Wasn't that the underlying reason she'd agreed to return to the US capital in the first place, to be near her grandmother, to let some of her success rub off on her? Maybe she just needed the right opportunity, and with *Mamó* helping she should be fine, right?

"Okay," she said finally, then added a more dignified, "Yes. So... what do I do first? When do I get started?"

"Why not tomorrow? Be at the embassy at nine o'clock." *Mamó*—or was it the ambassador?—smiled, apparently pleased with her granddaughter but possibly also at her continued powers of persuasion.

"Tomorrow? But I've got the store, and Jelly. What will I tell her?"

"These are the types of hard decisions you must learn to make. I'm sure your friend will get by fine without you." Her grandmother got up to signal the meeting was over. "Don't be late, Margaret."

Maggie thought about Jelly's offer and about being co-owner of Bella Bella. Well, she didn't really think that selling and sewing clothes was going to be the rest of her life, did she? She suddenly realized something. "I don't have a car, so I'll need to take the Metro. I'm not sure—"

"I've already thought of that," Ambassador MacCarthy interrupted. "I'll send another car for you tomorrow at eight thirty."

"Oh. With the same driver?"

Her grandmother's brow furrowed. "Why? Was there an issue?"

"Oh no. He was fine. I mean, it was fine."

Her grandmother took her hand and squeezed it. "I think you've made the best decision for a new life, Margaret. I will see you here tomorrow. Nine o'clock. Now, Desmond will summon a taxi to take you back to your shop." She turned without waiting for a response and disappeared around a corner, her footsteps echoing down the hall.

Suddenly alone, familiar doubts began creeping around Maggie like old ghosts. She always made a mess of things. Every time she tried to get ahead, to be successful, it all came crashing down, and she either did something stupid or something stupid did something to her.

She stiffened, drawing up a little courage. Not this time. This time she would make her family proud.

* * *

Jelly studied the engraved card that Maggie handed her after returning from the embassy. "*Two* accents over his name. Now that's sophisticated." She handed the card that Valéry had given Maggie back to her. "Does Valéry LaBonté have the abs? I bet he has the abs."

Maggie scrunched up her forehead. "The what?"

"*The* abs, girl. A six-pack. An eight-pack. Name like that he's got to have the abs." Her voice dropped to a whisper. "All those high-class guys with accents have the abs. Got to have the abs!" she suddenly shouted, pointing her finger in the air.

"Jelly!"

"Abs, abs, abs!" she sang. "Gimme them abs! Gimme them abs!" She broke down in laughter.

"Jelly, it's not like that."

"Not like what?"

"Like a... a cheap novel."

"I don't know, girl. Have you ever read one of those cheap novels?"

"Of course not."

"Well, I have, and there's one thing they got that you just might need."

Maggie sighed as she began folding scarves. "And what's that?"

Jelly leaned close and whispered, "Abs!"

Maggie allowed herself a slight smile. "I do not need 'abs.' I do not need four-packs—or whatever you call them. I need a man of... of sophistication."

"Like that guy who took you to that fundraiser last month?"

Maggie rolled her eyes. "That was my grandmother's idea. He was an exception."

"That's a nice word for it. I'd say he was flat-out weird."

"He wasn't that weird, he was just a little... patriotic."

Jelly dropped her hands to the desk and stared at her. "Girl, he was wearing a dress."

Maggie scowled. "It wasn't a dress, it was a kilt. It was a formal function, and he was a representative of the Scottish brigade, and it was a very nice function and he was nice too. There were lots of men there in kilts." She finished folding the scarves and started on a pile of hand-painted tees.

Jelly took a sip of her coffee. "All I know is if I'd been wearing a killer dress and heels and my date showed up in a shorter skirt than mine, I'd have 'kilt' him too." She laughed at her own joke. "And what's your excuse for Snooty Mc-What's-His-Name? The guy who took you to that fancy dinner and fed you cow udders and sea urchins. No, let me correct that—*tetines* and *uni*."

"He had a refined palate."

"As I recall, you puked up your palate in the bathroom. He didn't even bring you home. He just stuck you in a taxi."

Maggie tilted her head and looked at her. "So you have to sift through a few duds sometimes. But I don't think it's too much to ask that a woman want to find a man with some charm and sophistication."

For some reason she thought of her driver, Adrian, waving his stained red tie at her.

"And abs?"

"*And* that a woman can aspire to something in her life beyond just working in—" Maggie closed her mouth and refocused on folding the tees.

"In a what, girl?" Jelly put her hands on her hips. "You know how hard I work here. I may not be making a lot of money yet, but it's my own place and it's growing, and not a lot of people can say that about what they've done."

"I know. I didn't mean it that way." Maggie held up her hands. "I love working here. It's just I think there might be something more for me, you know?"

"If you find something that's better than living your childhood dream, then let me know, 'cause I'm doing it and it feels pretty good. And I think you know what I mean."

"What *do* you mean?"

Jelly gestured at a rack of custom clothing. "I told you, you're a natural here, girl. You've got the creativity, the style, you know how to work the customers. I didn't offer you a partnership because of your crazy accent."

"I appreciate that Jelly, I really do." Maggie stopped her sorting and stared out the window at the people going by on the street, most of whom she would never see again, all of whom she knew nothing about, each with their lives, their hopes, their anxieties. "Sometimes I think I would be happy just staying right here in the shop, where it's safe and I can do what I like. But there's another part of me that needs to know if I can make it, if I can be something more."

"If you ask me," Jelly said, "sometimes the something more isn't as good as the something you already have."

"Maybe. But I feel like if I don't try, I'll never know. And this is the best shot I've had yet. And it's probably my last. It would be nice to show my family that I'm capable of contributing to society in a way that doesn't end in a pony stampede or dove poop."

"Of course you're capable." Jelly gave her a quick hug. "Just know I'll be here no matter what happens. Unless it's the FBI again. In that case, I never met you."

"Oh, Jelly, I know I can always count on you."

Chapter Eight

THE NEXT MORNING WAS COLDER, reminding Adrian that winter still had some bite left. A brisk March wind rattled the trees, and he was wearing his heavier jacket, hopefully for the last time. The weather was supposed to improve again tomorrow. Yesterday's late-afternoon call for the full-time job driving Miss MacNally—*Maggie*—had been the first good news he'd had in days. As he waited outside of Bella Bella, he wondered what he was going to do with Charlie when summer vacation hit and he didn't have school to fall back on as a babysitter.

His cell phone buzzed. He checked the screen, worried it was her school. Was there another problem with her inhaler?

It was his driving service office.

"Hello, this is Adrian." He couldn't remember the dispatcher's name. Had to learn that soon.

"Hi, Mr. Adams? This is Carol from the dispatcher's office."

"Hi, Carol." He filed her name away for future reference.

"Two things. First, just checking on your pickup, if everything's okay?"

"Going fine. I'm here waiting for her now."

"Good, and I wasn't sure if you knew, but our drivers all wear blue ties. Home office likes you to match the Capital Transport logo. We put a tie in the glove compartment for you. Good luck."

The phone beeped and the conversation ended.

Adrian was tying on the new royal blue tie when Maggie came out the front door, wearing a short walking coat, leggings, and a bright flowered scarf wrapped around her dark hair. It seemed a bit old-fashioned, but then he realized it also seemed to fit her perfectly for some reason. She paused, then quickly walked to the nearby hickory tree. Leaning over briefly, she said a few words and tossed what looked like peanuts towards the trunk. He had to smile as the squirrel with the stumpy tail came out from behind the tree and began stuffing them into his cheeks. He went back to working on his tie.

"No red tie today?" she said innocently as he finished adjusting his collar, then struggled with the knot.

"It had tea stains on it, remember?" He gave the tie a final tug, then held the door for her while she got in.

He smelled light perfume and spotted what looked like a sprig of cherry blossoms in her dark hair. The scent of the flowers caused a sudden memory of Karen to trip through his mind. He was surprised to feel a flash of sweat break out on the back of his neck.

He squeezed the thought away and jogged around the back of the car, noticing the flashing meter for the space behind his. Time was up for that car, and *uh oh*, here came the enforcement officer. A woman in a yellow-vested uniform moved down the row of parked cars with her handheld ticketing device.

Adrian fished out a couple of quarters and plugged the stranger's meter, then continued on to the driver's door of his own car and got in. "Ready, miss?"

"That was quite nice of you," Maggie said.

"What's that?" Then he realized. "The meter?"

"Yes. You didn't have to do that."

Adrian noticed the still open glove box, closed it quickly, and tried to stuff the tea-stained red tie he'd left lying on the front seat into the crack between the cushions. "No one likes to start off their day with a parking ticket." He started the car. "I figure why not help someone out."

Maggie simply smiled.

"To the Irish Embassy, correct?" He pulled into traffic after his regular safety check.

"Yes, please."

Although he knew the route, he punched the "go" button on the already-programmed GPS. Maggie was staring at the picture of Charlie that Adrian kept as the screensaver on his phone in the center of the dash.

"Is that your little girl?" she asked.

"Yes. That's Charlie, my girl." Then as he always did, he explained the name. "My wife wanted to call her Charlotte, which was her grandmother's name. We compromised and made it her middle name, then that turned to Charlie for some reason and it stuck."

"I think it fits her." Maggie smiled. "She's a pretty girl."

"Thanks. She gets it from her mother. At least she didn't get the Adams family nose."

"Oh?"

Adrian turned briefly so she could see his profile and pointed at his nose. "This. My brother and I blame my dad's side of the family. Our uncle has a honker the size of a toucan."

Maggie suppressed a laugh. "I would never have noticed. I think it's a distinguished nose."

"Well, thank you, miss."

"Oh, please, call me Maggie. This whole miss thing bends me sideways. Not used to it."

"Sounds good, Maggie. And please call me Adrian." He turned onto Wisconsin to make his way to Massachusetts.

"Very well, Adrian. Do you have any other children?"

"Nope, just the one pixie." Then he thought, *might as well get it over with.* "My wife died when Charlie was three. We were planning on more, but..."

"Oh, I'm so sorry. That must have been very difficult."

"It is what it is."

Their gazes met in the mirror, and Maggie smiled at him. "That's funny. I mean, not really funny *funny* of course, but we have an Irish saying: *Tá sé mar atá sé.* It translates to 'It is what it is.' But my Gaelic isn't very good, so don't quote me on it."

"I don't think I could."

"My grandmother would claim I butchered it. My granddad called the saying the Irish soul."

"Well, I must have some Irish soul, 'cause it rings true to me."

"Maybe you do at that." She cocked her head, and their gazes met in the mirror again. "How did you become a driver? I mean, is this your full-time job?"

Adrian slowed for some jaywalking tourists crossing the road. "I was going to go through FLE training—federal law enforcement. Things like Homeland Security, Defense Intelligence, US Marshalls."

"Sounds exciting."

"It can be. Probably not as much as people think, though. My dad was actually in the Secret Service for a while. He got to meet Ronald Reagan once. Then he met my mom and decided to settle down. She was from Quebec, stationed here as a liaison with the Canadian Security Intelligence Service."

"Ooh, how romantic. A 'two spies meeting from different countries' kind of thing."

He chuckled. "I suppose so. She insisted my brother and I learn a little French. I suppose to give us some culture. It does come in handy. I had a client about a year ago, a nice old widow from Montreal, who insisted we talk in French once she found out where my mom was from."

"Aw, that's cute. So, is everyone in your family in government work?"

"I suppose so. My brother is a Diplomatic Security Service officer. I guess you could say it's kind of the family business. Although I don't think Charlie's going to be too interested. Biggest thing on her mind right now is the school play, and after that, playing house with her stuffed animals."

"You might be surprised. Sometimes children follow right in their parents' footsteps."

"We'll see. That's pretty far down the road. In the meantime, we have more serious problems to address at home, like a crooked front tooth and a Hello Barbie whose head keeps falling off."

"Those things can be just as exciting, in their way."

Adrian gave a nod. "You might be right. At the moment, we're doing fine, going day by day." He was getting uncomfortable just talking about himself and his problems. "So what brings you to DC?"

"Oh, new opportunities, new experiences. I went to college here. Then I went back to Ireland for a while, but I've never seemed to be able to stay in just one place." She laughed, but it sounded more sad than amused.

"Uh-huh. Any family here?"

"Just my *mamó*—my grandmother."

"The one who speaks Gaelic better than you?"

"Yes, she's... well, she's actually Ireland's Ambassador to the US."

Adrian raised his eyebrows and nodded. "Impressive. And you must work for her?"

"I suppose I do, now. She offered me a position yesterday. I'm not really sure what it will entail. Don't tell anyone, but I'm a little nervous about it."

"I'm sure you'll do great."

"I wish I was as confident." He heard her sigh. "My track record has been a little shaky."

"Everyone has a few bad job experiences."

"Not everyone has to explain to the FBI why they thought the Algerian embassy delivers pizza."

Adrian chuckled. "True. Well, my dad used to say, 'as long as anyone didn't die, everything's fine.'"

"Did he ever say anything about how to clean up after three-hundred birds stuck under a tent?"

Now he had to stifle an outright laugh. "Not that I can recall."

They turned into the short, curving driveway in front of the embassy.

"Anyway, thanks for the encouragement," Maggie said as she gathered her things.

Adrian got out to get her door, which she was already opening. "Ma'am," he said, as he helped her out.

"Miss," she corrected, stumbling a bit on the curb. He was glad he had his hand on her arm.

They locked eyes for a brief moment, which he somehow managed to find embarrassing.

His fingers tingled, and he cleared his throat, stepping back. "Again, just text or call when you're ready for a pickup."

"Thanks for the ride," Maggie said, looking away, then back at him.

Adrian watched her go. Definitely unique. Then he shook his head, clearing the thought.

On to the next job, right?

He walked to the driver's side of the car and got in. Adjusting the mirror, he took a deep breath, smelling the lingering scent of fresh cherry blossoms. But now instead of thinking about Karen and feeling sad, he thought of Maggie smiling at him, her head tilted, the lilt of her accent.

Suddenly feeling guilty, he shifted the car into drive and pulled out into traffic.

On to the next job.

* * *

Maggie entered the front door of the embassy with a little more confidence. Talking to Adrian had strangely helped, and this time she also knew which path to take to reach her grandmother's office. She showed herself up the gently curving spiral staircase.

In the second-floor hallway, she greeted Desmond, who gave her more of a sneer than a smile. Great. He obviously doesn't like me being here. Maybe because the ambassador had asked him to help her granddaughter at her new internship? Probably smacked too much of nepotism.

Maggie hoped this didn't mean she'd failed before she'd even started. She wasn't sure exactly what her grandmother would be having her do, but she was sure the ambassador wouldn't keep her in the dark for long. She was right.

"Good morning, Margaret. How did you sleep?" *Mamó* was sitting behind her wide mahogany desk. Each item was neatly in place—stacks of paper carefully arranged, folders organized, pens even in a row. Her grandmother was definitely one for order.

"Okay, I suppose. I'm a little nervous, to be honest." She laced her fingers together as her grandmother rose.

"Not to worry. So you're probably wondering what it is you'll be doing here."

That was an understatement. Maggie nodded.

Her grandmother reached for a small folder on her desk. "Have you heard of the Diplomats Gala? The gala is an annual event, a fundraiser for the diplomatic community to help fund the Embassy Adoption Program. Tickets for a single table start at ten thousand dollars."

Maggie swallowed. "Sounds very important."

"It is, and it's also very helpful. We help thousands of children every year find homes and families. This year our embassy, along with the British, French and Belgian, is in charge of the organization and planning for the gala."

Something in Maggie's mind clicked. French Embassy? That was where Valéry said he worked.

Her grandmother continued. "Plans have already been underway for some time, of course, but there is still plenty of work to be done, including the decorations and other particulars for the night itself. Normally I would have Desmond assist with the project, but I thought since you have some expertise in that area it would be a good fit for you."

Maggie was thinking. "It sounds like a very important project. Are you sure it's something I should be involved with?"

"It's what you think that concerns me. I've noticed in my career that there are two kinds of people. Some jump into life with both feet, and others need just a little push, shall we say."

Maggie wasn't sure if she was being complimented or insulted. "Well, of course, I'd be happy to help—to do what I can."

"Good. I believe you'll be assisting with the choice of decorations and with organizing the music." She pulled a card from under a paper clip attached to the folder. "The gala organizer is a very nice gentleman named Valéry LaBonté. He's attached to the French Embassy." She handed Maggie the card.

As she eyed the familiar-looking fleur-de-lis, her heart skipped and she tried not to seem startled. "Okay. Of course. I'll get in touch with him immediately."

The ambassador smiled. "Good. And report back to me later today with what you'll be doing. I will be out of the office traveling periodically the next few weeks, but Desmond can assist you with other particulars such as budget, procurement procedures, and so forth." She moved to the door. "I don't need to remind you what an important opportunity this is for you. You'll be working with a variety of embassies. It's quite exciting."

"I know, yes. It will be grand. I can't wait to get started," Maggie said, a little over-enthusiastic. "I'll call this"—she pretended to study the card—"*Valéry* immediately."

"See that you do. Good luck, dear." Her grandmother came to give her a rare hug.

Maggie left the office in a swirl of emotions. She was happy, to be sure, that she was going to be part of such an important project, but she was surprised to be working with Valéry. That seemed to be something of a coincidence. I mean, just meeting him a few days ago and now this. A happy accident, she supposed, already starting to plan.

She'd need to talk to Jelly about decoration ideas. Then there was the music—something classy, for sure, and an ice sculpture—*definitely* a swan. But no doves. She made a mental note on that one. This was going to be easier than she thought. Maybe she was cut out for the diplomatic life after all. She'd just needed the right opportunity.

Well, if this wasn't it, nothing was.

She followed Desmond downstairs to a small corner off the reception area and sat at her chair behind a small but official-looking desk. Not as grand as the ambassador's desk, but it was a start.

Desmond smacked the folder down in front of her. "Let me know if you have any questions."

Maggie had a million, but he was gone before she could even open her mouth. She briefly thought about calling Adrian to tell him the good news. The thought made her smile, but he was probably busy with other jobs, and anyway she had a job to do herself now. A political one.

She took the card her grandmother had given her and dialed the number on the bottom, using the embassy phone and her most professional voice. "Valéry, hi, it's Maggie—Margaret. We met at the Red Zone the other day. You won't believe the coincidence..."

Chapter Nine

DINNER AT THE YOUNGER ADAMS HOUSEHOLD was becoming a fairly traditional Saturday night visit for Adrian and Charlie. This was the first time since winter had melted away that they and his brother's family were venturing outside to grill and for the kids to reclaim the swing set. The single cherry tree in Danny and Beth's backyard was just starting to bloom, pink blossoms peeking from the stark brown branches, promising new life as they did without fail every year.

"More coleslaw?" said Beth, offering Adrian a dripping scoop from a green salad bowl.

"Sure, thanks," he said, not wanting to hurt her feelings but knowing it would probably just end up being quietly dumped in the trash.

He loved coming over to his brother's house, but it was well known in the Adams family that Beth's cooking was a recipe for an extra Alka-Seltzer at midnight. But at the same time, it was also what strangely endeared Beth to everyone, although the jokes did fly when she wasn't in earshot. His brother did just that as his lovely wife made her way back inside the house to the kitchen.

"Did I ever tell you about the time Max got a hold of some of Beth's chili?"

Adrian's mouth dropped open. "No way." Max was the Adams family's lovable mutt, half Schnauzer and half stomach. Locks were the norm on the family trash cans.

"Yeah, she had made an extra batch—don't ask me why—and had to throw some away because the freezer was full or something, and Max got into it."

"Ouch," was all Adrian could say as he took a swig of his Dr. Pepper.

"I was up half the night cleaning chili-fied dog diarrhea off the kitchen floor, the hallway floor, everywhere. I swear I could see little flames coming off of it."

"Now *that's* why I don't have a dog," Adrian exclaimed.

"Not yet, maybe, but how long are you going to be able to hold out from the puppy princess?" Danny nodded at Charlie, who was happily playing tag with her two cousins around the backyard swing set.

"As long as it takes. We were going to get one, you know, before Karen died. But now we're just not home enough. Hard enough chasing one puppy around." He jerked a thumb toward Charlie, who seemed to scream gleefully in reply, twirling on a swing.

"So...how's the new job going? Congratulations, by the way."

"Thanks—fine. Actually, I think I like her... I mean it, the job. It should be good. The company is pretty on top of things. They've got—"

"Okay, what do you mean, *her*?"

"I meant *it*—the *job*. The *her* is just the girl—the woman—I'm driving at the moment."

Danny nodded. "Now we're getting somewhere."

"Oh, c'mon, it's not like that. I mean, it's my assignment. I can't be, like, going after a client on the job."

"So you'd like to, huh?"

"Why do you always read into everything?"

Danny shrugged. "I'm a reader. I like books. What does she look like?"

"You're not going to let this go, are you?"

"Nope."

"Fine. Well, she's Irish."

"I don't know what 'Irish' looks like. Does she have green skin?"

"No, she doesn't have green skin, she doesn't River Dance, she doesn't eat Lucky Charms. Her name's Miss MacNally."

"Miss?"

Adrian shrugged. "It's what she prefers." He saw his brother's un-convinced look. "Don't worry. She's normal." He pictured her chatting to the squirrel with the stumpy tail. "Mostly, anyway."

"Mostly?"

"Well, she's not crazy or anything."

Danny let out a sudden burst of laughter.

"What?"

"Sorry. You said 'crazy' and it just popped in my head. You're 'Driving Miss Crazy.'"

"I said she *wasn't* crazy."

"Who's Miss Crazy?" a little voice piped up. Charlie had appeared by Adrian's side munching some potato chips.

"No one's Miss Crazy, Charlie."

"Except your dad's new client," Danny said with a smirk.

Charlie grew wide-eyed and looked up at her dad. "She is?"

Adrian pulled his daughter onto his lap. "No, Charlie, your Uncle Danny is being his usual goofy self. No one's crazy."

"Okay." Charlie seemed to be convinced, hopped off her dad's lap and returned to her cousins at the swing set.

"Sorry, bro," Danny apologized. "So, what does she look like?"

"Miss MacNally?" Adrian waved his hand. "She's fine. At least, this French guy seems to think so."

"What French guy? Her boyfriend?"

"He's nobody." Adrian wished he'd kept his mouth shut. "She met him for lunch yesterday. I drove her back to the Irish embassy afterward. She works there."

"So, good looking?"

"Nah, his eyes are squinty and he wears too much cologne. Not my type at all."

"Nice... you know what I mean."

Adrian hesitated. "Yeah, I guess you could say she's cute."

"Cute?" Danny laughed. "What is this, junior high? She is over sixteen, isn't she?" he said with mock caution.

Adrian rolled his eyes. "Okay, *pretty*. There. I'm driving around a very pretty woman who's not a girl and isn't sixteen and has an Irish accent."

"Oh ho, so now she's *very* pretty. Now we're getting somewhere."

"Can we change the subject?"

"Nope. You like her?"

Adrian knew that he could get some ridicule for his answer, but he also knew that his brother would only be a teasing jerk up to a point.

"Well, yeah, I think I kinda do."

Danny said nothing, letting his brother continue if he wanted.

"I mean, it's fun driving her, for the job and all, but I have to say I like talking with her." He held up his hands. "I mean, you can always use more friends, right?"

Danny smiled. "Sure can. What's her name?"

"Margaret—Maggie. MacNally," he added.

"Good Irish name. I like those Irish accents."

"Tell me about it. She went to college in DC and she's been back in the States awhile, but there's just enough accent left to make it interesting."

Danny raised his eyebrows slightly. "Well, big brother, things may be looking up. New job, new friend of the female persuasion."

"Maybe."

"Hey, Ady, I'm not saying this girl's 'the one' or anything dumb like that, but I'm glad to see you're even thinking about being with a female who isn't Charlie."

Adrian said nothing, then checked his watch. "Speaking of which, better get her home to bed. She has another long play rehearsal tomorrow afternoon. You'd think they were training these kids for a Broadway production, not a second grade play."

His brother yawned, checking his own watch. "Okay. Same time next Saturday?

"Sure, if the schedule works. Not sure if I'll be working."

"Right, your new job." Then he thought. "Hey, why don't you bring Miss Crazy? Our kids would love to meet her."

"Maggie? No way. She's my client, remember? Besides, you'd just make some lame joke about 'always being after me Lucky Charms' or something." He shook his head. "Don't need it."

Danny smiled. "Probably right. But think about it. She sounds like a nice girl. Either way, see you next week?"

"You got it." Adrian gave his little brother a brief hug, then headed to the swings to retrieve Charlie, who protested that it was way too early to leave yet. He then became the "best dad in the universe" when he gave her five more minutes, which he knew she would try to stretch to ten.

What a pixie.

Beth came out to gather her own protesting kids, and for a moment his heart ached for someone to be able to do the same for Charlie. Someone like his new client, with eyes that crinkled at the corners when she smiled at him. *Maybe that's why I'm thinking about her so much. Maybe I'm really that lonely, and it's time. Maybe.*

* * *

By the time Jelly joined Maggie at a table in the back corner of the Red Zone on Sunday afternoon, Maggie had been working on the gala all weekend.

"So let's see this party list of yours," Jelly said.

Maggie handed her friend her clipboard full of notes, brochures, and printed web pages.

Jelly scanned the clean checklist on top, then gave out a low whistle. "You sure you got the budget for this, girl?"

Maggie shifted in her seat. "I know some of those things are expensive, but this *is* a thousand-dollar-a-ticket gala. People will be expecting something special. You know, romantic and out of the ordinary."

"Mmm-hmm. Okay, looks like you got your table decorations, centerpieces. You got music on here?"

Maggie pointed. "I'm having just background music while everyone arrives, but I need a string quartet. You know, like in *Titanic*, where

Kate Winslet and Leonardo DiCaprio danced on the stairwell." She closed her eyes. "Now *that's* romantic."

Jelly snorted. "Romantic? Maggie, that man froze and died at the end of that movie."

Maggie made a face. "You know what I mean." She sighed. "I want this to be perfect, just like that movie."

Jelly raised an eyebrow. "Um, and you do know that ship sank too, right?"

Maggie scowled. "I'm serious, Jelly. If I don't get this right my grandmother will have my head. And maybe some other parts."

"All right, all right. Just remember *perfect* isn't as always as perfect as it seems. Believe me, *good enough* can be a lot less hassle." She saw the line item for the ice sculpture and gave another whistle. "And less expensive. Looks like you've got everything here except—" She stopped. "Oh my word, does this say horse and carriage? You got a horse and carriage for this party?"

"Not yet, but I will." Maggie was busy searching her phone for string quartets on a local talent agency's website. "It's a gala, remember? You don't expect ambassadors to just ride in any old car to a gala, do you?"

"Well maybe you should get your cute new driver to take them. Unless you're afraid some lady ambassador will steal him from you."

"Oh, shush."

"Just sayin'. There might be more than one way to get the abs."

Maggie ignored her. "No, we're staying with the horse and carriage." She pulled another folder from beneath the clipboard and began going over the list of table decorations.

Jelly shook her head. "Okay, but you know horses poop, right? You sure you want something pooping at your party?" She laughed at her own joke. "Get it? You're going to have an actual party pooper at your party."

"Very funny. If you want to be serious then help me choose the tablecloths. I want them to match the curtains at the venue, but I can't find the best color."

"Okay, alright, I don't want you to lose your head. Or other body parts. Let me see."

They spent the next hour going over colors and fabrics from the pages and samples Maggie had found. Jelly did her best to steer her in a more practical direction, but Maggie was determined to make this a gala to remember.

"You sure your grandmother's going to go for all this?" Jelly asked for the tenth time. "I don't quite see her as someone who likes a big party."

"Oh, *Mamó* could use some loosening up. It's probably been too long since she's seen what a real ball should look like."

Jelly stifled a laugh. "I doubt if that woman ever danced in her life. Her legs would probably snap off."

"Oh, you don't know her like I do. I've seen her dance before, in Dublin, when I was a little girl."

"No way."

"Sure, and she was pretty good too." Maggie had seen her now distinguished grandmother twirling and smiling at an Irish *céilí* dance. This was before her grandmother was caught up in politics, when Maggie's grandfather was still alive. He was the life of every party, she remembered, kind of like her mother used to be.

She stopped those thoughts to return to her work. She flicked through a talent brochure "Ooo... What do you think about an 'aerial champagne bartender'?"

Chapter Ten

IT ONLY TOOK A WEEK FOR MAGGIE to get a good glimpse of how busy her new role at the embassy was going to keep her. Desmond was an efficient although surly taskmaster, helping her learn the basics of the embassy routine. She always got the feeling he was watching her with a sneer, but he seemed to do that with everyone, so she chalked it up to his personality.

Her days centered around gala preparations, and she was more determined than ever to do a good job—and impress her family.

She was at Bella Bella, thinking about the centerpieces and helping Jelly go over store inventory on the computer, when a mismatched pair of men entered the shop. One was wearing a shiny, ill-fitting dark suit and carrying what looked like a violin case, and the other younger guy was in worn jeans and a Washington Nationals baseball cap. Both men looked slightly uncomfortable, scanning the displays, as if the women's clothing were about to suddenly come to life and pounce on them.

"You expecting someone?" Jelly asked, motioning at the strangers.

Maggie popped up from her chair. "Are you the gentlemen from the talent agency?"

The man in the suit stuck out his hand. "Yes, ma'am. Smokey Hills Quartet—well, minus two. My name's Walter and this here is Lucius."

The other man nodded a greeting.

Maggie was already excited. And relieved. She was pretty sure the Smokey Hills were near Tanglewood, a venue well known for its classical offerings every summer. This group might be the perfect fit.

She hadn't expected helping to organize a Washington gala would be easy, but it was proving to be even more challenging than she had thought. As overwhelming as it appeared, she was committed to doing well at her assignment, not only to show her grandmother she could, but maybe more importantly to show herself she could finally do something worthwhile and important, and do it right.

The first man cleared his throat. "The, uh, talent agency said you were looking for a quartet?"

"Oh, yes, definitely. I've had an awful time finding one. Most of them seem to be booked for some reason." She hurried to the back of the counter where she kept her clipboard of gala notes.

"Yes, ma'am, wedding season and lots of dances this time of year." He cleared his throat again. "I was actually just heading to do a wedding now, so if we can make it quick I'd be obliged."

Maggie nodded, quickly returning. She didn't want to lose out on booking them. The Smokey Hills Quartet must be sought-after if they were doing a wedding on a Friday afternoon. She felt lucky to find them, especially since no other quartet seemed available. She looked at her scribbled notes. "I assume you have the usual instruments?"

"Yes, ma'am. Four of us on strings."

"That's fine. Excellent," Maggie said. "And you have Saturday the twenty-third available? The gala begins at seven thirty p.m., and we would need you to play from then until approximately"—she checked the schedule—"eight forty-five p.m."

Walter nodded agreeably. "No problem, ma'am. We got that whole day free, 'cept in the morning we might have to do a shivaree for Pete's cousin John." He flashed a knowing glance to his friend. "But only if he makes it to the wedding Friday night." The second man smiled knowingly as Walter leaned in closer to Maggie. "S'got a bit of a drinkin' issue and left Louisa at the altar twice already."

Maggie smiled and nodded, vaguely aware of what a "shivaree" was. It was probably just another local word for a wedding celebration. She knew it was French, so she made a mental note to ask Valéry next time they spoke. "Good, so I'll send you the music. It will be mostly the classics—Schubert and Mozart. Are you familiar with them?"

The man thought. "Well, we don't have nothin' by the first guy, but Mozart I know. He write the Tennessee Waltz, Lucius?"

His companion shook his head. "Naw, that was Pee Wee King. I think Mozart wrote the Kentucky Waltz."

Maggie, although slightly confused, just nodded. "Well, as long as there are at least a few waltzes. So we can see you on the evening of the twenty-third?"

"Yes, ma'am, it's a done deal." Walter stuck out his hand for a shake.

Maggie then had him sign a contract she had ready on her clipboard, pleased and proud to have at least one major task done.

Now, only about a million other details to handle…

* * *

The man behind the counter at Peak Talent Agency was looking at Maggie's list of requirements. "A horse carriage. I see, and would you like it to turn into a pumpkin after the 'ball' is over?"

Maggie looked up from her phone. If that was sarcasm she didn't appreciate it. Who wouldn't want a carriage at a gala? It would be perfect. Just like the ice sculptures she had planned. "Yes, a horse and carriage. Do you have anything like that? I've seen them in some of the parks."

The man smirked. "Those are mostly private businesses, but I can put you in touch with someone who may be able to help." He looked on his computer and wrote down a number on a card and handed it to her.

"Thank you. And now I need someone who makes ice sculptures."

"Ice sculptures?"

"Swans, if you please. And I want the best."

"The best? Well, that would be Azad. He's excellent, but he doesn't speak much English. He's from Azerbaijan. I'm afraid the cousin who usually translates for him is away. Now, we do have a few locals who are fairly good—"

"No, no." Maggie waved her hand. "Azad sounds perfect. If he's the best, he's who I want."

"Very well." He tapped on his computer keyboard as she peered over his shoulder. "Here's his address, and I'm including the details of your needs." He tapped some more. "I've translated them online as best I can." A sheet slid out from a copier on the desk behind him. "The address might be a little difficult to find, though. Would you like me to call you a carriage?"

She narrowed her eyes at him. "Thank you, I'll manage." She gathered her purse and phone from the counter.

"If there's anything else you need, a golden goose, a fairy godmother, just let us know."

Maggie was already heading to the door. Sarcasm. Definitely.

She just smiled. Things were falling into place beautifully for her vision for gala. Nothing was going to go wrong this time. She was sure of it.

* * *

An hour later, she stood at the front door of a slightly dingy restaurant in Columbia Heights, peering through the glass. It had taken more than thirty minutes, three wrong turns, and a dying phone battery to get here after leaving the last Metro, and she still wasn't sure if this was even the right place. The scent of spices and strong coffee wafted out of the front door as a couple sidestepped past her.

She double-checked the address the agency had given her, then the map on her almost-dead phone. Kavaka Kebabs smelled like it might serve Azerbaijani food, although she wasn't really that familiar with what Azerbaijanis ate. She almost wished she'd called Adrian to drive her.

No, you can handle this.

She pulled open the door by its greasy handle. The room was dark but somehow still pleasant. It was empty except for a couple who glanced up from their table, then went back to their quiet conversation in a corner. Swirling balalaika music played from the overhead speakers. As her eyes adjusted to the light, a swarthy man with dark hair and a neatly trimmed goatee approached, wiping his hands on an apron.

Maggie smiled. "I'm here about ice sculptures."

He looked at her blankly, apparently not speaking English.

She tried again. "I'm looking for Azad?"

"Azad!" he shouted, along with some other words she didn't understand, then returned to his place behind the bar. A taller and thinner version of the man appeared through the swinging kitchen doors.

"You make ice sculptures?" she prompted.

"Eyes shrulplure?" he said, obviously not understanding. Then he nodded as comprehension sank in. "Yays, yays," he said, followed by something obviously in Azerbaijani.

Maggie had planned ahead for the language issue. She pulled out her phone, ignoring the flashing red two-percent-battery warning, and thumbed through the screen until she found her translation app which she'd already set to the Azeri language.

"Okay, yes, um…" She tapped in "ice sculpture," then looked up and carefully said, "*Booz hay-kel.*"

Azad squinted at her for a moment, then nodded, followed by more Azerbaijani.

Maggie had no idea what he was telling her. "Sorry, that's the extent of my Azeri, I'm afraid." She passed over the sheet she had gotten from the agency with the details of the event.

Azad read it and nodded again, pointing at the details. "Then?" he asked.

She smiled, the universal communication tool. "Yes, please."

Fortunately, this time he seemed to understand. He marked down the information in a black notebook he pulled from his apron. The sheet included his price range, so she was hoping he wouldn't vary from that, but she'd deal with that later.

Azad looked up. "What make?"

Maggie twisted the paper from the agency towards her. She saw the date, time, and place, but now realized Mr. Sarcasm had neglected to put down that she wanted swans. Back to the phone app, she stared down at a black screen. Her phone was dead.

She'd seen the "swan" translated on the computer screen at the agency. What was the word again? She knew it was short and began with a Q. She wrinkled her nose. Okay, next option. She took a pen from her purse, turned the paper over, and began sketching as best she could. Two swans facing each other, wings raised majestically. The feet looked more like claws and she forgot to curve the necks, but she couldn't erase with a pen.

His brow furrowed in thought. He wasn't getting it. "Cue?" she said, hoping her slim memory of the word would help make the connection.

He looked up at that. "*Coo-chay?*" he questioned.

"*Coo-chay?*" Maggie repeated. Hmm. She supposed that could be it. She'd better make sure. She made the swooping shape of a swan's neck with her arm, then flapped her arms. She remembered the swans at the pond at her grandparents' country house and the way the birds had chased her when she was a child, so she added some snapping motions with her hand. "*Coo-chay?*" she said, hoping he would finally get it.

Azad nodded, seeming to understand. "Yays, yays. *Coo-chay.*" He held up two fingers.

"That's right. A pair of swans. And the price?" Maggie hoped she wouldn't have to twist herself into a dollar sign for this bit.

"Prize?" Azad said. "Yays, yays, umm…" He thought for a moment and then wrote a number down on the paper. "Okay?"

Maggie saw the number with a dollar sign in front and knew he had understood. It was in her price range, so she nodded. "Yes."

Azad nodded back, then turned to his partner and rattled off something else she couldn't understand punctuated with "*coo-chay*" at the end. He made another note in his book, and the other man shrugged, returning to cleaning the bar.

"*Tank you,*" Azad said with a bow.

"No, thank *you*." Maggie smiled at him, but was just as pleased with herself.

Another task ticked off her list. This was going to be the best gala this city had ever seen.

Chapter Eleven

TWO WEEKS OF GALA PREPARATION at the embassy had left little time for Maggie to do much real work at Bella Bella. She felt bad for Jelly, but she was sure her friend realized how important this opportunity was to her, and she would make it up to Jelly somehow. Maybe once this gala was over, they'd go out on the town. Maybe she and Valéry could convince Jelly and Gerard to finally step out together.

She and Valéry had certainly been spending a lot of lunch and dinner time together, bouncing from one fancy restaurant to the next. It was fun—Valéry seemed to know every waiter in the city—but it was getting a little tiring. Sometimes she wished they'd just sit on a park bench somewhere and split a hot dog, but she knew he'd never go for that. Besides, which wine goes with hot dogs?

Maggie clutched her small purse and eagerly stepped out of the side door that led down from her and Jelly's apartment. Adrian was to pick her up again this morning. Every day, she found herself looking forward to the drive as one of the best parts of her day.

There was something easy and natural about him, as if they had been life-long friends who were just now catching up. With Valéry, it did seem like she always had to be on her best behavior. It was nice to just be able to relax with Adrian and not worry about whether she was using her salad fork for her main course, or calling Valéry's lawyer friend an "avocado" in mangled French.

And there was his car, right on time. Early, in fact. She tossed the squirrels a quick handful of peanuts and walked towards the waiting car, noticing a small face smiling out the window in the back seat where Maggie usually sat.

Adrian rushed around the car to the curb. "Sorry, Maggie, but is it okay if we have an extra passenger this morning? Charlie was running a fever, and I really want to keep an eye on her. Normally, I would never do this, but I couldn't reach a sitter and—"

Maggie waved her hand. "No, no it's fine. I'd be happy to share a ride with Miss Charlie. So, do I still sit in the back?"

"Maybe you should sit up front with me? I don't want you to catch her germs. Again, I'm sorry."

"Think nothing of it."

Adrian reached for the door for her, but first she tapped on the back window where Charlie was plainly watching. The little girl waved and rolled the automatic window down.

"Hello, Charlie." Maggie leaned forward, smiling. "My name's Maggie. Is it okay if I ride with you today?"

"Sure." Charlie smiled back. "Dad told me about you. You're pretty."

"Well, thank you, as are you. Mind if I take the front seat?"

"Sure. I'm supposed to be sick, so don't touch me."

"Okay, I'll be careful," Maggie said solemnly. After she got in the car, Adrian closed the door and jogged around the front to the driver's door.

"Dad says I should call you Miss MacNally."

Adrian did his usual mirror check and pulled into the traffic.

"Why don't we make it Miss Maggie instead?" Maggie said.

"Hi, Miss Maggie."

Maggie turned in her seat. "Hi, Charlie. I'm sorry you're sick today."

Charlie shrugged her little shoulders. "S'okay. I get to miss school and be with Dad."

"Well, that sounds like fun."

"Are you Miss Crazy?"

Adrian almost swerved into the opposite lane. "Charlie!"

Maggie sat silent, eyes narrowed.

"But Uncle Danny said you were driving Miss Crazy," Charlie continued.

Adrian's voice was strained. "I'm sorry, Maggie. It was just a joke. I mean, it wasn't a *joke*. My brother was trying to *make* a joke."

"I understand," Maggie said quietly. Miss Crazy? Is that what he thinks of me?

"Really, Maggie, it's just a misunderstanding. I'm sorry. Charlie, no more Miss Crazy talk, okay?"

Charlie seemed to sense the tension in the car. "Okay."

Adrian made a right turn onto the now-familiar route to the Irish Embassy. "Charlie, did you drink your orange juice?" He was obviously changing the subject.

"Yes, Dad, I drank my orange juice and I wiped my nose and I didn't use my sleeve this time."

"Okay, just checking."

Maggie's mood softened. Regardless of his "crazy" comment, she could feel the warmth of the relationship Adrian obviously had with his daughter. Charlie must miss her mother, though.

"Are you a princess?" Charlie blurted.

"What, dear?" Maggie said, not understanding.

"You sound like Merida. She's a Disney Princess."

Adrian glanced at Maggie. "It's your accent," he explained. "Charlie, Miss Maggie comes from Ireland, so she just sounds a little different than us."

"Well, I think she sounds like a princess."

"Oh, Charlie," Maggie said, "that's about the sweetest thing I've—"

"You don't look like her, though. She has red hair, and it's long and curly." Charlie wiped her nose with her sleeve and returned to playing with her iPod. "But I like yours better."

"Well, that's even sweeter, then. Thank you, Charlie."

"Where's Rireland?"

Adrian smiled. "Ireland is near Great Britain, in Europe, sweets. It's also near Scotland, where Merida comes from."

"Cool. So do they talk the same as us there?"

Maggie fielded that one. "Pretty much. We do have some different phrases, though. Like, different ways of saying things. Like that there"—she pointed to a food delivery truck parked on the side of the road—"we'd call a lorry in Ireland. Or if we frighten someone, like if I jumped out from behind a tree and scared you?" She pretended she was lunging at Charlie with her fingers out. "We'd say 'you put the heart crossways in me.'"

"'You put the heart crossways in me.'" Charlie repeated the phrase as if she were memorizing it. "Cool." She seemed satisfied with that information, but then studied Maggie's face, her head cocked to the side. "My mom's dead now," she said matter-of-factly. "We're sure she's in heaven, though."

"Charlie!" Adrian looked surprised—and embarrassed.

"Oh, sweetie." Maggie wasn't really sure what to say. "I'm so sorry." She turned in her seat so she could look at Charlie. "That must be so hard. I lost my grandfather a few years ago."

Charlie's eyes grew wide. "Really? That's scary. Where did you lose him? I lost my dad in Target once. I had to have a fat lady named Doris help me find him." She leaned forward and whispered loudly, "She had three chins and smelled like cats."

Maggie was struggling to keep from bursting out laughing. "Really?"

"Yup. Then I think she got mad at me because I tooted."

"Charlie..." Adrian said in warning.

"Grandpa says 'better out than in,' Dad."

"Well," Maggie said in as serious a tone as she could manufacture, "that's not very ladylike, is it, Charlie? I mean, what would the boys at your school think?"

Charlie wrinkled her nose. "Boys suck. I like puppies and kitties—puppies better. Mrs. Dewmeyer has a new puppy and she brought it to school. It peed on the carpet by the reading chair."

Adrian sighed. "Okay, Charlie, I think that's enough about tooting, peeing, sucking, and so on."

"It's life, Dad, that's what you always say. Everybody poops, everybody pees, everybody—"

"Charlie," Adrian interrupted. "Tell Miss Maggie about your play."

Charlie wrinkled her nose in thought, then brightened. "Oh, yeah! We're doing *Snow White* and I get to be a squirrel and Ricky Comdon has to be the prince and Marisha Sooners is Snow White and he has to kiss her!" She started giggling. "He has to kiss her on her face in front of the whole school!" She made exaggerated kissing sounds—*moom moommwahm mwah*—and giggled some more.

Maggie laughed. "That sounds like a lot of fun to me. When is your play?"

"Next month, after school." Charlie obviously had an idea. "Can you come? Pleeeeease?"

"Miss Maggie is going to be pretty busy," Adrian said, giving Maggie an apologetic glance.

"Please!" Charlie insisted again.

"Well, I'd love to, but we'll see," Maggie said.

Charlie seemed to take that as a yes. "Good. You can see how bad Marisha is as Snow White. She tries to sound like you, like 'Ooh, the prince!' and stuff, but she's *terrible.*"

"Okay, Charlie, I think you've dominated the airwaves enough for a while."

"Hey, Dad, maybe Miss Maggie can help me practice my part." Her head turned toward Maggie again. "None of the boys wanted to be dwarfs, so all of the dwarfs are girls. The boys only wanted to be trees and stuff."

"We'll see, Charlie," Adrian said this time.

"Grown-ups always say we'll see and then most of the time I don't get to see it."

Maggie was thoroughly enjoying the conversation.

Charlie continued, "Dad plays the prince when we practice. He's pretty good. You can play the Snow White part, but don't forget, there's kissing."

The car swerved sideways for a second time, jostling them briefly all to the side.

"Charlie, I—" Adrian shook his head. He apparently couldn't believe what was coming out of his daughter's mouth.

Maggie was now laughing out loud. "That's quite all right. You know, Charlie, I have some experience playing a princess."

"You do?" Charlie's eyes grew wide.

"Mmm-hmm. I played Cinderella at my primary school."

"Cool. Did you have to kiss a boy? Ricky Comdon has buck teeth."

"As a matter of fact, I did. His name was Lionel. I don't remember his last name, but he was very handsome. All of the girls thought he was the most handsome boy in the class."

"And you *kissed* him? On his mouth? Eww." She pulled the corners of her mouth down in disgust.

"Well," Maggie said, "not on the mouth, more like on the cheek. But it was my first kiss."

"Cool. Dad, what was your first kiss?"

Adrian appeared caught off guard. "My what? Oh, um… oh, I don't really remember."

"Oh, come on," Maggie said, "everyone remembers the first time they tried to 'lob the gob' on someone."

"Lob the gob?"

Maggie laughed. "Sorry. Irish expression. Kind of means 'steal a kiss.' And you haven't answered the question."

"Yeah, Dad, don't be lame. Miss Maggie said hers."

"Okay, alright, let me think."

"You have to think about your first kiss?" Maggie teased.

"Just hang on. Remember, I'm driving here." He made another turn. "Okay, so if you must know, it was Patty Chardeau in kindergarten."

"Oh my, you were a fast mover."

"Right, I was a fast mover. But if you must know, Patty kissed *me*."

"Where?"

"On the playground."

"No, I mean where on your *face*."

"Smack on the jaw, ladies."

Charlie's eyes grew wide. "Ooh, Dad. Go, Dad. Yay Dad!" She began making dance moves in her booster seat.

"Hey, I thought you were sick, little girl."

"Not sick enough for *luvvvvv*, Dad."

"Okay, that's enough of that."

Both Charlie and Maggie were now giggling together.

"And fortunately, thank goodness, here we are." He pulled the car into the turnout at the embassy and stopped at the steps in front of the iron doors.

"Can I ride with Miss Maggie tomorrow? I think I'm going to be sick then too."

"No, you little faker. Tomorrow you'll probably be back at school. I have a feeling this fever is a one-day thing." Adrian got out to get the door for Maggie.

Maggie turned in her seat. "It was very nice to meet you, Charlie. I hope I see you again sometime soon."

Charlie grinned. "Me too."

Maggie got out, turned to give a wave to Charlie, who waved back, then she headed up the steps of the embassy. She couldn't help but chuckle. That had been the most fun she'd had in a long time.

* * *

"I really like her, Dad," Charlie said as soon as Adrian was back inside the car.

"I like her too," he answered without thinking.

Charlie leaned forward. "Like, you *like* like her, or just *like* her?"

Adrian wished he'd kept his mouth shut. "We're not having this conversation."

" 'Cause if you *like* like her that means you have to marry her. That's what Uncle Danny says."

"Uncle Danny can… Uncle Danny is sorely mistaken."

"I guess you'll just have to find that Patty girl and marry her, then."

Adrian found himself actually wondering about Patty Chardeau from kindergarten for a moment. That seemed a little desperate, he realized.

But something else tugged at his thoughts, something he'd been unwilling to entertain until now. Something he hadn't considered until he'd seen Maggie and Charlie together, laughing, teasing. He hadn't seen Charlie react like that with a woman in forever.

The familiar flash of nervous sweat crossed his neck again.

What if Uncle Danny was right?

Chapter Twelve

"BETTER HURRY UP, GIRL," Jelly called up the stairs of Bella Bella to their shared apartment. "That man will be here any minute."

"Coming." Maggie headed down the stairs in a flurry, wearing a new blouse, black capris, and a flowery scarf. "Too much?" she asked her friend.

Jelly looked her over. "Just right."

"Are you sure?" Maggie checked her makeup in the mirror in the back room, then tried to straighten a wisp of her always-unruly hair.

"Plenty good for him."

Maggie caught something in her friend's tone. It reminded her of Adrian's reaction whenever he drove her to meet Valéry. "You don't like him?"

Jelly paused. "No, no, he's fine. Now, you won't be out too late tonight, will you, dear?" she asked in mock worry.

"You know this is only lunch."

"Mmm-hmm, but he's taken you to lunch before. How many times is it now?"

"I'm not keeping count." *Twelve?* Valéry was very attentive.

"Well, remember, lunch can lead to dinner and dinner to *ooh-la-la*." Jelly wagged her finger.

Maggie tossed her head. "We'll see."

"Well, just be careful around Mr. French. I get the impression he's a fast mover. If you know what I mean."

Maggie thought of her conversation with Adrian about his first kiss. "I do, and I don't agree. Valéry is a gentleman. He always has been." That much was true. "Did I tell you he's taking me to La Flamme de la Picardie today? I've always wanted to go there. They're supposed to have the best *escargots à la bourguignonne*."

Jelly made a face. "Snails taste like buttery little pencil erasers. Noooo, *thank* you."

"Well, I'm looking forward to it." Maggie checked her watch for the fifth time in the last three minutes. "I'm not sure when I'll be back. I'm going to the embassy this afternoon"

"No problem." Jelly began organizing a rack of blouses. "Missed seeing that cute driver of yours yesterday."

Maggie looked up. "I met his little girl." She leaned against the doorframe, fidgeting with her hands behind her back. "His wife died. I haven't asked him directly, but I think it was cancer or something."

"Oh, dear. That's so sad, girl."

"He's pretty protective of Charlie."

"You met his son too?"

"Oh, sorry, Charlie is short for Charlotte. She thought I was a princess."

"Mmm, well, so might you be someday, you keep hobnobbing with all those diplomats like you've been. Just remember us peasants when you're saying hi to all the queens and kings at your gala."

"Oh, Jelly, stop your teasing. I'll always be your old college roommate." She raised her chin and stared into the distance. "No matter how important and influential I become," she added airily.

"Well, my advice is maybe a little more like that little girl and less like her princess. Maybe spend more time with her cute dad before you get too solid with Mr. French." She arched her eyebrows, waiting for a reaction from Maggie.

Maggie frowned. "Why do you keep calling him cute?"

Jelly laughed. "'Cause he *is*, girl. And I see you looking at him when he's walking around the car."

"I do no such thing. Wait, are you spying on me?"

"I prefer to call it snooping, and it doesn't change the fact that you were checking him out."

"Well, of course. He's an attractive man. You know how I appreciate beauty."

"'Beauty'?" Jelly laughed. "Girl, beauty is for flowers. That man is *hot*."

"Jelly, why are you trying to complicate my life?" Maggie turned and looked both ways out the front door to see if she could see Valéry's car coming.

Jelly stopped her sorting and came to the door. "I'm not trying to complicate—I'm trying to facilitate. Hey." She touched Maggie's shoulder. "I'm just saying sometimes the things you really might need are right in front of you. So don't throw away all of your options to chase after some guy with a fancy accent. Just because he sounds like a dream guy doesn't make him one."

"I thought Americans were supposed to chase their dreams."

Jelly waved her hand in dismissal. "That's what all those Disney movies have done to us. Reality can be a little different. But maybe more exciting?"

"Well, maybe just let me chase my dream a little before I have to come back down to earth."

Jelly nodded. "Sure thing. I'll be here waiting when you get back. The bobbin on the Juki machine is rattling again. Guess I'll finally need to get a new one."

Maggie suddenly realized something. "Jelly, I need to apologize for not being here as much. Planning the gala is running me ragged."

Jelly waved her hand. "I know, I know, don't you worry. I did fine before you got here. It was just all the drinking I had to do to get through a day. I'll need to remember where I stashed that whiskey bottle."

Maggie slapped her friend on the arm. "Oh, stop."

Jelly cleared her throat. "Um, there is something—a favor, I guess, I'd like to ask."

Maggie tilted her head. "Sure. Anything."

"Well, seeing as how you're going to be at a schmancy ball among DC's finest, I was wondering if maybe you'd let me design a dress for you."

"For me?" Maggie touched her heart in surprise. "Jelly, that's a terrific idea. Everyone will see it. Of course I'll do it." She gave her friend a tight hug.

"Well, thanks. I'll show you what I'm thinking later, when you get a chance."

A car pulled to the front of the shop. A now-familiar stylish black BMW with diplomatic plates. For a moment, she thought it was Adrian in the front seat, and her heart jumped. But it was Valéry's driver, with him in the back.

"He's here." She took a last look in the mirror and headed for the front door.

The driver was already out of the car and opening the rear door. Valéry, still in his seat, was looking at his phone.

"You go have fun with your abs man. I'll be here when you get back," Jelly called out.

"Oh, I will," Maggie said sarcastically as she opened the shop door to go out. "I'll see you later this afternoon." She gave her friend a quick wave and was gone.

* * *

Even after all these weeks, she still wasn't used to being chauffeured around town like some dignitary. It just seemed a little pretentious somehow. Valéry sat beside her, pointing out various local landmarks on the way. It didn't matter that she already knew most of them from going to college here and previous trips to the downtown area. Valéry always acted as if he were her guide. So what if it could be a trifle irritating. He was only trying to be helpful.

That was Valéry. Always helpful. He had a wealth of suggestions about managing all the gala details too, particularly when it came to the budget. She really didn't know what she would have done without him.

His driver stopped at the entrance to the restaurant, silently exited the car, and came around to Maggie's side. As he held the door of the BMW for her, she gave a nod of thanks, which he returned silently. His silence made her uncomfortable, as she was so used to the banter she and Adrian shared.

Valéry let himself out and joined her, leading her by the arm under a striped burgundy awning with bright brass supports.

La Flamme de la Picardie was a fairly new restaurant to downtown DC area, an area that took its dining very seriously. If you couldn't find it here, it probably didn't exist—Malaysian, Afghan, Laotian—the American capital had it all. Fine dining was a benefit of living in DC, one she'd been enjoying often with Valéry.

The waiter, who was already waiting for them, showed them up a set of stairs carpeted in red to the second floor where they were led to a two-person table near a window. The room was bright and airy, with gentle new age jazz playing somewhere in the background. The tinkle of glasses, the occasional titter of laughter—all indicated that this was a place of culture and discrimination. Aside from the Corinthian columns of some government building visible across the street, you could almost imagine you were in Paris.

Paris. How many times Valéry must have visited there, probably dining on the Rue de Rivoli, drinking French coffee, sealing diplomatic deals over sidewalk lunches in Belleville. Even though Paris wasn't that far from Ireland she'd never been. Her parents, though, had been there, of course. So had her grandmother. Maybe she'd get to go there sometime soon after all.

"So, what do you think?" he asked, straightening his napkin.

"Oh, it's fabulous."

"Sometimes you have to wait weeks for a table." He gave a Gallic shrug as if to indicate that he had some pull with the management. "But we deserve the best, no?" He motioned to a waiter and asked him a question in French.

Maggie caught the word *vin* and assumed he was asking for the wine list. She turned out to be correct when the waiter returned with a list in his hand.

Valéry perused it, pursing his lips in thought. "I usually like the Sauvignon Blanc with lunch, especially with *crevettes*—it is exquisite. How does that sound?" He handed the menu back to the waiter, who waited.

Maggie realized he was talking to her. "Oh, it sounds... exquisite." If she could have kicked herself, she would have. *Exquisite?* He had just said exquisite. She sounded like a parrot.

Valéry indicated to the waiter the wine he wanted, then snapped the list closed, "*Les escargots à la bourguignonne aussi. Pour deux.* "After the waiter hurried he off, he explained. "Oh, I am sorry. I took the liberty of ordering escargots for two. The snails, that is. I hope that is satisfactory?"

Maggie's French was rusty, but not that rusty. Of course he was just being helpful again. "Oh, yes, of course. I've heard great things about the snails—the *escargot.* I usually don't have them at lunch, though, so this will be a treat."

The waiter arrived with the wine, uncorked it, and deftly poured it into each of their glasses. Leaving the bottle at the table, he disappeared once more.

Valéry raised his glass. "To you, *chérie.* May your plans for the gala be as successful as you are beautiful." He took a long drink.

"Oh my. Thank you. I've never been toasted— I mean..." She raised her own glass. "*Merci.*" She took a sip of the wine and had to resist spewing it across the table. It tasted like vinegar that had been soaking in an old shoe under a chicken coop. She finally managed to swallow the vile stuff, all the while trying to maintain a smile. "Wow," she managed, clearing her throat. "So good it takes your breath away."

Valéry seemed pleased. "Yes, it is from a vintner near my family home. They have grown the same grapes for hundreds of years."

They must have used some of those hundred-year-old grapes for what she'd just choked down.

"Someday maybe I will show you my home city," Valéry continued. "It is beautiful. In the summer the grapes fill the air with the sweet scent of new wine. In the winter the snow fills the rolling fields like clouds." He waved a hand. "But I am only talking about me. I want to know more about you." He took another sip from his wine. "We have focused so on the gala, but I still feel as if I don't know you completely. Before this, what is it that occupied you here? What brought Maggie MacNally to this city of Washington, DC, to the American capital?"

"Mostly a plane," Maggie said with a small laugh, then cleared her throat. She realized he'd never really asked about her past in any previous conversation. "No, really, well… obviously this is one of the most powerful cities on earth. I mean, just think how many important decisions happen just on one day here."

"Indeed. I might say I have been privy to many of these myself. I consider it a privilege to be able to be some small part of it." He grinned. "But you know, this, no? Your grandmother, the ambassador, she is also very successful in her work."

"Oh, yes. I'm very fortunate to be a part of her team."

"And the plans for the gala are still coming along well?"

"I believe so. How could it not be with you as the chairman?"

He raised his glass again. "You are too kind. But I must say I do enjoy the small role I get to play at each year's event." He took another sip of his wine.

Maggie wondered how he kept from gagging.

He continued, "I'm pleased that you are doing so well in your new job. The gala is a very important step for you."

"Oh, I know. I'm taking it very seriously. I'm still a little worried about the budget, though. Are you sure I'm not spending too much?"

He gave a dismissive wave of his hand. "Do not worry. The event is always very successful. Money is never a problem. In fact, I find that the more grandiose the gala is, the more successful."

"Well, I am keeping within the budget Desmond gave."

Valéry shook his head. "I have worked with Desmond before. I find his budgets are just a guideline. And you are a very creative woman. I think you should think about how much this could do for your career."

"Well, you're the expert, certainly. I did have this idea for a horse and carriage to take passengers on a short sightseeing loop around the venue. I was reconsidering, though."

"But why?" Valéry smiled. "I don't believe that's ever been done before. It would be most impressive."

Maggie grimaced. "It would also be most expensive. I'm worried about the cost now that I have the quote. Perhaps I should talk to my grandmother"

Valéry's mouth pinched. "No need. I am the chairman. You will learn as you go that where donations are concerned, the money will come." He looked into her eyes, then took one of her hands in his, his smile returning. "Trust me."

Maggie felt uneasy, as if she were somehow breaking a rule. But surely Valéry knew what he was talking about if he had done it before. Besides, she was doing something right with her life for once, and it wasn't ordering Turkish pizza or calling someone a chicken anus. "Well, if the gala *is* a success, it will certainly be due to you."

"Ah, you are too kind. More wine?" he gestured to the bottle.

"Oh, no! I mean, I still have some here in my glass, see?" She raised it to show him, then pretended to take a sip. It even smelled bad.

Lunch continued—soft violin music in the background, pleasant but not very deep conversation. After the waiter took away their dishes, Valéry rose, indicating lunch was over, and took a last sip of wine. Maggie got up as well, and he took her hand, leading her through some curtains to the small veranda that overlooked the street. Green ferns and flowers spilled over clay pots on the railing, scenting the air. The spring air was chilly, too cold really for the plants to survive, so she assumed they brought the pots in every night. She could see the spike of the Washington monument in the distance, reminding her of the history and importance of this city.

Which she was a part of now, if just a tiny one.

"*Ma chère,*" Valéry said, moving closer to her. "I must make a confession. I have not been entirely honest with you."

"Oh?" What was he talking about?

"Yes, when I first met you at the coffee shop, I thought I had only met a very attractive young woman."

Very attractive? Her heart thumped, not so much from attraction but nervousness. He moved even closer, and her nose tickled from his cologne. She had a sudden fear she was going to sneeze in his face.

"But now, seeing you work, and how well you are doing, I know you are destined for something more than just beauty."

"Really," she said, then looked down, blushing. Maybe Jelly was wrong and this was her dream guy after all.

He raised her chin with his right hand, cocking his head as he looked in her eyes.

"Yes," he said softly, his face moving closer.

Was he going to kiss her? Did she want him to? After five lunches she'd been wondering when he might try...

For some reason she couldn't close her eyes. A nearby car horn blared twice. They separated, the moment ruined. Or was she relieved?

"Sorry," a familiar voice called up through the window from a car below. "Wasn't sure if that was you." Adrian waved. "Hey, Valerie."

"Va-*lay*-rie," Maggie corrected him automatically. "What are you doing here?"

"I'm here for your pickup," he said to Maggie.

"Pickup?" she said, as she quickly untangled herself from Valéry.

"Yes, one thirty. I believe that's what you said. One thirty outside of the Flaming Pickle."

"La Flamme de la Picardie," she corrected him again. "And I texted you earlier that I would not be needing your services today."

Adrian checked his phone, then shrugged, looking sheepish. "So you did. My bad. Please, carry on as if I weren't here."

"I wish you were not," Valéry muttered.

"Sorry?"

"Please, yes, you may go now. Immediately." Valéry frowned down at him. "As you heard, Miss MacNally has no need of your services now."

Adrian nodded and waved. "Got it."

The engine started.

Maggie turned back to Valéry, whose eyes were narrowed. "He's really harmless. I—"

"Perhaps I should speak to the ambassador about this driver of yours? He seems rather... incompetent."

"So, seven thirty tomorrow morning, right?" Adrian called out, interrupting again.

"Please, Adrian," Maggie said, "can we discuss this later?" She didn't want him to get in trouble. It wasn't just that he was her driver. In the last weeks, he'd become more like a friend, and she didn't want him to jeopardize his job like this.

Adrian waved. "Seven thirty it is."

Valéry smiled as he pulled away, although he was obviously not amused. "These American *boys*, huh? They like to play games. Someone should inform the service he works for, no?"

Maggie forced a smile. "No need. I'm sure he was just trying to help. So...can you drop me at the embassy?"

"Of course. And I must say that I haven't had a more pleasant lunch in a long time." He bent to kiss her cheek.

Maggie felt his lips brush her skin, dry and scratchy like sandpaper. "Me either." Because what else could she say?

At least Valéry was a perfect gentleman, something she hadn't experienced in a long time. And handsome; that certainly helped. She should he glad he seemed interested, but she was almost relieved that kiss hadn't happened. Well, at any rate she was finally experiencing a real life with real opportunities. She even believed she deserved it. *Finally.*

Things were going well in spite of Adrian's attempt at—whatever he was attempting. She frowned, then felt her face almost reluctantly soften into a small smile. *Flaming Pickle.*

Chapter Thirteen

AT SEVEN THIRTY THE NEXT MORNING, as Adrian waited outside Bella Bella, he had the feeling Maggie might be miffed about his antics yesterday. But he couldn't help himself. There was still something about that French guy that had his jerk-meter going off the scale. When she mentioned she was having lunch with Valéry again, he'd decided it wouldn't hurt to be there at the restaurant in case she needed an escape route. Well, it seemed like a good idea at the time.

Not so much now. Maggie said only a short good morning to him, and she immediately got in the back seat without waiting for him to open the door. A bad sign, considering she'd taken to riding in front with him most days.

Fortunately, Adrian had brought along reinforcements.

"Hi, Miss Maggie!" Charlie piped in her little voice from her booster seat next to Maggie.

"Charlie! I thought you would be in school already."

"The teachers have some thing they do this morning, so we get to go in late."

"Well, I'm glad I get to see you again."

Adrian slid behind the wheel. "Maggie, I didn't get a chance to say… to apologize for yesterday."

"I understand," Maggie said, cutting him off. She turned to Charlie. "Have you been practicing your Irish?" Charlie had wanted to know more about "Rireland," so Adrian had let Maggie teach him a few more phrases to share with his daughter.

"Mmm-hmm. Yesterday Dad dropped the sugar bowl and broke it, and sugar went all over the floor, so I said, 'that's a fret!' I don't think he got it, though." She whispered to Maggie, "He didn't think it was funny."

"Oh, there's a lot of that going around."

Adrian tried to catch her expression in the rearview mirror. He wasn't sure if she meant him or Valéry.

"Miss Maggie, can you help me practice my play? Remember, it's Snow White and I'm a squirrel."

"Maggie likes squirrels," Adrian offered.

Their eyes met in the mirror.

Charlie continued. "Well, I really wanted to be a dwarf, you know, but a squirrel's okay because I get to wear a tail, but then I also have to be with Randy Melcorn. He's the tree."

"Hmm. And you don't care for Mr. Randy Melcorn?"

Adrian didn't need to see in the back. He could picture Charlie's horrified face.

"No way! He throws rocks at girls at recess and he says 'crap' too."

"Sounds awful," Maggie said. "In my experience, you should always stay away from mean boys. Of course, sometimes, the girl is just in between the boy and some other boy he doesn't like."

Adrian was too busy watching traffic this time to catch if she was directing that at him. He slowed the car. There was new construction ahead stopping traffic and he'd probably have to detour a few blocks out of his way to get around to the embassy. "Crap," he muttered under his breath.

"Crap, Dad!" Charlie said brightly. "Crap, crap, crap!"

"Charlie!"

"Dad doesn't like it when I say crap."

Maggie gave a little snort of laughter that she tried to disguise with a cough.

Charlie giggled. "Sorry, Dad." But she kept laughing.

"Charlie, you know that's not polite," Adrian said sternly. "I don't want to hear it again."

"Okay," she said softly, although Adrian could see Maggie in the mirror winking at her, which appeared to give Charlie an idea. "Dad, can Miss Maggie help me with my part after play practice today?"

"Oh, sweetie, I don't think that's an appropriate thing to ask Miss Maggie." He had gotten so used to interacting with Maggie almost as a friend that he'd forgotten she was his client.

"No, actually, that would work out well for me," Maggie said. "I'd be happy to practice with you, Charlie."

Adrian was surprised, but she *was* still the boss, and if she wanted to help… "Okay, if you're really sure, I could pick you up at four at the embassy, which should give us just enough time to get Charlie after practice at four thirty."

"That's just fine. If you like, we could practice at the Red Zone."

"Okay, if you're really sure."

"All right," Charlie said, beaming. "It's a date."

* * *

The three of them were gathered around a table at the coffee shop, one girl sipping her Irish tea and the other an Italian cream soda that the owner, Gerard, had whipped up for her, and which she now pronounced as her favorite drink in the world.

Adrian decided on a simple black coffee and took his seat next to Charlie, who was already taking over the conversation.

"Okay, here's my part," she said, instructing Maggie. "I'm supposed to tell the prince where to find Snow White. Okay, Dad, you're the prince."

Adrian looked up, surprised. "What? Me?"

Charlie's head flopped back in impatience. "Yes, Dad, we need you for the boy parts."

"Boy parts?"

"Yes," Maggie contributed slyly. "I don't think you're ready for the man parts yet."

"Good one," Adrian admitted, then took the script Charlie handed him. He shuffled through the pages, then found his line.

"So, I start here where you come in?"

"Yeah, I'm Swishy the Squirrel."

Adrian chuckled. "Of course you are."

Charlie cocked her head, annoyed. "C'mon, Dad, this is serious. You want me to get to college, don't you?"

Maggie covered a laugh with her hand. "Yes, please, Dad, let's be serious."

Adrian held up his hands in submission. "Okay, okay. What's my line here?"

Charlie pointed at a spot on his paper. "You start here where it says 'I am a noble prince.'"

"Got it. Okay, 'I am a noble prince, come looking for—'"

Charlie shook her head. "No, Dad, c'mon. Do it like you do at home, with the voice."

Adrian shot a glance around the room. "Charlie, I don't think this is the right place—"

"Miss Maggie will do her voice, won't you, Maggie?"

"Me? Sure, of course."

"No fair," Adrian said. "She already sounds like a princess." He glanced at Maggie. "I mean, she already has the accent and everything."

Charlie rolled her eyes. "Don't be such a chicken, Dad."

Adrian relented. "Fine. Okay. Fine. Let's see…"

"'I am a noble prince,'" Charlie said helpfully.

"Don't rush me. Maggie was Cinderella in school. I'm just an amateur." He found his place. "Okay, 'I am a noble prince, come looking for fair Snow White.'"

"'Snow White? She ain't here,'" Charlie said in her best squeaky squirrel voice.

Adrian pointed at his script. "C'mon, it doesn't say 'ain't.'"

"I'm improvising, Dad. Ms. Marple says all great actors need to know how to improvise."

"Well, let's just stick to the script, okay?"

Charlie rolled her eyes. "You're squilching my creative juices, Dad."

Maggie had just taken a sip of tea, and she choked over a burst of laughter. She hid her face in her hand, shoulders shaking.

"Right," Adrian said. "Do your line, Swishy."

"Okay. 'Snow White? She *isn't* here!'" She glared at her dad, then continued, "'Have you tried looking in the haunted glade?'"

"'I have searched all the forest, but to no avail.'"

"'Why do you search for her, O prince?' Dad, wait, what's a glade?"

"It's part of the forest—now keep going."

"'Why do you search for her, O prince?'"

"'She is the fairest in all the land, with raven black hair and skin of snow.'"

"Hey, that could be Miss Maggie."

Adrian looked up, meeting Maggie's eyes. "Sure could. I'm sure she was the fairest in all the land in her forest."

Maggie dipped her head, bowing. "Thank you, kind prince. At least maybe in my 'glade.' From whence come you?" she asked, eyebrows raised.

Adrian made a grand gesture with his hand. "I have come from afar, from a kingdom called...Canada. Hast thou heard of it?"

"Dad?"

"Canada? Such an exotic sounding land must be a magical place." Maggie leaned closer and said in a low voice, "Tell me... are there *dragons* in Canada?"

"Dad? Miss Maggie? Hello?"

"Aye, fair maiden," Adrian whispered back. "Fierce dragons. Dragons with claws of iron and teeth of steel—"

"Dad, you're kind of weirding me out."

"Dragons that would as soon rip the heart from your chest as say hello. But..." Adrian looked at his fingernails nonchalantly. "I have no fear of them, for their scales have tasted my sword."

"Okay, Dad, please stop. You're way off the script."

Adrian sat back, palms out. "I thought Ms. Marple wanted you to improvise."

"I don't think she wanted us to just make the whole thing up, though. Like, there aren't any dragons in Snow White." She stuck out her chin in thought. "Although that would be really cool."

Adrian sat up straight. "You're right. Okay, from the top."

"Wait, maybe we should go to my other part at the end. Where there aren't any dragons and stuff for you to make up."

Adrian raised his hands. "Suit yourself. What page?"

Charlie ruffled through her pages. "Page twelve, where Miss Maggie can be Snow White."

"Oh, good. My own part."

Charlie eyed her, squinting. "You aren't going to make up more parts are you?"

"Me? No. Promise. Where do we start?"

"Okay, so this is the part where I help the prince find Snow White in her box in the forest. So I go 'Prince! Prince! Here she is! We have found her! Snow White at last!' Then the narrator says some stuff and you go…"

Adrian launched in with, "'Indeed! She is as fair as the stories have said, fairest in all the land.'"

"'But she is asleep, noble prince! How will you awaken her?'"

Adrian cleared his throat. "'With a kiss, of course. It is the only thing which can break the spell the evil witch has placed on her.'"

"Okay, then you lob the gob on Snow White, but you don't have to do that here, 'cause it's kinda gross."

Adrian cleared his throat. "Thanks. I mean, that's fine." He tried not to look Maggie in the eyes.

"Then Snow White says…"

Maggie caught her cue and spoke: "'Where am I? And who are you, fair prince?'"

Adrian continued, "'I am Prince Valiant'—*Valiant*? Really?"

"Keep going, Dad."

"I am Prince Valiant! I have come to rescue you from the witch's evil curse."

"'With a kiss…'" Charlie prompted.

"'With a kiss,'" Adrian continued.

Maggie picked up her cue. "'Thank you, noble prince. The spell has been broken and I am free. I will always be in your debt.' And, by the way, you're really hot.'"

With that both she and Adrian burst out laughing, laughing too hard to have time to think the situation was at all embarrassing. He hadn't laughed that hard in a long time, and that warm feeling pulsed in his chest again watching Maggie's sunny, effortless laugh.

All Charlie could do was shake her head in disgust. "I can't take you guys anywhere."

Chapter Fourteen

ADRIAN PEERED THROUGH THE WINDSHIELD. "This is it. Sign says Strathmore Dance Academy." He pulled the car into a serendipitous parking space in front of a wide two-story brick storefront that had been converted into a dance studio. "Do you know what time you'll need to be picked up? Charlie's at my brother's, so it can be any time. I mean, I'll be here whenever you need me again." He was slipping into being too comfortable with Maggie again.

Or too uncomfortable. After the play practice with Charlie, he wasn't sure how to treat her. She was his boss, but she also felt like something more. Need to keep things on a professional level.

Maggie bit her lower lip. "The lesson was for three thirty. I'm not really sure. Can you come inside while I find out?"

"Of course." Adrian put the car in park and turned it off.

Inside, Maggie approached an empty front desk. Adrian could hear the lilt of waltz music reverberating from a nearby room.

"Hello? Ms. Strathmore?" Maggie called out.

A thin, athletic older woman strode into the room, wearing lavender leggings and a tight-fitting sweatshirt. Her face was severe and angular, indicating not too many smiles had attempted to crack it. Graying hair was pulled back and packed tightly in a bun on the top of her already pointed head, making her face look even longer. Her sharp gray eyes seemed to catch everything and approve of not much. Adrian had to shake the feeling he was back in grade school about to be reprimanded for whacking Shannon Wheeler with a stick at recess. He unconsciously stiffened as she caught his eye.

"Yes?" she said.

Maggie introduced herself, then said, "I'm here for my first lesson?"

The woman fixed her gaze on Maggie and nodded. "Yes, Miss Mac-Nally, welcome." She looked Adrian up and down. "And this is your partner?"

Adrian's eyebrows shot up. "Me?"

Maggie cut him off. "Mr. Adams had agreed to assist me for this first lesson, yes." She grabbed Adrian's hand and squeezed it, hard.

"Ow," he muttered, surprised at her grip.

"I see," the prim instructor said, sizing up the situation. She clapped her hands suddenly.

Adrian and Maggie both jumped.

"Let's get started," she said. "There are dance shoes in the nook here if you need them." She frowned at Adrian's feet. "Which you will. I will await you in the practice room."

And with that she sailed out as gracefully as she had come in.

"I'm sorry. I was going to ask you before today, but I was afraid you would say no." Maggie was begging Adrian before he could say anything.

Adrian put his hands on hips. "Really? And you expect me to drop everything now and help you learn how to rumba?"

"It's not the rumba. It's the waltz."

"And why couldn't your pal Valéry help you out?"

She bit her lip. "I didn't ask him." She saw his look. "I don't know how to waltz, and I'm sure he does. I just wanted to make sure I didn't look like a total idiot before I have to dance with him at the gala…" She trailed off.

Adrian said nothing, unsure of what to do.

"Please," Maggie begged again, moving closer. "I don't know anyone else."

Adrian rolled his eyes. "You sound like Charlie asking for another cookie."

"*Please?*" she repeated, softer, her eyebrows raised and chin lowered. He sighed, not oblivious to her attempt to use her feminine wiles. "Fine. Sure." He looked around the room. "So what do I have to do?"

Maggie clapped her hands once. "Grand! Okay, so as Ms. Stratworth said, you can find some dance shoes in the nook over there. I'll wait for you in the practice room once I change." And she flitted off carrying a drawstring bag to a room marked Women.

Adrian trudged to the nook she had pointed out, where there was a shelf of boxes of various sizes of dance shoes. He found a pair in his size and sat down on a bench to switch out his shoes.

What was he doing? *Always Mr. Nice Guy.*

* * *

Maggie was waiting for him in the dance room, wearing a black leotard under a short pink skirt. One wall of the large, wood-planked room was all mirrors with a long barre running across it, like for ballet.

Great. He shuffled to meet her in his slippery shoes. He'd be able to see himself screw up all afternoon.

Ms. Strathmore was waiting, feet crossed, hands on hips. "In this session we will learn the classic waltz," she said in a firm voice. "Not the twist, not the boogie-woogie, not the jitterbug, and not"—she made air quotes with her fingers—"the hip hop."

Adrian suppressed a laugh, disguising it as a cough.

Ms. Strathmore scowled at him. "You may have never taken dance before, but I assure you, once I have completed your training, you will not only have mastered the art of the waltz, you will excel at it."

"She makes it sound like we're about to storm the beaches at Normandy," Adrian whispered out of the side of his mouth.

Maggie smiled, until she saw Ms. Strathmore glaring at her.

"The waltz is one of the most graceful of the dances—elegance in movement if you will."

"I won't," Adrian whispered again, then gasped from the sharp elbow Maggie jabbed in his side.

"We will begin in closed position. Step forward, please, Mr. and Mrs. MacNally."

"Um, Maggie and Adrian," Maggie stammered. "We're not married... or a couple. We're just friends. I mean, well... driver and passenger."

The instructor took this information in silently, her face expressionless. "Very well," she said. "We begin by having the gentleman grasp the right hand of the lady and place his hand on her waist."

Adrian stepped forward, hesitating, then put his hand on Maggie's slender waist. He raised his right hand and let it hang uncertainly in the air.

Maggie tilted her head expectantly. "You aren't too afraid to hold my hand, are you? I don't have cooties or anything."

"Of course I'm not afraid. I'll hold a hand if I want to."

She wiggled her fingers. "Here you go."

"You don't just grab it."

"Go on. Touch one finger. Any finger."

"I will."

"Oh, here, I'll do it for you," she said, grabbing his hand.

Adrian twitched his hand under hers. "If you're going to do it right, here." He interlaced his fingers with hers, then closed them.

"Your palms are sweaty."

"No, they're not."

"Are you nervous?"

"No. It's just hot in here. They must not have heard of air conditioning."

"So your palms *are* sweaty."

"No, it's just hot in here."

"It's not that hot. It's early spring, not July."

"It's hot enough."

"Shush, please," Ms. Strathmore said sternly. "Proper position for the hands is the gentleman grasps the lady's hand thusly." She placed their hands together, Adrian's fingers wrapped around Maggie's. She then went to start the music at a CD player on a small desk nearby.

Adrian could feel the heat from Maggie's back where he held her, felt her pulse in his hand. She seemed as reluctant to catch his eye as he was hers, but they were too close not to. Maggie seemed just about to say something when the speakers began blaring music of a lively waltz.

"We will now address the position of the feet," Ms. Strathmore announced.

The next fifteen minutes were spent on the basics, with them slowly learning simple steps, movement, and staying with the music.

After a few tries, Maggie tilted her head and looked at Adrian with suspicion. "You've done this before, haven't you?" she said, trying not miss a step.

Adrian shrugged. "Well, I did take lessons once. But that was a long time ago." He couldn't tell if she was mad.

She stepped on his foot. "Why didn't you tell me?"

He thought about saying, *you didn't ask.* "I really wasn't sure if I was going to remember." The last time he'd danced like this had been at some lame recital at the end of a ballroom dancing class Karen had convinced him to take. He was surprised by how much he remembered. Maggie muffed a step and stopped, pulling at her shoe.

Ms. Strathmore intervened with, "Miss MacNally, come," and she motioned with her hand. She grasped Maggie's hand, then waited for the beat of the music to come around again. "Follow my lead."

And off they whirled, leaving Adrian alone. He took the chance to move to the side of the room and plop onto one of the benches, wishing he had a water bottle. He rubbed his neck as he watched the two women circle around the floor, stopping occasionally to give and receive instructions.

Adrian realized he hadn't held a woman's hand in—what? Had it been the four years since Karen? It shouldn't have been a big deal, but somehow it seemed like it, and he couldn't decipher whether it was because Maggie was just a woman or because... she was *Maggie*.

He watched her pirouetting with the instructor, halting yet somehow graceful at the same time. The older woman patiently led her in the simpler steps of a waltz, her frown scrunching into a wince every time Maggie unintentionally stepped on one of her toes.

Adrian smiled inwardly, unearthing a feeling of... what? Attraction? He had been attracted to beautiful women since Karen died, of course, but this was different. This wasn't just beauty, he thought, seeing her smile, then almost laugh, as she began to catch on to the steps. There was something beyond attraction he was feeling. Safety? *Home?*

"Okay, we're ready for you to step in again," Ms. Strathmore announced.

It took Adrian a second to process the command. He grimaced as he got up from the bench, catching Maggie's eyes. *You owe me.*

She beamed back a look that seemed to say thank you.

Ms. Strathmore clapped her hands briskly. "You have managed to assimilate some of the fundamental steps of the waltz. Now it is time to explore the *spirit* of the waltz. Allow me to demonstrate."

And before he knew what she was doing, the wiry instructor had grabbed Adrian's right wrist, raising it high in the air, then grasped his waist with her spindly right hand, which gripped him like a vise.

"Mph!" he managed to say before she began whirling him across the floor to the boisterous, bouncing music.

She called out instructions as they went. "Notice the position of my feet to his, Miss MacNally. You must let your partner move you across the floor gracefully, not clomping around like some blundering football player."

Adrian was too busy trying not to step on her toes, or his, for that matter. The few waltz lessons he'd had were years ago, and he'd danced as the man, not the woman. He just about fell over trying to think backwards.

Ms. Strathmore seemed unaware of his discomfort. "Relax and let me lead you in the ecstasy of rhythmic bliss." A quavering cello began a solo as the song reached its peak. Without warning, Ms. Strathmore, stopped, dipping Adrian backwards until his back almost snapped, then held him midair in her unbelievably strong grip, her wizened face just inches from his, smiling. He had the horrible fleeting thought that she was going to kiss him, but just as suddenly, she pulled him up to his feet, all the while keeping her iron grip on his wrist and back.

Maggie jammed her palm in her mouth, no doubt to keep from bursting out in laughter.

"And that is how you accept your partner's lead, Miss MacNally. Now you try."

Adrian welcomed the change of partners. One more dance like that and he'd need medical treatment. Maggie rejoined him while Ms. Strathmore went to start the music again. This time they quickly found each other's hands, thumbs together, eyes locked, waiting. The music began, Ms. Strathmore counted *one-two-three* and they were off. Now their feet moved together, the lessons having taken some hold, with only a few missteps.

"Good, good," Ms. Strathmore called out. "Hover, hover. Don't rush the beat."

Adrian soon found himself surprised by how smoothly they now moved together, almost instinctively. Maggie might not have waltzed before, but she had certainly picked it up fast, almost anticipating each move. He found himself still locked on Maggie's eyes as they glided across the glossy wooden floor. She in turn gave a slight smile, obviously enjoying the dance, finally letting a little instinct take over.

"Adrian?" she said.

"Yes?"

"Thank you."

* * *

The rest of session was spent in foot-numbing repetition of steps. Maggie could almost feel the blisters forming on her feet. Tonight she suspected she would have dreams of hundreds of hatchet-faced dance instructors clawing at her face while soaring waltz music played a soundtrack to her nightmare. Finally, the instructor clapped her hands and indicated the lesson was over.

"Well done, students," she said, nodding her head in approval. "You have done better than I hoped."

"Thank you," Maggie said, her hand still in Adrian's. They had danced so long together that it no longer seemed strange that their fingers were linked.

Now that the music had stopped, they both jumped back, hands at their sides.

Adrian, smiled at her, then wordlessly shuffled to the bench at the edge of the room. She followed, tired but with a glow of something that caused her to smile at him too. It had been work, it had been painful, it had even been embarrassing at times, but it had been *fun*. More fun than she'd had on any of her lunches with Valéry—or on any date she could remember. But this wasn't a *date*, of course. She took a seat by Adrian with a groan.

The sound of a man clapping slowly echoed across the nearly empty room. "Very nice, very nice," said a French-accented voice, moving closer. "You have definitely taught them well, Madame Strathmore."

Maggie turned to see Valéry slowly approaching them. Why was he here?

The teacher turned as well, giving a small nod of her head. "Thank you, *monsieur.*"

"Not at all. I apologize for the interruption. I am Valéry LaBonté. I am here for Miss MacNally."

Maggie's brow furrowed. *For me?*

Valéry took the hand of the instructor and kissed it. Her face actually cracked a smile. She bowed again. "*Merci,*" she said, then gestured towards Maggie and Adrian. "We have managed to make some progress, but there is more work to be done, certainly." Her smile disappeared as she flashed a stern glance at Adrian.

He stared back innocently.

"In that case, I would be happy to continue your practice, if that is agreeable to you, Madame Strathmore? I am most familiar with the waltz."

The older woman smiled for the second time. "Of course."

"Margaret?" Valéry extended his hand toward Maggie, who took it reluctantly, glancing at Adrian.

"Well, I wouldn't want to... " She hesitated. She still wasn't sure why he had showed up. All of a sudden she felt exhausted, the workout from dancing catching up with her.

"Nonsense. We have at least thirty minutes until we need to be at the restaurant. We might as well use it wisely."

Maggie stared at him.

Valéry raised his eyebrows. "You do remember our dinner date for this evening?"

Maggie's shoulders dropped as she gave a small laugh. "Of course. Yes. At the...uh... " She bit her lip.

"Le Petit Chateau."

"Le Petit Chateau," she repeated. "The Little Hat."

"*House*," Adrian said helpfully from his bench.

Maggie gave him a glance. "House, of course. Can't wait to go to the little house."

"Of course," Valéry purred, eyes squinting. "Then shall we dance first?" He turned to look at Adrian who was now wrestling off his shoes. "That is, if you are finished?"

Adrian looked up at her, ran a hand through his hair, and stood. "No problem. I need to pick up Charlie from my brother's anyway. Just need to get my shoes." He looked around, spied his street shoes, and went to pick them up.

Maggie felt a sudden tinge of guilt. "Adrian, I'm so grateful," she called after him. "Thank you so much for helping me."

"Yes, thank you, *mon ami*, for your assistance." Valéry smiled at Maggie. "It will make Margaret all the more spectacular when we are dancing at the gala, no?" He lifted her hand and gave her a small twirl.

She forced a small smile and tried not to get dizzy. "Well, I have a long way to go, but I think I might be able to make it through at least one waltz without crushing anyone's toes."

"Nonsense," Valéry said. "You will be the princess of the ball."

She looked for Adrian, but he had already disappeared from the room.

* * *

Adrian went to the side room where he'd left his coat and sank down a bench to change his shoes. "You will be ze *princess* of ze *ball*," he muttered, mimicking Valéry's French accent. "Whatever."

He heard the sound of approaching footsteps on the hardwood floor. "I won't be a moment," Valéry called back to Maggie. "Then you can show me what you have learned."

Adrian couldn't see the French diplomat, as a short wall divided the main entrance area and the small alcove where he sat, but he could hear Valéry speaking in French, obviously talking on his cell phone. Adrian strained to decipher the words. Although Valéry's voice was low, he could still make out most of the French.

"So, you've taken care of the numbers? Make sure that there isn't a paper trail—shred all of the documents when you're done." A pause. "No, I'll make sure she doesn't know." Another pause. "Because I'm with her now. She won't, and they won't. Just get ready to do the transfer after the gala is over. Yes, yes, even bigger than last year."

The conversation ended, and Adrian held his breath, hoping that Valéry didn't decide to come around the corner. He exhaled as he heard the footsteps retreating, moving away on the hard wood floor, back to the main room.

"Okay, *ma chère*, show me what you have learned."

Waltz music began playing, bouncing off the hard floors and walls of the dance room.

Adrian continued slowly putting on his shoes, brow furrowed, pondering the cryptic conversation he had just overheard. Transfers? Documents? And he was obviously talking about Maggie. Something was definitely up. But what?

* * *

Maggie clumped up the narrow stairs to her and Jelly's apartment, which tonight felt like she was climbing the Himalayas wearing lead shoes. She hadn't realized how strenuous dancing could be. Slumping through the door, she shuffled into the kitchen, glancing into the small living area. Jelly was sitting in her favorite chair, feet up, reading and listening to some light jazz. Maggie shrugged her purse off her shoulder and onto the kitchen table.

"How was dance class?" Jelly looked up. "You get your cha-cha on?"

Maggie blew out a breath. "I feel like I've run a marathon. Ms. Stratworth, the instructor, certainly puts you through the ringer. Then Valéry took me to this new restaurant, and *then* he insisted on walking me around Embassy Row. We must have walked two miles. She rubbed her eye. "I'm wrecked," she said, and went to the fridge to get a bottle of water.

"Sounds like a night."

Maggie got her water and unscrewed the cap. "And then some." She took a long drink.

"So, now you're ready to dance the night away with Mr. French at the big ball?"

Maggie shambled to the small living area and plopped into a chair, kicking off her flats. "I'll be happy to just make it through one dance so he doesn't think I'm a total flop." In a singsong voice, she orchestrated with her hand." *Right foot back... left foot side... right foot back.* Yeesh."

Jelly smiled. "That bad? And how did your *partner* do? Did he agree to help you out?"

Maggie made a face. "He was just fine, the stinker. He's already taken lessons, so he was ahead of me." She took a sip of her water. "I suppose that made it easier."

"Mmm, that's all it was, just 'easier'?"

Maggie glanced at her friend. "Yes, just 'easy.' I told you, I don't need any more complications."

"I see, I see... I can understand how it might be difficult to handle two handsome studs in your life at one time."

"Adrian isn't a 'stud.' He's a..." She searched for the right word.

"Thoroughbred? Hunk? A *fine* thing?"

"Oh, please stop." To Maggie's surprise, she was beginning to blink back tears.

Jelly quickly rose, came over, and sat on the arm of her chair. "Hey, girl, you know I'm just teasing, right?"

Maggie sniffed, then rubbed her eyes. "I'm sorry. It's just been a long day."

Jelly pulled a tissue from a nearby box and handed it to her.

"The gala's in less than two weeks," Maggie continued, "and my grandmother has me running ragged. I just don't need any more complications." She sniffed.

"Course not." Jelly squeezed her arm. "You just need a quiet night. Take a bath, get your batteries recharged."

Maggie stood up and wiped a last tear from her eye. "I know. It's just nerves. I want things to go so well. They *need* to go well."

"They will," Jelly reassured her, nodding. "I'll start the bath. You make some of your schmancy Irish tea. You're just... *banjaxed*—is that the word?"

Maggie smiled at her friend's attempt at Irish slang. "Tired, yes, *definitely* that." She gave her roommate a short hug. "I'll be better in the morning." She shuffled to the kitchen, grabbed her copper kettle and filled it from the sink, then put it on the stove burner to boil.

Jelly went to fill the bath.

In a few minutes, the water began roiling in the pot, steam brushing Maggie's face, helping to sooth away the stress. What was that all about anyway? She had to get herself in order. Adrian had just flustered her.

She opened and closed her hand, remembering the feel of her fingers in his, the way it had felt to float across the floor in his arms.

No, this is silly. Adrian was her friend, her driver really. Nothing more. She had more important things to take care of if her plans and job weren't going to come crashing down like spinning plates.

She stiffened straight, her face set in resolve, both hands on the edge of the counter. *No. Not this time.*

Chapter Fifteen

"YOU'RE RIGHT," DANNY SAID through a stuffed mouth. "These fries are incredible. What do they put on them?"

"Some special spices, not sure." Adrian took a big bite of his own burger as his brother grabbed an extra napkin. "I can't believe you've lived here all your life and have never been to Ollie's Trolley."

The two were sharing a rare lunch together, as their schedules usually didn't allow for the time, but the small burger diner in downtown DC was right on the way to Adrian's next appointment, and Danny had a few minutes before the start of his next shift.

"So," Danny said as he finished another bite, "the job still going okay?"

"Pretty well. It's steady, at least. And I've made some connections that might lead to something even better."

Danny arched his eyebrows. "Really? I thought you liked driving Miss Crazy?"

"Danny, don't ever call her that again, okay?"

Danny's expression fell. "Hey, sorry. I forgot. I just meant, I thought you liked the job you had."

Adrian knew his brother's apology was sincere. "Well, sure, I do, but I don't know if it's going to ever be a full-time job. I still have to supplement with some other clients. And I expect when Maggie moves up the ladder someday, she'll get her own car and I'll be looking for steady work again."

Danny wiped his hands on a napkin. "She that good?"

"Well, from what she says it sounds like she's shooting to be an ambassador or something someday."

"Wait—this is the girl who talks to squirrels and nuts, right?"

"No, not the nuts, just the squirrels."

"Oh, okay. I was worried for a sec she might be a little, you know"—he made air quotes with his fingers—"weird."

Adrian shook his head. "No, she's not weird. She's more what you might call a contradiction. One moment she's going on about how excited she is about this gala thing she's working on—how the Sultan of Swangbangy and the Emir of Hoopla is going to be there. Then the next second she's snapping a cherry blossom from a tree and putting it in her hair or having a happy fit because she got extra sprinkles on her ice cream cone. I half expect a bunch of bluebirds to come flying in and land on her arms while she starts singing a happy working song."

"She hasn't started making dresses out your curtains yet, has she?"

"Not *yet*. But we have mini blinds."

"Ouch." Danny took a swig of his drink. "Well, bro, looks like you've finally found a live one."

"I haven't *found* anything. I'm just her driver."

"Drivers don't call their clients by their first name and play handsome prince and Snow White."

"What? How did you hear that?"

Danny smiled. "Charlie texted Alice."

Adrian nodded. "And your daughter told you."

Danny laughed. "Modern communication, bro. Nothing is secret anymore, especially among cousins."

"Apparently."

"Well, don't count her out just yet. Sounds like Charlie is enamored with her."

"That may be, but as far as romance goes, Maggie seems to have her eyes locked on some dude from the French Embassy."

"French? Same guy you mentioned before?

Adrian grimaced. "Guy looks like he just swallowed a pompous cat who just swallowed a sour mouse."

"Perfect hair?"

"Of course."

"I take it you don't like him."

Adrian shook his head. "He's nice enough to her, I suppose, but something's not quite right about him. Not sure what yet."

"Your 'Spider-Sense' is tingling?"

"Something like that."

"Mmm. Sounds like you'd better keep a close eye on her."

Adrian furrowed his brow, then realized what his brother meant. "I don't think she's interested in the barely employed dad of a sassy seven-year-old. She's looking for a guy like this Valéry dude—someone successful. And rich. And sophisticated. And good-looking. Who has his own car."

"Jerk."

"Right, and I'm not the kind of guy she's going to—"

"Okay, stop right there, 'cause I know you're going to say, 'Oh, I'm just a poor little limo driver with no money and no future and a girl to look after. No one is going to want me.' "

"Is that how I sound, my voice all high and squeaky?"

Danny ignored him. "I'm saying before you count yourself out, why don't you give her a chance to decide. She's a big girl."

"Who talks to squirrels."

"Who talks to squirrels. So, remember the time we were kids and sleeping in the basement 'cause we were doing a *Nightmare on Elm Street* marathon? And we heard the bed squeaking upstairs in Mom and Dad's room, and we froze, 'cause we kind of knew what was going on, but we didn't want to say anything because it was so freaky? And you had to go to the bathroom upstairs really bad, but you were afraid to because you had to go by their room to get there, but you went up anyway, but Dad was already in the bathroom? Then you looked in their bedroom door and saw Mom was just jumping on the bed?"

"Yeahhhhh... so what does that have to do with anything?"

"Nothing." He took sip of his Coke. "I just love that story."

Adrian rolled his eyes. "Well, as always, I enjoy our little talks, but for now I'm sticking to the plan."

Danny took the last drink from his Coke, his straw gurgling in the ice. "Well, just be careful you don't play too may sides against each other, or you might end up losing the whole game."

"Thank you, *sensei*, but I think I've got it covered. If this other job works out, it'll mean Charlie and I can at least stay in the house."

Danny looked at him quizzically. "You're not telling me something."

"Well..." Adrian hesitated, having said more than he had intended. "I don't want you guys to worry. The medical expenses... you know, from Karen?"

"Yes?"

"The insurance isn't going to cover as much of what's left as I expected. Something about 'policy changes' or some other crap."

"Is it really that bad? You know, Beth and I could help you out—"

Adrian waved his hand. "No, no, you guys have enough to worry about already. You've got kids, and your hamster is losing his hair."

"Wait—how'd you know that?"

Adrian smiled. "Modern communication, bro. Works both ways. Look, we'll be fine, really, especially if this new thing works out."

Danny checked his watch. "Man, sorry, Ady, I have to go. I really want to talk more about this."

"Sure, but don't worry. And don't tell Beth, okay? She has enough to worry about with your bald hamster."

Danny laughed, his eyes crinkling. "No problem." He gave a short wave to Adrian and made his way to the exit.

Adrian gathered the wrappers, dumped them in the trash, and headed for the door with his to-go drink.

I hope I have it covered. Lot's of balls in the air. He really did want what was best for Maggie, and as much as they seemed to be getting along well together, he didn't want to keep her from the success she seemed to crave.

And then a thought popped in his mind, something his dad always used to say: To be happy in life you must learn the difference between want and need.

Easier said than done, Pop.

Chapter Sixteen

SATURDAY MORNING, a few weeks later, Maggie finished a brief late morning session at the embassy where she was helping file and shred documents. She was finding out that diplomatic life had a large amount of average, even boring aspects to it. But she supposed that was just a part of starting at the bottom. She was sure things would get much more interesting given time and a little more experience.

Jelly had dropped her off at the embassy on her way to the fabric store before Bella Bella opened, but she had no ride back to their apartment. At her small desk, she began gathering her things. She thought of walking the six blocks to the Metro, but then decided to text Adrian instead.

Just wondering if you were about and could give me a lift today. At the embassy. She hit send.

A few moments later Adrian's response dinged back. *Sure thing. Pick-up in a half hour okay?*

Thanks! she texted.

She decided to spend the time going through some old email. Even though she hadn't worked at the embassy very long, she was already feeling behind. Every day was a new project, or procedure to be learned, or one of a hundred different little tasks that made it difficult to concentrate on the gala preparations. Desmond was helpful but usually surly, and it didn't help her concentration that she knew he was less than happy with her invading his territory assisting her grandmother. It was definitely different than working at Bella Bella with Jelly. That had been hard work too, but laughter and camaraderie had eased the aches and stress from a day's work.

She sighed. She wished she could have both, but if she was going to have a real career, she had to soldier on.

She stopped for a stretch and a yawn, then tackled another stack of receipts. The hardest part of organizing for the gala was keeping up with all the paperwork. Or lack of it, sometimes. Desmond and Valéry had a habit of just giving her verbal instructions on various needs, and when she would ask about pricing or the budget they would reply with a vague "we'll take care of it later" comment. It seemed at odds with their usual efficient manner. She knew she was still new at this game, but she couldn't help think a better paper trail would make her job a lot easier.

It was almost thirty minutes on the dot when Adrian arrived outside the embassy with Charlie in the back seat of the BMW, happily listening to something on her iPod. She flashed a huge smile and waved when she saw Maggie.

"Miss Maggie! Miss Maggie! Hi!" she called after rolling down her window.

"Mind if I hitch a ride?" Maggie called back, returning her wave.

"Yes! Get in the car, lady!"

Adrian gave a disapproving glance to his daughter in the back seat. "Be nice, Charlie." He opened his door as if to get out to get Maggie's, but she stopped him.

"Oh, no, I'll find my way. You stay." She stepped around the front of the car and got in the passenger side.

Adrian put the car in gear and checked all of his mirrors, as usual.

"Are you going to the art place with us?" Charlie asked hopefully.

"The art place?"

"She means the National Gallery," Adrian said. "She has to do a report for school." He turned to his daughter. "Charlie, I'm sure Miss Maggie has other things to do today. We're just going to drop her off at home and be on our way."

"Please, Dad? Please, Miss Maggie?"

Maggie was finding it harder and harder to resist the little girl. "I haven't been there for a while. What are you going to see?"

"I have to pick a picture and write about it. It'll be fun if you come along."

"Sounds interesting." It *did* sound interesting, and it would just be an afternoon. And it would mean a lot to the girl. "You sure it's okay, Adrian?"

"Fine with me."

"Okay, I'm in," Maggie said as they pulled away.

It wasn't like it was a date or anything. It was just Adrian and Charlie. And it might be a good break from all the worries.

* * *

After a sugar-laden lunch of tarts and croissants and mandatory milk for Charlie, the three made their way up the wide, flat steps and through the imposing pillars to the main entrance of the National Gallery, America's repository of its most famous and important art. They passed through the huge open rotunda and into one of the smaller sections, where images of dour-faced women in ruffles in gilded frames seemed to disapprove of their stares.

"So, I have to pick one of these pictures?" Charlie asked.

Adrian checked a sheet. "Yeah, your teacher says pick one and then do a report on it. What you feel when you see it, why you like or don't like it, that sort of thing."

Charlie wrinkled her nose as she looked at the paintings on the wall. "Well, I don't like any of these old ladies. Can we find something else? Do you think they have any funny kitten pictures here?"

Adrian smiled. "We'll see. It's a big museum. Let's keep looking."

The three sauntered their way through the various rooms. There were rooms filled with paintings of beautiful, lush landscapes, rooms with elegant still lifes, rooms with castles and dying toreadors, but none seemed to trip Charlie's fancy. Finally, they arrived at a room of French impressionist paintings.

"Ooh, here's a Degas," Maggie said, looking closely at a nameplate on a painting of girls at a dance lesson. "He's my mum's favorite. We had one hanging in our front hallway."

A real one? Adrian thought. Could be. Maggie hadn't talked much about her parents, but he knew they were fairly prominent politicians in Ireland.

She came over to the painting he had been studying. "What's this one?"

Adrian read the placard next to the painting. "Georges Seurat. *The Lighthouse at Honfleur.*"

The painting was of a small lighthouse on a bay. Next to it was a building, and a boat was on the beach.

"Hmm. Honfleur—that's in northern France," Maggie said. "Painters love that place." She studied the painting. "Can't say I think much of this one, though."

"Oh, I don't know. It's a good example of pointillism."

Maggie's eyebrows arched. "You know about art?"

Adrian nodded. "I had to take an art appreciation class in college."

Charlie was squinting at the painting, a frown on her face. "It's all just kind of messy blue and orange smudges."

"Right, but you're seeing it up close. It's looks better farther back."

Charlie's frown stuck. "Well, it still looks just like smudges to me." She looked around the room. "I like that one over there of the girl with the cat better."

The painting was of a small girl in a blue chair with a cat on her lap.

"She looks like she's watching TV but she's bored," Charlie said.

"Well, why don't you sit over there on the bench and write about her? Here's your notebook." Adrian handed her a spiral notebook and pencil from her backpack, and she went over to the bench and began staring at the painting. He returned the few feet to where Maggie was leaning in closer to the Seurat painting.

"I love how some impressionists painted using just dots of paint that seemed like a mess of brush strokes up close, but farther back, it became a clear image. Each dot, even though it looks kind of insignificant, helps complete the whole picture. Here." She took Adrian's arm and brought him close to the painting.

"Don't get too close or you'll set off the alarm," he warned.

"I won't." She pointed at a section of the painting. "See how it's just a bunch a smears. You can't even tell what it's a painting of."

He leaned back from the painting, looked at Maggie and smiled. She was still leaning forward, eyes squinting and lips pursed as she studied the painting.

"Mmm," he said. "Sounds kind of... metaphorical?"

She leaned back, then their eyes connected.

"I think that's right. Metaphorical." She moved closer.

"Metaphysical?" he asked, still locked on her eyes.

"Meta—"

A piercing, chirping alarm interrupted them. Adrian jumped back as if he had been shocked, for a brief strange moment wondering if it was because he had gotten too close to Maggie. Then he remembered. "Where's Charlie?" He and Maggie whirled to look. Charlie wasn't at the bench where they had left her.

"There!" Maggie shouted over the din of the shrieking alarm, pointing at a painting.

Adrian saw Charlie standing, wide-eyed and frozen in front of the painting of the little girl with the cat. A man in a security uniform strode quickly into the room, saw the culprit was no threat, then quickly spoke into a microphone on his collar. The alarm ceased, but still seemed to ring in Adrian's ears.

He rushed with Maggie to Charlie, who looked like she was about to melt into tears.

"I didn't know you weren't supposed to touch it," she said in a tiny voice.

* * *

After about twenty tense minutes in the National Gallery security office, complete with profuse apologies, some scolding, and assurances that this would never happen again, Maggie followed an embarrassed

Adrian and a subdued but apparently none-the-worse-for-wear Charlie back into the main gallery area.

"Well," Maggie offered, "this has turned into quite an adventure."

"You could call it that," Adrian said, obviously not amused. He checked his watch. "Look, why don't we look around the gallery just a little more and then maybe head for home? It's already been a day."

"Dad, I'm thirsty."

Adrian pulled out a gallery map he had folded in his back pocket. "There's a concessions place one floor down. While you look more, I'll get some bottles of water. You'll probably have to wait to drink it outside anyway." He cocked his head at Charlie. "And no touching anything, right?"

"Okay," she said quietly.

"I'll be right back."

"I'll make sure she's okay," Maggie assured him as he left. She saw Charlie's somber face and took the little girl's hand. "C'mon, Charlie, let's take a look around." Time to change the subject. "So how's the play coming? Are you learning your part for Swishy the Squirrel?"

Charlie swung their linked hands as they walked past the stern faces of America's founding fathers. "Yeah, I'm kinda getting it. Randy Melcorn keeps messing up his part as the tree, which messes me up and then Ms. Marple gets mad and makes us practice it again. I wish I had one of the other parts, like the queen or the mirror or something."

"Well, every part is important, you know. You just have to do yours as well as possible."

Charlie looked up. "Was it fun being Cinderella when you were in the school play? She's the star."

Maggie bit her lip. "Sometimes it's more fun not to be the star. I liked making up plays with my friends best. We used to pretend we were different people from different countries. My favorite was when I would pretend I was a cowgirl from Texas."

"Really?"

Maggie nodded. "Oh, yes. We would even go to stores and buy something from the counter and pretend we were from America to see if the owner noticed."

"Cool! What did your voice sound like?"

"Oh, it's been years, Charlie…"

"Do it here."

"I don't know Charlie." Maggie looked around.

"Please! It will help me learn how to do my play better. Ms. Marple is always saying how a good actor needs to learn how to improvise."

"Well then, little missy," Maggie said, mustering her best cowboy twang, "why don't we mosey on over thar to that thar paintin'."

Charlie giggled. "That's so cool! Do it again."

Maggie ambled with her to a large painting of a man on a rearing horse. "Well, look thar, little missy. Kinda reminds me of mah grandpappy's horse Clementine."

Charlie giggled again, and a middle-aged woman in a bright pink pantsuit slowed and stared at them.

Maggie put her hands on her hips. "She'd always be a-rearing up like that if'n she didn't have her, uh… oats."

"Really?" the woman said, approaching. "I was just trying to figure out why the horse is rearing." She looked at a brochure in her hand. "The guide says the rearing horse usually means the rider was killed in battle, but General Beauregard here died in his sleep."

Maggie knew she'd look like a complete idiot if she dropped her cowboy twang now. "Um… well, back home in Texas, they say a horse that's a-rearing is a shore sign it ain't gonna rain for three weeks."

"Really?" the other woman said again in surprise. "That's so interesting. My friend is from Galveston. Louise! Louise!" She motioned over a short, round woman in a flowered blouse.

"Oh, that's okay," Maggie said. She had no idea where Galveston was, but she realized her twang had slipped and recovered with, "We was just fixin' to leave—"

"Nonsense. Louise is always going on about how much she misses Texas—hasn't seen a Texan in a week. She'd love to say hello, wouldn't you, Louise?"

"Hello. And you are…?" The woman looked expectantly at Maggie.

"Howdy, ma'am. Name's Margaret. Pleased to meet y'all."

Charlie looked on in amazement, as if she were watching the best TV show ever made.

"Margaret here's from Texas too, Louise."

Louise's face brightened. "Well, it is a pleasure," she said in a syrupy-sweet drawl. "What part of the great state are y'all from?"

Maggie thought quickly. "Oh, here'n thar, hither and yonder, all over those parts. Mah daddy was an oil rig driver, so we kept a-movin'." She swung her arm for emphasis.

Louise's eyes widened. "Your daddy was a trucker? What company? My daddy drove for King of the Road for over thirty years."

Maggie kept her grin but began to sweat. "Well… Lot's of 'em, *all* of 'em, seems like. Y'all know how it is." She nudged Louise with her elbow.

Louise laughed a big hearty laugh. "I sure do. Say, your daddy ever get to Galveston?"

"Why, he musta coulda, ma'am. Spent many a summer up thar on the panhandle, during the summer, that is."

Louise looked confused, her eyes squinting. "The panhandle? That's up north. Galveston's on the Gulf."

Maggie was beginning to panic. "*Pan*handle? No, ma'am, I meant he *manhandled* those rigs all the way down thar to Galveston. Down thar in the *south* of Texas. The great state of Texas, yes, ma'am."

"I see." Louise obviously didn't see at all. She spied Charlie and bent down to see her. "And who's this sweet thing?"

Maggie opened her mouth—

"Mah name's Eloise," Charlie said in a tiny twang, "and I'm shore pleased to be a-meetin' you, ma'am!"

"Well, I'm sure pleased to meet you too," Louise said as she shook Charlie's little hand. "What a darling little girl."

Maggie could only smile and was about to say thank you and make a hasty exit when Charlie piped up again. "Thank you kindly. And this is mah momma, Miss Mistletoe."

Louise straightened up, her eyes squinting again. "Mistletoe? I don't believe I've ever met any Mistletoes from Texas."

"Mah momma grew up in Rireland, ma'am. She's a princess!"

Maggie knew she needed to extricate herself from this conversation. She grabbed her phone out of her purse and pretended to answer. "What's that, honey?" she said to no one. She covered the phone with her hand. "It's mah man, Dirk." She spoke into the phone again. "Hey there, sweet thang. Yes, sir, me and Eloise was just fixin' to leave." She put the phone away and gave a short salute to Louise.

"It was shore nice to meet y'all, but my man's a-waitin'. Might oughta git this sassy pony to the little cowgirl's room." She shook the slightly dumbfounded Louise's hand vigorously with her right hand, grabbed Charlie's hand with her left.

They passed around a column, and Maggie pulled Charlie into a corner where they both plopped onto a marble bench, giggling.

"Omygosh, that was *so* cool!" Charlie said, totally excited. "Let's go find someone else to do it to!"

"Oh no, Charlie, that was a little too much for me." Maggie wiped her sweating brow, then giggled some more. "But it was a little fun, huh?" She felt almost out of breath.

Charlie was still going on. "Did you see her face when I said 'Mah name's Eloise'?" She started laughing.

"Okay, Charlie, okay. We had some fun, but… just don't tell your dad, okay?"

"Just don't tell your dad what? Where have you been?" Adrian was carrying two bottles of water.

"Oh my gosh, Dad. Maggie did this thing—there were these two ladies and she pretended a voice and they didn't know. It was *so* funny!"

Adrian raised his eyebrows. "What ladies? Where?"

Maggie grinned sheepishly. "Oh, we were just having a little fun pretending. You know, just kind of practicing for the school play?"

"Dad! Dad! I said my name was Eloise and—"

"Okay, Charlie, I think that's enough," Maggie said, hoping the little girl would stop. She didn't, of course.

"—and then Maggie said 'I hear my *man* calling' like she was talking on the phone to you and then she called you 'sweet thang' and it was *so* funny."

"Sweet thang?" Adrian said.

"Oh, no," Maggie said and laughed nervously, "I didn't call *you* sweet thing. I was just pretending to... I mean I wouldn't have called *you*... Is that my water?" She grabbed the bottle out of his hand, unscrewed the cap and starting gulping it, purposely avoiding his eyes.

"I see," Adrian said. "Well, *this* 'sweet thang' would appreciate it if you didn't involve Charlie in any of your crazy escapades in the future. And I don't think you should be drinking water in here. I don't want more trouble with security."

"Oh, Dad, it wasn't that bad. We were just having fun. Miss Maggie was just showing me—"

"Miss Maggie needs to remember that kids should be kids and grown-ups should be grown-ups and not involve kids in not trying to act like grown-ups."

Maggie felt her face flush, but raised her chin. "And maybe sometimes grown-ups need to loosen up and act a little more like kids."

Adrian stared at her for a moment as if he were going to say more, then rubbed his face. He handed Charlie her backpack. "Okay, well, we can talk about that later. It's already been a big day. Time to get going."

"Look, I can take the Metro home," Maggie said. "I don't want to bother you—"

"You're on our way." He led Charlie by the hand down the steps to the main exit.

Charlie looked back over her shoulder. "C'mon, Miss Mistletoe!" she called out to Maggie.

"Miss Mistletoe?" Adrian said.

Charlie was more than happy to explain.

Chapter Seventeen

"SO, HOW DID IT GO TODAY?" Adrian held the car door for Maggie as she slumped into the back seat. She blew a strand of hair up from her forehead, then sprawled back, rubbing one ankle on the other as he closed her door. He was doing a late afternoon pickup from the embassy and taking her home. With only two weeks left until the gala, he already knew the answer to his question. Her body language said it all.

"They have me running ragged, what with gala planning and paperwork. I've never seen so many documents and applications and forms." She threw up her hands.

"Welcome to bureaucracy, huh?"

She held up three fingers to his mirror. "I went through *three* Magillicuttys today."

"Is that a brand of shoe or some Irish drink?"

"Neither. It's a person."

"That's definitely a lot of Magillicuttys."

"And I've got bills for the gala coming in. You know how much fifty-five sequined tablecloths cost to rent?"

"No idea."

"Three thousand dollars." She shook her head. "I could *sew* them myself for less."

"I don't suppose you could just use plastic?"

"And all of the decisions. Do you want *silver* beaded charger plates or *gold* beaded charger plates, or clear glass or acrylic, or round or square."

Adrian nodded. "That *would* be a difficult decision, especially since I have no idea what a charger plate is."

"And what color votives to get—"

"Not sure what a votive is either."

"And candelabras—"

"Candelabras I've heard of."

"And *round* chafers or *square* chafers—"

"Nope... lost me again."

"And glassware!" She threw up her hands. "I've half a mind to just chuck the whole thing and hide under my desk until it's all over." She stopped and wagged her finger at him again. "And don't say anything about my half a mind."

Adrian kept his eyes on the road. "Just try not to get too overwhelmed. Remember, it's your first time organizing something this big. Just take it one thing at a time." He paused. "So, Valéry's helping you, right?"

"When he can. His duties at the French embassy keep him pretty busy."

"Hmm." He glanced at her in his rear view mirror. Her face was the picture of stress. *I can't believe I'm actually going to say this.* "Well, maybe he should be helping you more. I mean, he's supposed to be the expert, right?"

"I need to show I can handle it. I'll be fine."

"I know, but you were just saying—"

She fixed him with a steely gaze. "I said I'll be fine." She raised her chin, then looked out the window. "It was just a busy day, okay?"

He dropped it, having already learned how stubborn she could be. Time to change the subject. "Mind if we make a small detour?"

She immediately brightened. "Charlie?"

"She wants to go out for ice cream after play practice. I promised her she could ruin her dinner just this once." He took a stab at a peace offering. "Ever been to Duffy's?"

Her eyes widened. "The ice cream shop? I have, but not for years."

"Well, I'm sure Charlie would love to have you come along." He could feel his neck warming again. *Am I asking too much?*

"And I'd love to come along," she said. She suddenly began rummaging in her purse. "That reminds me, I got a small gift for her. I hope you don't mind?"

"Sure, what is it?"

She held up a small, pink, fluffy squirrel. "I saw it at the drugstore near the embassy and thought of her. Isn't it cute? I thought since she's a squirrel in her play, you know?"

He smiled, fascinated by how she could go from a frustrated woman to an excited girl in seconds. "She'll love it."

"I can't wait to give it to her."

"Okay, then get ready for a happy girl and a graham cracker, honey, and hot fudge sundae with rainbow sprinkles."

* * *

Duffy's was a little out of the way from Adrian's usual routes and their home, which was why it was always such a treat for Charlie. Usually there was a line out the door, and today was no exception, even for late afternoon. Fortunately, there was a brick-lined patio outside with a few cozy tables under the trees where they could wait for the line to die down. The three of them sat down, Charlie between the two adults, legs swinging under the wrought-iron black chair, chattering about play practice as she hugged her new squirrel she had instantly named Swishy.

"And, oh my gosh, you should have seen Randy Melcorn. He fell over when he put his tree costume on and couldn't get back up." She giggled uncontrollably. "It was so hilarious."

Maggie laughed too. "It sounds like your play is going to be a big hit."

Charlie scrunched her face. "I don't know. We still have to learn our singing part, and all of the boys are being jerks about it."

"Well, that's what boys do," Maggie said, glancing at Adrian. "What song are you singing?"

Charlie thought. "It's something about the forest and the birds watching out for Snow White or some stuff. We haven't really learned it yet." Her chin dropped. "I really wanted to practice it with Dad."

"Gee, that's too bad," Adrian said.

"Well, we could sing another song," Maggie suggested.

Charlie's face instantly brightened with an idea. "We could do the "I Know" song. Dad sings it with me sometimes when I can't sleep."

Adrian was appalled. He was going to have to start teaching Charlie she couldn't just blurt out everything that popped into her head. "I don't think Maggie is going to want to sing with you."

"C'mon, Dad, I can teach her. Miss Maggie can do the other part and I can do the trumpet thing. I never get to do the trumpet thing."

"Charlie, you know how bad I sing."

"Oh, c'mon, everybody can sing," Maggie said. "Some people just might do it better than others."

"Well, then I must be one of the others."

"Well, you can at least try. Charlie, you'll help me, won't you?"

Charlie stood up from her seat, excited. "Sure!"

Adrian sighed, knowing his daughter wasn't going to let this go. "Okay, well, then why don't you just teach Maggie first?"

Charlie turned to Maggie. "Okay, so I start..."She looked up as if trying to remember the words. "'*The other night, dear, as I lay sleeping...*,'" Charlie sang in her light, airy little girl voice.

"Oh, I know this song," said Maggie suddenly. "My grandfather used to sing it to my grandmother."

"You know it?" Adrian asked, surprised.

"Yes, it's 'You are my Sunshine', right? He sang it for her on one of her birthdays. It was *so* cute."

Charlie had stopped singing. "Dad, you need to do the other part with me."

"I don't know if I remember the words."

"Sure you do. We just did it last week. You always sing it with me."

Maggie jumped in. "Maybe I can help." She clasped her hands together and scooted her chair closer to Charlie. "So, Charlie, you start."

"*The other night, dear...,*" Charlie sang brightly.

Adrian glanced around at the customers milling around the busy ice cream shop, then cleared his throat nervously, singing tentatively, "*The other night, dear...*"

"Louder, Dad."

"That's not loud enough?"

"You do it louder at home."

He looked around again at the people sitting at the other tables, some catching his eye then looking away. He could see Maggie watching him as well, not sure if she was going to laugh at him or not. "Okay, alright. You start it again."

"*The other night, dear...*"

"*The other night, dear...*" Adrian sang in harmony.

"*As I lay sleeping...*" they sang together.

Maggie's head tilted. She picked up the words to the first verse, singing along with Charlie.

Charlie watched Maggie as she reached the chorus. "You are my sunshine, my only sunshine..."

Maggie joined in, her light voice matching Charlie line for line.

"The customers are starting to stare," Adrian whispered when they took a breath. He motioned his head at the full tables around them.

"Who cares?" Maggie whispered back, then returned to singing. Charlie was oblivious, her sunny girl voice dancing in the spring air, head bobbing.

Adrian sighed, watching them both, two little girls, large and small, singing a meaningless ditty, heads together. A tinge of sadness touched him as he thought how Charlie would never get the chance to sing with her mom, yet the guilt that usually followed such a thought didn't fall on him this time. Who was he to deny their girl this joy? He found himself humming again.

"No, do it like your trumpet part," Charlie insisted.

Adrian tentatively switched from humming to mimicking a trumpet, trying to remember the solo part he had made up one night with her. He hoped no one he knew was at the ice cream shop today. Charlie and Maggie kept singing, watching him as they finished the chorus.

"Please don't take my sunshine away..."

As the chorus finished, Adrian found himself fixated on Maggie's bright blue eyes, the edges creased from her smile. "Uh, that's all I—I don't remember the next verse," he stammered, his courage disappearing.

Maggie tilted her head, then seemed to catch herself. She looked at Charlie. "That's okay, right Charlie?"

Charlie hopped off her seat. "Yup. Dad you sounded good. Can we get the ice cream now? The line isn't as long." She pointed towards the storefront.

Adrian welcomed the distraction. "Sure thing."

All three stood as Charlie grabbed her dad's hand, then reached almost instinctively for Maggie's, who took it, seeming surprised but pleased. An older couple approached them, each holding an ice cream cone.

"Excuse us, but we just wanted to tell you what a lovely family you have," the woman said, smiling. "I'm sorry, but we heard you singing. That's one of Ben's favorite songs." She nodded toward her husband.

Adrian glanced at Maggie. "We're not actually—"

"That was our song," the man said. "Well, the Lennon Sisters sang it back then, but it was the song playing on the jukebox when we first met."

The woman tugged at her husband's arm and began moving away to a larger table where a group of seniors sat. "Well, we won't keep you. We just wanted to say thank you." And they headed off to join their friends.

"Well, that was sweet," was all Adrian could think to say.

"Dad, what did they mean by 'our song'?" Charlie asked, looking up at him.

"Hmm? Oh, that's just something two people say when they have a song they both like."

"So now you and Maggie have song just like them!"

"What? Well, I don't know…"

"Cool!" Charlie said, then tugged at their hands. "C'mon, we need to get the ice cream before the line gets long again." And off she went, singing, "*You are my sunshine…*"

Maggie smiled at him, and Adrian smiled back, humming the tune under his breath.

Chapter Eighteen

"OOPS, I'M SO SORRY," Maggie said as Valéry hopped back from under her waltzing misstep.

"No, no… no apologies. Here, let us try again, and make sure you follow my eyes, not my feet, *d'accord?*" Valéry retook her right hand, his face a grimace more than smile.

Maggie forced herself not to look down but follow his lead. She waited until the next appropriate beat and let him guide her into the steps, the light waltz music filling the white marble-tiled drawing room of the Irish Embassy.

Normally used for small meetings or receptions, the high ceilings, stately white wood-trimmed walls and large ornate gold-framed mirrors made it almost seem like a small room in a palace. Old oil paintings lined the walls, late afternoon sunlight filled the tall, white-curtained windows, and a set of French doors flanked by tall boxwood topiaries led out onto a small stone-balustered veranda that connected with the street on the side of the building.

Maggie completed a circle of the room, eye to eye with Valéry. She was wearing a simple gray dress with leggings, and Valéry was in his customary refined suit and tie, jacket removed.

"Excellent, Margaret, your lessons have been very helpful," Valéry pronounced. "Just make sure you watch my eyes, no? Just trust me and I will lead you." He gave one of his seemingly perpetual smiles, deep brown eyes sparkling.

Valéry had insisted on practicing one more time before the gala next week. He was a pretty good dancer, but she was disappointed that she had to concentrate a lot more than she expected. It hadn't been nearly as smooth as her last dance with Adrian at Ms. Strathmore's. She must have forgotten more than she realized.

The song came to an end and Valéry even attempted a twirl, which Maggie, to her surprise, pulled off almost gracefully, returning to his arms, where he drew her close.

"See? Just trust me," he said, still clasping her hand in his. His face drew closer.

"Knock, knock!" a familiar voice said.

Maggie dropped Valéry's hand as her partner's smile disappeared. "It's not five already, is it?" she said.

Adrian was leaning into the room from the doorway. "Well, not quite yet, but I thought I'd just let you know I was here."

"Fine. Well, as you can see I'm not quite ready, so if you..." And she gestured with her head for him to leave.

Adrian looked puzzled. "If I...?"

Maggie tried to sound professional. "If you would please wait out on the entryway, thank you?" She didn't want Valéry noticing Adrian had arrived at the wrong time again.

Adrian's eyebrows rose. "Oh. Sure, of course. You kids carry on. I'll be out here. Just outside the door." He smacked it for emphasis, then slowly backed out of the doorway.

Valéry had been observing the exchange with an annoyed expression. "Your driver, he doesn't always take the hint very well, no?"

Maggie turned back to face him. "Hmm? Oh, I suppose not."

He pursed his lips. "Well, having been here in the States for a while, I have had a variety of experiences with the American... *boy*." He waved his hand in dismissal. "They like to stick their noses in where they're not wanted, no?"

Maggie nodded. "I suppose so."

Valéry laughed. "And I suppose it is difficult not to stick your nose into business when it is so large."

Maggie tilted her head. "Hmm?"

Smirking, Valéry reeled off something in French and still smirking, explained, "I'm sorry. It is a joke. 'His nose arrives fifteen minutes before he does.'"

Maggie nibbled her bottom lip as she got his meaning. "I think Adrian's nose is kind of distinguished."

"Hmm, yes. A distinguishing characteristic, like the animal—the one with the long *nez*?" He gestured with his fingers, pulling away from his nose.

"An elephant?" she asked uncertainly.

"*Non*. The one who eats insects."

"An anteater?"

He looked delighted. "*Oui*, anteater." Just then his watch alarm began beeping. He glanced down at it, then back at Maggie with a small smile. "Five o'clock. I believe our time is now actually up."

Maggie rocked on her heels. "Well, thank you for the refresher course."

"My pleasure." He took her hand and raised it to his lips.

"Five o'clock, kids!" Adrian popped his head in the doorway again. "Whoops! Okay, that's definitely my bad." He quickly popped out again.

Valéry's eyes narrowed as he leaned in to give Maggie a peck on the cheek, then released her hand. "Until tomorrow, then, *chérie*? Lunch is all arranged."

She straightened a lock of hair. "Yes, until tomorrow."

"Oh, I almost forgot. I have a little gift for you." Valéry strolled to a brass coatrack by the room's entrance and returned carrying a gold garment bag. Sparkly pink fabric peeked out of the bottom. "I took the liberty of finding a dress for you for the gala." He unzipped the front of the bag. Inside was a glowing pink cocktail dress. It was strapless and looked awfully tight.

"It's beautiful," Maggie said graciously as she touched the fabric. She looked up. "But I can't accept it."

He waved his hand in dismissal. "Nonsense. I insist. It is a Victoria Beckham, by the way."

Maggie's eyebrows rose. Victoria Beckham? Those were incredibly expensive dresses! "Oh, Valéry, that's too much." She didn't want to insult him, but it felt a little presumptuous.

He smiled. "Not at all. Your grandmother provided me your approximate measurements. We will need to have it fitted of course, but there will be time for that later." He re-zipped the bag, then strode back to the coatrack by the door and hung up the dress.

Maggie bit her lip again. The strapless gown was definitely head-turning but not quite her style. Plus, she'd promised Jelly she'd wear *her* dress. She'd have to find a way to tell him later.

Valéry had returned. He cocked his head and smiled. It dawned on her that he smiled a lot. But she wasn't always sure it was because he was happy. "Lunch tomorrow is at Adagio. I have managed a table with Senator Talbot. He always has the most marvelous stories of his time as a presidential aide."

"Of course, yes. Tomorrow at Adagio."

Valéry nodded. "I will pick you up. No need for *him*." He gestured with his head towards the doorway, indicating Adrian.

"Of course," Maggie said.

"Until tomorrow, then?"

"Until tomorrow."

He smiled, turned, and made his way out of the room without a glance at Adrian, who was standing in the doorway, hands in his pockets.

Adrian cleared his throat. "So, are you ready to go?"

"I may stay here for a bit. I have a lot of work to do."

Adrian crossed toward her. "Hey, Maggie, I'm sorry. What you do on your own time..." He stopped. "It's just that—"

"It's fine. No apology necessary." She didn't want to discuss Valéry with him, so she walked to the French doors and swung them open, letting in the late afternoon spring breeze. Outside, the sound of traffic mixed with a street performer playing a violin somewhere down the block.

After a moment, Adrian followed. "Your lessons—you two seem to be doing well. Looks like you'll be ready for the big dance in a few weeks." He folded his arms as they both looked out at the street.

Maggie rolled her eyes. "Yes, if he has any toes left by then. He'll need to be wearing steel-toed shoes if he's going to make it through the night."

"Oh, come on, give yourself some credit. I saw you. You're doing fine. Believe me, he won't mind a few crushed toes as long as he gets to dance with you."

She glanced at him and then back to the street. "Well, we'll see."

"Just remember what Ms. Strathmore would say." Adrian imitated the dour instructor's stern voice. "'Dancing with the *feet* is one thing, but dancing with the *heart* is another.'"

"Maybe Valéry should dance with Ms. Strathmore."

"Are you kidding? She'd want to lead and end up snapping his back with a dip."

Maggie laughed at that. "I just can't seem to get the hang of when to go back with my left foot if he's leading with his right."

"Well, first is always watch your partner's eyes. Then remember to visualize the box, like she said."

She turned to face him, then looked down. "So, if your feet are like this…" She placed her feet between his. "Then I'm supposed to always go back when you go forward?"

"Or forward when I go back."

The street violinist ambled down the street, closer to the embassy, now playing a three-quarter-time piece that waltzed through the warm air.

"Here, let me show you," Adrian said.

Maggie raised her eyebrows. "Here?"

"Just to make sure you have it down. For the gala."

"But there's no—"

"There's music. Out there." He gestured with his head towards the open doors to the street. The violinist continued to play, his violin case now open on the sidewalk at the bottom of the steps, ready for commuters to toss in coins.

Maggie relented. "Okay. Sure." She drew closer to him, hands raised for him to take.

"Let me know if my anteater nose gets in the way," Adrian said.

Maggie's eyes widened. "I... he was just..." was all she could stammer.

Adrian just took her right hand in his, brushed a strand of hair from her temple, then put his hand on her waist, ready to begin. "Not all of us bourgeois types are ignorant losers," he said, waiting for the right beat in the music in order to start. "I know a little French. Remember? My mother was from Quebec."

Maggie could feel her cheeks reddening and couldn't look at his face. "I'm so sorry. I didn't mean—I mean, Valéry, he..."

"Look up here, watch me."

She did, her feet following his.

"Good. My brother used to get teased more than me," Adrian continued. "Nicknames like Toucan and Pinocchio." They spun slowly around the room, the music drifting through the doors from the street.

"That's terrible," Maggie said.

"Not a big deal, really. Our mother used to say 'Just remember, *cher garcon*, nobody can change what they look like on the outside, but they *can* change what they look like on the inside.'"

Maggie smiled into his eyes. "That's very wise." Then she looked around at the walls slowly passing by as Adrian led her out through the doors onto the veranda. "We're dancing," she said, surprised.

"*Oui, cherie*," Adrian said, mimicking Valéry's baritone voice. The violinist's piece came to and end. They slowly lost the beat and then stopped, still holding each other.

Adrian looked down. "To be honest, until we took those lessons, I hadn't danced since Charlie's first grade father-daughter dance."

Maggie smiled. "Really? I would like to have seen that."

"I have to say I was pretty good. She mostly stood on my shoes, though."

"She must have been very convincing. To get you to dance."

Adrian nodded. "She has her ways. Don't most women?"

"Oh, we do, we do." She found herself looking up at his face again. "It's how we get our way." Her heart was pounding slightly, she realized. The violin started to play again, a romantic, Romani tune. A few lingering cherry blossoms drifted down from a tree above them.

"And what are your ways?" Adrian asked softly. His hand was still around Maggie's waist, warm, comforting.

"Well, you remember this one, right?" She slowly intertwined her fingers into his right hand.

"That one I remember, yes." He drew her closer.

"Sometimes we bat our eyes," she said, their faces now inches apart.

He shook his head slightly. "That never worked for me."

"How about sweet nothings?"

"Mmm, closer."

"Closer?" She raised herself slightly on her toes.

"*Very* close," he said as he pulled her to his chest.

"Just don't let your big nose get in the way," she whispered as his face moved to hers.

The kiss was as natural as if she were, well, kissing someone she had known for years. Eyes closed, Maggie felt Adrian's warm hand cradling her neck, while the scent of the cherry blossoms, the violin still playing lightly on the street, the breeze in the trees, the birds, all of it seemed a small symphony playing just for them, never to be repeated, but never to be forgotten. She felt a strange buzzing in his chest, and briefly wondered if her heart felt like that to him. It certainly felt like that to *her*.

Then she realized it was his phone. She opened her eyes and saw his were open as well. They parted suddenly.

"Sorry, I—"

"I shouldn't—"

They both spoke at the same time.

Maggie wasn't sure which one of them seemed more embarrassed. She straightened some hair, which hadn't been out of place until she had touched it.

"I didn't mean to... I mean, my phone. It's Charlie..." Adrian trailed off. "She's probably done early from play practice again. I hate to do this, but I don't think I can take you home."

Maggie cleared her throat, then dropped his hand and began smoothing her dress. "Of course. Yes, you need to do that. Right now would certainly be a great time for it, and I can"—she looked around the street—"take the Metro back to the shop, no worries."

"Okay, well, I'd better get going." He stepped toward the street, then stopped. "You're sure you're okay getting back?"

"Oh, yes, sure, I have my pass and my... legs... and I'll be just fine walking. Just down the block, I think..." She craned her neck down the street. "Yes, there's the station and I'll just go to it."

Adrian turned. "Okay, then, I'll, um, okay." And he jogged down the stairs and toward his car.

Maggie followed slowly behind him and stopped at the bottom of the stairs. The violinist was playing a new song, now slow and slightly mournful. She wished she had some coins to toss in his case. Or a hundred dollar bill.

She pressed a hand to her heart. Still buzzing.

Chapter Nineteen

ADRIAN'S PHONE DINGED on the kitchen table. He read the message and frowned but also felt relieved. It was from Maggie.

"What is it, Dad? Aren't we going to pick up Miss Maggie on the way to school?" Charlie was sitting on the opposite side of the table finishing the last few spoons of her Cheerios, legs swinging under her chair.

Adrian forced a smile. "I guess not today, sweetie. Maggie says she took the Metro already this morning." He powered off his phone and slid it into the holder clipped to his belt.

"Aw, man. I wanted to do more play practice with her. I almost have my squirrel part memorized."

"I know, honey." He swallowed a sip of his coffee. Cold. "I'm sure we'll see her sometime this week."

But after yesterday's complicating interaction on the veranda, he wasn't terribly sure about that. What had he been thinking? He hadn't gone there to kiss her, but the dancing, her smile. Something about the way she looked at him. He shook his head. He didn't know about her, but he hadn't slept too well last night, a variety of emotions jumbling his thoughts. Confusion, fear, excitement, even guilt. Yet none of them had provided him with a clear picture of what, if anything, he should do next.

Maybe it was best to just let it go. They were adults—lots of stress, spending lots of time together. Just one of those things. No big deal, right?

He took the last gulp of his coffee and stood, feeling calmer. Maggie was probably thinking the same thing anyway. He found his keys in the cubby, then went to help Charlie get her lunch ready. *Probably.*

* * *

Maggie was sitting at her meager desk at the embassy, processing visitor requests for tours when Desmond breezed by, nose in a folder.

He stopped, looking surprised. "You're here early this morning."

"Oh, yes. Early bird and all that."

"Of course," Desmond said. "Um, since you're here..." He approached her as he pulled some papers from a folder. "I have some new work orders for the gala. I was wondering if you could sign off on them for me?" He pointed to a signature line at the bottom of the first page.

Maggie squinted at the top page, then flipped through the sheets underneath. "I'm sorry, what are these for, exactly?"

Desmond shifted his feet. "Oh, nothing really. Just extra orders for cups and plates. Just a formality, really."

Maggie found it hard to concentrate on the jumble of forms as she sifted through them. She was finding it hard to concentrate on anything this morning after a restless night of little sleep. She sighed. Well, it must be okay if it was from Desmond. She took her pen and signed the top sheet.

He took the pages and placed them back in his folder. "Well, good morning," he said, and scurried on his way.

Maggie tried to stifle a huge yawn and failed, then shook her head to wake herself. She felt a little like a coward for not having Adrian drive her in this morning, but she just didn't need the complication of not knowing how he would react. They *were* adults after all, and just because you kissed someone didn't mean there was necessarily anything there. And Adrian knew she'd been seeing Valéry. She had been seeing him, right?

She opened her next folder of visitor requests and pulled out the stack. If she just let a few days go by, things would return to normal. She didn't have time to think about it more anyway. Desmond had returned.

"Ambassador MacCarthy would like to see you, please. In her office?"

"Of course." Maggie stood up, hoping it was some good news to change her mood. Her grandmother had just returned from two weeks of brokering some trade negotiations with Silicon Valley, then back in Ireland for a few days. She made her way up the white marble spiral stairs to her grandmother's office, then knocked on the open door.

"Margaret, come in." She motioned with her hand to a seat in front of the desk.

"Good morning, Ambassador."

Her grandmother smiled at the use of her formal title. "I hadn't expected you here so early this morning. Is everything alright? You look a little pale."

Maggie managed a brief smile. "Me? I'm fine."

Her grandmother nodded, seeming unconvinced, but went on. "Margaret, I can't tell you how proud I am of how well you're doing with the preparations for the gala. I know I've been unable to assist you personally these weeks, but Monsieur LaBonté tells me you are doing a fine job."

Maggie blushed, surprised at the unexpected praise. "It has been a lot of work, I must say. That's very kind of Valéry—Mr. LaBonté to say."

"You will do well to model his abilities. I believe he has quite the future in diplomacy."

"Yes, he's been very helpful."

Her grandmother nodded. "I'm glad to hear that, which makes me believe you will, with his help, also be able to handle this new challenge."

New challenge?

Her grandmother stood and came around the desk. "Now, as you are aware, the gala is one of our most important events of the year, not only because it benefits so many children and organizations, but because of the cooperation it fosters among our many European brothers and sisters."

Maggie tapped her foot and tried not to bite her lower lip as she waited.

"You might be aware that the Queen of England has been planning a visit to the United States for some time." She sat on the edge of the desk, eyeing Maggie closely. "Now, I don't want you to be alarmed, but we've just received word that the gala will be on her agenda while she's here in Washington."

"The...gala? The *Queen?*"

"Yes. Now, obviously, we'll need to make some additional preparations."

The gala? *My* gala? Maggie's mind was already shooting off in a thousand different trajectories. She'd need a red carpet and—what did they call those long trumpets they used in the movies to announce the queen?

Her grandmother took her hand. "Margaret, now stay calm. Don't start putting the cart before the horse."

Horse? Should she get a white horse for the carriage? The carriage that still needed to be arranged...

The ambassador seemed to see the fear on Maggie's face. "Margaret, now, we've dealt with this type of thing before, and it shouldn't change your plans. There will be a few modifications, but Mr. LaBonté can handle most of those."

Maggie cleared her throat. "Of course. I'm sure there won't be any problems we can't handle."

Her grandmother patted her hand. "Good girl. Now, there is one other thing. Regarding your driver, Mr. Adams?"

Thoughts of the Queen suddenly evaporated. "Yes?"

"Margaret, you know you need to have all of your wits about you, especially now with these knew circumstances?"

Maggie knotted her hands, waiting.

"I've been receiving reports that you are spending quite a bit of time with Mr. Adams. In a non-professional capacity."

Who had tattled to her grandmother? And what had they said? What was there *to* say? *Valéry? Or maybe Desmond...?*

"Now, I understand that you like to have fun," her grandmother said. "But don't you feel that Mr. Adams is somewhat of a distraction to your work?"

Maggie's jaw stiffened. "Actually, I think he's been quite helpful."

She sighed. "Margaret, you're a big girl. You understand our role. In order to succeed in this profession, we must all have focus. I simply believe that Mr. Adams is a hindrance to that focus for you. Now, I'm sure he's quite a handsome young man, and that is attractive to you. I'm still a woman, you know, even in the midst of all of this." She motioned at the imposing office.

Maggie's face was expressionless. "I see. And what do you suggest?"

"Certainly there are other competent drivers. I'll have Desmond make a phone call."

"That won't be necessary."

"Margaret, I'll be frank. Shouldn't you be directing your romantic interests to someone a little more ambitious?"

Something clicked. "Like Valéry, I suppose."

"He does come to mind, now that you mention him."

"And now that I mention him some things are becoming a little clearer." A little stubborn courage shot through her. "Were you the one who suggested he just happen to meet me at the coffee shop that morning?"

Her grandmother's face remained unchanged. "And if I had, what would have been the harm in that? You seem to have been enjoying his company these last few weeks."

"I prefer to choose my own friends from now on, thank you."

"Come now, Margaret, don't be upset. Surely you can see the sense in meeting a few men of a more... sophisticated culture.

"Like the one who wore a dress?"

Her grandmother scowled. "You know very well it's called a kilt." She waved her hand. "I'm not having this discussion. For some strange reason you seem bent on squandering a perfectly good opportunity just so you can play house with some chauffeur and his child. I don't think you understand the seriousness of this situation."

Maggie stood, her chin in the air. "I understand enough. I understand that Mr. Adams—Adrian—is a good man who's just trying to provide for his family." She put her hands on the edge of the desk. "He needs this job, *Mamó*. I won't be the one that disappoints him."

Her grandmother sighed. "As usual, you're being too emotional about this. You always did lead with your heart."

Maggie's ears burned. "No, *Mamó*, I'm not being emotional, I'm being *compassionate*—there's a difference. Sometimes I wonder if you understand that."

Her grandmother's expression remained calm. "You know, I could have him removed without your permission."

"Oh, I know, and I will tell you that if you do, I will quit this job and be on the first flight back to Ireland."

"Really?" *Mamó* lifted an eyebrow. "You would be that impulsive?"

"I call it being decisive—something I would think you would appreciate."

She laced her fingers together as she studied her granddaughter. "Well, I can see you've made up your mind. Although I think it's the wrong decision, I can appreciate your fervor. Mr. Adams can stay."

"Thank you. Now, can we talk about the gala? If the Queen is coming, there is a lot of work that needs to be done." Maggie sat down, her heart racing. She'd won an argument with her grandmother!

"I'll have Desmond prepare a list of some of the extra accommodations we already know about that we'll need to take care of. We will need to be in touch with our counterpart at the British Embassy. There will, of course, need to be more security, and..."

Maggie's mind was already dashing ahead as her grandmother continued on with the list. She felt a tinge of pride that she'd stood her ground. Maybe there was some of that old MacCarthy fierceness in her after all.

And the Queen of England was coming to her gala! This was the opportunity she'd been waiting for all her life. No more botched dreams. This was going to be the best gala this town had ever seen.

Chapter Twenty

ADRIAN WAS WAITING, arms folded in front of him, as Maggie exited the front door of Bella Bella looking very professional carrying a black leather briefcase. She gave a perfunctory smile as he opened the back car door for her.

"Hello."

"Hi."

Adrian held the door as she got in. He thought about saying something, then sighed as he moved around the back of the car to get to the driver's side.

The trip was uncomfortably silent, except for the hum of the car as he glided through the morning traffic. Adrian was uncertain of what to say, or if he should say anything, and if he did, would it just make things worse?

Then Maggie blurted, "Oh, um, I have some interesting news. About my job. Guess who's coming to the gala now?"

"Let's see... the Queen of England?"

"How did you know?" Maggie's voice dropped in disappointment.

Adrian looked in the mirror, surprised. "What? Really? You're kidding. I mean I was just kidding."

"Yeah, right. Did someone tell you?"

"No, I swear, I didn't know."

"Well, she's coming, and thank you for ruining my surprise."

"Maggie, that's great, really. But won't that be a lot more work?"

"Of course, but we'll be ready."

"I mean, just the security alone…"

"We'll be ready," she repeated, a little crossly. "Everything is under control. Except for the transportation. We still need to figure that out. And I still need to find a carriage."

"A carriage?" A vision of a pumpkin pulled by white horses popped in his head.

"And we'll probably need more tables. And I forgot to ask for more chairs when I called the event center." She sounded worried.

"Don't take this the wrong way, but are you sure you don't need some more help? I mean, surely the embassy has more staff."

"No, as I've said before, I'll be fine."

There was the stubbornness. "Got it." He made a turn. "Well, it sounds like it's all starting to come together, then. I mean, the actual Queen of England. Will you get to meet her?"

"I suppose I might…I don't know…" She sounded like she hadn't thought of it before.

"Well, if you do, make sure you let her know you're a princess."

"Oh, I will," she said.

Oops. He could feel the sarcasm in her voice.

The trip grew silent until Adrian remembered something. "Oh, yeah, about Charlie? Her play's next Thursday night. I didn't know if you remembered?"

"Oh, yes… of course. Um, Thursday night?"

"Yes, at seven, I think."

He could see her biting her lip. "Oh, well, gosh. I'm sorry, but I'm pretty sure Valéry has me meeting with the caterers that night."

He bristled at the mention of Valéry's name.

She paused. "Is there any other night?"

"No, it's just the one performance."

"Well, you'll tell Charlie I'm sorry, won't you? I mean, I really wanted to be there, of course." She sounded sincere.

Regardless of how she might feel about him kissing her, the bond with Charlie was strong.

"Sure, of course." He steered the car through traffic. "Don't worry, she'll be fine."

"Maybe you can tape it?"

"Yup. I'm sure I'll be just one of every other parent there with a cell phone stuck to his face videoing their kid."

"Okay, thanks. And you'll tell her I'm sorry?"

"I will. She'll be fine," he repeated.

And she would be, for the most part. Charlie was pretty resilient, but her Maggie connection was strong. Maybe he shouldn't have involved her in his life so much. He hadn't thought about how long was this job going to last. Once this gala was over she might not need a driver anymore. She might even move back to Ireland, who knew? He hadn't thought about what it would do to Charlie if she couldn't see Maggie anymore. He hated to admit it, but she had become almost a mother figure to her.

His heart sank a little. Well, maybe Maggie's busyness would be a boon—a way to wean Charlie off of her involvement in their life in case she did move on. Although he definitely didn't want that to mean spending more time with the Valéry guy.

He glanced at the mirror and saw the now-familiar curves of her face. A sudden pang hit his chest as he thought of not seeing her anymore, and it wasn't for Charlie. It was for him.

What was going to wean *him* off of Maggie?

Chapter Twenty-One

"CAN YOU FIX IT, DAD?"

Adrian was squinting at his daughter's broken necklace, trying to locate the problem. One of the links had twisted and broken away.

"I think so," he said. "Let me get the pliers."

"Please, Dad. I really want to wear it at the play next week."

Adrian had stepped out of the room to get the pliers. "It'll be under your costume anyway, won't it?" he called back from the hallway.

"Yeah, but I still want to have it on. It's my lucky necklace. Maggie got it for me from that Ireland store."

Adrian came back into the room with needle-nose pliers. "Why is it your lucky necklace? Because it's a four-leaf clover?" It was a small, golden shamrock with a green emerald in the center.

"'Cause nothing bad has ever happened to me when I've had it on."

"But you never take it off, so how would you know?"

Charlie's shoulders dropped in annoyance. "I don't take it off because I don't want anything bad to happen to me."

He winced internally from fear and a little shame. Was he being too over-protective? He touched her knee lightly. "Sweetie, nothing bad's going to happen to you. I promise. Now, is everyone ready for the play?"

Charlie kicked off her slippers and hopped up on the edge of her bed.

"I guess so. We've only got a few more rehearsals. Dad?"

"Hmm?"

"How come we haven't seen Maggie?"

Adrian continued to try to squeeze the broken link on the necklace, squinting as he fumbled with the pliers, tongue stuck between his teeth. "Well, she's been very busy. You know, she has a lot of responsibilities now, and she can't always be going off with us like she used to."

"Well, is she coming to my play?" Charlie asked, hopefully.

Adrian didn't want to get his little girl's hopes up. He knew Maggie wasn't going to be there. "We'll see, Charlie."

"You always say we'll see, and then—"

"I know, 'most of the time I don't get to see it.' "

She sighed, picked up the now-prized pink squirrel Maggie had given her a couple of weeks ago, and climbed into her bed, sitting with her back against her pillows.

Adrian gave a last squeeze on the pliers, then tugged on the necklace to make sure the clasp held. "There," he announced. "What do you think?" He handed the locket to Charlie, who inspected it carefully.

"Looks good, Dad." She looked up. "You can fix anything."

"Humphh. Not *everything*, believe me."

"Can you fix it so Maggie can come to my play next week?"

Adrian tried to change the subject again as he stood up. "So, which story tonight?"

"Ummm... the princess story."

"Again? I figure you'd have that memorized by now."

"I do. I just like it when you read it."

"Okay," Adrian sighed as he began looking through her bookcase for *The Magic Castle*.

"And I want the voices. Do the voices like you do, and do the one of the princess like Miss Maggie."

"Oh, sweetie, not tonight, okay?" Adrian found the familiar book at the end of the stack, well worn from countless nights of bedtime stories. He returned to Charlie's small bed and sat on the edge while she pulled her quilted pink bunny blanket to her chest.

"Please, Dad? Do the voices?" she pleaded, leaning forward.

"No, not tonight," Adrian repeated, a little more sternly than he probably should. "I have to get up a little earlier tomorrow, so Uncle Danny is going to pick you up for school."

Charlie was obviously disappointed and sank back into her bed. "Okay. Can you at least do the voice of the prince like yourself?"

Adrian smiled briefly. "That I can do." He began reading while she closed her eyes, little hands folded on her chest. "Okay. 'Our story begins in a castle, but not just any castle, a castle in a magic kingdom, and not just any magic kingdom, but a magic kingdom in the clouds.' "

Charlie listened to his familiar, safe voice, until her breathing slowed, grew deeper, and she drifted off to sleep.

Even though she was asleep, Adrian continued to read until he finished the story, and the princess was safely rescued from the castle, the evil witch was defeated, and the brave boy had completed his journey and had won the princess's heart. It was a pretty simple story, but Charlie loved it, mostly because he did funny voices for most of the characters. But not tonight.

His eyes rested on the smiling picture of Charlie's mom she kept on her bedside table. It seemed pretty easy in the storybook, he thought. Fifteen pages and then "happily ever after." Well, he'd had the "happily." It was the "ever-after" that had left with Karen. The books never seemed to include that chapter.

He yawned. Somehow the brightness had gone out of the room, and he was suddenly tired. Some nights the house he now shared with just one girl seemed to echo with too many memories. He rubbed his eyes, then closed the book and, leaning over, placed it carefully back on Charlie's little bookshelf by her bed. Still sitting on her bed, he watched her chest rise and fall. She stirred, then, still asleep, clutched the fuzzy squirrel that Maggie had given her closer to her chest. Adrian tucked the corner of the blanket around his daughter, then patted her arm.

"Don't worry, sweets," he said, even though he knew she was asleep. "We'll be fine."

Now he just had to convince himself.

* * *

Maggie dropped her shoes onto the kitchen floor of her and Jelly's apartment, then shuffled to the refrigerator for something to drink. *Like maybe a whole bottle of wine.*

She was running herself ragged trying to get the final details for the gala in place, and now, on the night she was supposed to have met with some caterers, Valéry had convinced her to go to a performance of *Carmen* with him, using some last-minute opera tickets he had procured from one of his embassy connections. Lately it was just go-go-go with him. It was after ten, and she had just gotten home.

Jelly opened the door a minute later, carrying a to-go cup from the Red Zone. "Hey, girl." She dropped her keys on the kitchen table. "Guess what? The girl from Regal Rags called today. She showed the designs and samples to her board and they loved them."

"That's great," Maggie said dully, pulling out a cold bottle of water from the refrigerator and holding it to her temple.

"Whoa." Jelly eyed her. "How did the evening's festivities go? Looks like you had a rough one."

"It was going pretty well, until the fight started."

"Fight?"

"Just a bunch of drunk hooligans outside the Kennedy Center."

"I thought you were just going to meet with some caterers or something."

Maggie bit her lip. "Well, I was, but something came up."

Jelly took a sip of her drink as they both crossed into the small living area. "Let me guess... was the something about six foot two, brown eyes, and smelled like a French cologne factory just blew up?"

Maggie wrinkled her nose. "He had tickets to the opera, and he really wanted me to go. *Carmen.* Have you ever seen it?"

"Hmm... I've seen Elmer Fudd sing 'Kill the Wabbitt' on Saturday morning cartoons. Does that count?"

"Not really."

"Wow. Sounds like a great evening. Opera *and* a fight."

"Jelly, it was a once-in-a-lifetime opportunity."

"Oh, I don't know. Stick around this neighborhood long enough, and you'll see plenty of fights."

"You know what I mean."

"Mmm-hmm. So how is this gala going then?"

Maggie sighed. "The gala is going as planned. Valéry is making sure we're getting everything we need." *And then some.* "He definitely has a lot of influence."

"Mmm, I can see that. Sounds like he's taking care of everything."

Maggie could tell her friend had more on her mind. "What do you mean?"

Jelly sighed. "I don't know, Mags—and don't take this wrong—but there's just something about that guy that sets off my jerk radar."

Maggie's eyes narrowed. "Really? Sounds like you and Adrian have been sharing opinions."

Jelly shrugged. "Maybe. Seems like Adrian might be on to something too."

Maggie put her hands on her hips. "Great. So all of my friends think I'm playing out of my league. I don't deserve to finally experience some of the finer things in life, is that it? I thought we were all supposed to run after our dreams in America."

Jelly put up her hand. "Whoa, hey, not saying that. Just trying to look out for you, that's all. Remember? That's what friends do?"

"Friends also try to be happy when their *friends* are happy, or so I thought." Maggie flopped back into her favorite chair and pulled her knees up to her chest.

"That's true. But I can't say I'm seeing a lot of happiness going on here."

"I'm happy." *Aren't I?*

Jelly put her palm out. "Look at yourself, girl. You're all knotted up. Just seems like if you were really happy you'd be more… happy."

Maggie sighed, rubbing her forehead. "I know." She looked at her friend. "Am I really doing the right thing? I mean, this is what I've wanted my whole life—to finally be a success. To make a difference, to be with a man of sophistication, to not..." Her voice trailed off.

"End up working in a dress store?" Jelly came to her friend, kneeled down, and folded Maggie's hands in hers. "Sophistication, success—those are just words. All I can do is see what I see, and right now I see a girl who seems to get *less* happy the closer she gets to what she says is going to make her *more* happy."

Maggie considered that for a moment. "It does seem that way."

"I'm not saying working here was any easier. I mean, how many Saturday nights did we spend in the back room listening to my crazy jazz station while we sewed our fingers off in order to make just a few more scarves to sell."

"But it seemed so much more... fun."

"You got that right. I don't think I ever laughed harder than when you sat on that pincushion. You're working just as hard now and I hardly ever even see you smile much anymore."

"I'm too tired to smile."

"We weren't too tired on those Saturday nights."

Maggie sighed. "Maybe."

"And then there's men."

Maggie sighed more deeply. "Yes, there's always men."

"So there you are. On one side you got your sophisticated, super-cute French whozit taking you to a street fight tonight, right?"

"It wasn't a street fight. It was just an altercation outside of the theater."

"Right. And on the other side you got your boring, down-to-earth, dull American guy who took you to an art museum?"

"Who, Adrian? Well, yes, but that was for his little girl."

"And your hoity-toity, hunky European playboy went to what college, again?"

Maggie frowned. "He didn't have time for college—his father got him a job straightaway in the French Embassy in Paris."

"And your dull, everyday, average American dude graduated college at... remind me again?"

Maggie sighed. "George Washington."

"George Washington, right, and he only knows three languages, you said?"

"Okay, I think you've made your point, Jelly."

"I don't think I have if you're still pining over a man who feeds you snails on a regular basis, but you can't give the time of day to the one guy who made you laugh so hard tea came out of your nose."

"But Valéry seems so..."

"Perfect?" Jelly snorted. "How many old Hollywood movies have you been watching, girl? The princess doesn't ride off on the white horse with the knight anymore. We're lucky if we find a guy who even owns a white Corolla and doesn't live with his mother." She softened. "Look, I know how much finding the right guy means to you, but all I'm saying is maybe you've been missing what's right before your eyes."

Maggie suddenly thought of the day with Adrian and Charlie in the museum, and the Seurat painting—all the artistry, the subtle beauty, and all she could see were the misshapen, imperfect dots. Maybe she *should* step back and take another look. Not just at Adrian, but her life.

Chapter Twenty-Two

MAGGIE STUFFED THE DUSTY BOTTLE OF CHAMPAGNE Jelly had given her into the bucket of ice she had placed on one of the tables in the gala event room. Jelly said it was a cheap gift an old boyfriend had given her, but as long as it popped and was fizzy, it should probably serve its purpose. Tomorrow was her big day, and she felt a little celebration was in order for all of the hard work she had put into make the event a success. She'd be too busy tomorrow to probably even eat, so she would need to get any frivolity in tonight.

Workers were already filling the halls with drapery, bunting, tables, everything needed to turn the space into something fit for a queen. A *real* queen. Right down to the red carpet Maggie had insisted on having that led to the small dais where the Queen was expected to deliver a short address.

It was the first time she felt that the hard work—the running around the city, the scheduling headaches, even the late nights going over expense reports—was all worth it. It all felt so right this time. No FBI visits, no bogus pizza calls or misprinted posters. Definitely no doves.

She left the champagne to chill as she walked down the carpet, imagining what it would be like if she herself were the Queen, all eyes on her, waiting expectantly for her gracious words. She gave a small laugh.

"Well, you seem awfully bubbly this evening, Miss MacNally."

Maggie turned to see Adrian carrying in the last of the boxes of votive candles from his car. She rocked on her heels happily. "Bubbly? Well, I suppose so. I suppose I am, at that." She straightened the small pink ribbon in her hair, then motioned to the table. "Won't you sit?"

"Sure, I can take a break." Adrian put the box down on the floor, dusted off his hands and his pants and followed her to the table. Workers bustled around them unpacking boxes and testing the sound system microphones.

"I must say, all the plans are coming together. It's weird, really. The past week or so everything has just kind of fallen into place. I mean, companies have been contacting *me* to see if they could help."

Adrian sat at the table. "Well, congratulations. You worked really hard. I'm happy for you."

"Thanks. I wanted—"

Now, music blared over the speakers, before quickly subsiding into the background. *Kiss me while I'm dancing, kiss me with romancing eyes...*

For a moment her gaze locked with Adrian's. Her heart thumped. Probably just nerves.

Then he looked away. "Well, I'm sure it will be a great success," he said as he stood.

"You're not going already?" She nibbled her lip.

"I just figured once I had dropped off the candles you wouldn't be needing me anymore."

"But you'll miss the surprise."

"Surprise?"

Reaching behind the cherry blossom-studded centerpiece on the table, she slid forward the bucket of iced champagne and the two plastic cups she had stashed there.

Adrian sat back down. "Fancy."

"Not really." She shrugged sheepishly. "Sorry about the cups. The real champagne flutes are around here somewhere."

"Did you end up getting the gold ones with the silver rims or the pink ones with the gold stems?"

"Neither. Just plain silver." She wiped some dust from the bottle. "It's taken a lot of decisions to get here. So, no reason two friends can't enjoy a glass of champagne to celebrate, right?"

Adrian raised his empty cup. "No reason."

"I've taken the liberty of procuring the finest of champagnes, imported all the way from"—she squinted at the label—"New Jersey. It's not French. I'm afraid. Then, it couldn't be any worse than the stuff Valéry's family bottles."

"That bad?"

She held her nose and made a face.

Adrian took out a penknife and removed the foil from around the cork. He took a look at the label. "Dom DeLuise Cuvee Rose Magnum. Sounds great. *Much* better than anything French. Want to do the honors?"

* * *

Adrian watched her fiddle with the stubborn champagne cork and listened to her chatter about the final gala preparations. The flowers she was having flown in from Maui for tomorrow night. The matching table skirts she had had custom made from some Spanish cloth she had found at some artsy fabric shop in Palisades... She'd gesture to make a point, then go back to wrestling with the cork, her smile illuminating her face.

He listened to the slight Irish lilt in her voice, smelled the familiar fresh scent of her hair, and then there was something, something deeper that he couldn't describe. A sense of, not perfection, but just ... *rightness* was all he could think of, if he was even thinking at all.

And just like that, like seeing a picture that had been hanging in his house for months but now for the first time he was truly seeing it, there it was. So beautiful and natural and real he wondered why he hadn't seen it before, and he wanted to tell her he loved her.

He loved how she blew her hair up from her eyes with the corner of her mouth without realizing it. How she bit her lip when she was nervous. He loved how only one of her eyes would crinkle when she laughed, and how her laugh sounded like a bright, snowy Christmas morning when you've just come down the stairs and first seen the presents under the tree.

He loved how she pronounced "been" like "bean" and that she said "darn" like she was from Texas, and that she talked to squirrels, and that she never swore because it wasn't sophisticated, and how even now she was struggling to open the champagne bottle by twisting it between her knees because she didn't care that the workers setting out the centerpieces were starting to stare.

He didn't care about Valéry's reaction or how it would affect his job. There were other jobs, but there was only one Maggie.

He was going to tell her he loved her, because he had to do it now or he would never have the courage to do it again. He was going to tell her he loved her. He leaned closer. "Maggie, I—"

With a yelp, she jerked loose the cork. *Pop!* It shot from the bottle and hit him straight in the eye.

* * *

The young ER doctor finished checking the red welt over Adrian's eye. "You're lucky. About a half inch lower and you could have lost that eye."

Maggie was pacing fretfully in the ER exam room. "Adrian, I'm so sorry. I'm *so* sorry," she repeated, then covered her mouth with her hand. She looked like she was almost in tears.

"Hey, don't worry about it. Like the doctor said, I was lucky you weren't a better shot."

She folded her arms. "How can you joke about this? I almost blinded you!"

The doctor gave Adrian a sheet of instructions. "If you notice any double vision, blurriness, anything out of the ordinary, call the number on this form, okay? The nurse at the front desk can check you out." He shook Adrian's hand and left the curtained exam area, on to his next emergency.

"Hear that?" Adrian whispered. "The nurse is checking me out."

Maggie gave him a cross look. "I wish you would take this seriously."

Adrian raised his eyebrows in mock surprise. "But...you always said I needed to loosen up a little."

She gave him a mean smile, then came closer to his exam bench where he was still perched. "Are you sure that cork didn't rattle your brain?"

He smiled, remembering what he was going to tell her before the champagne cork had interrupted him.

He tried to look confused. "Pretty sure, Francine. Are the kids waiting outside in the bus?" He gave her a glazed look. "Where's my tennis racquet? I'm supposed to go bowling later..."

She opened her mouth, then just swatted his arm. "I swear, mister." She shook her head at him. "You sure they didn't give you anything?"

He rubbed his arm and smiled. "Nope. Anyway... I was going to tell you something, you know, before you shot me in the eye."

"Yes?" Her blue eyes searched his face.

"Um, well, the moment was... I mean, it was kind of—"

Her phone buzzed and chimed in her purse. She pulled it out and looked at the screen. "I'm sorry, Adrian. I really should take this. It's probably about the gala."

He waved his hand. "No problem. I'll just stay here and look for my bowling ball."

"You mean your tennis racquet." She smiled and touched his hand. "Hello?" she answered the phone as she left the exam area.

So, was he going to go through with this? He looked in a nearby mirror, gingerly touched the angry red welt over his left eye, then straightened his hair and his collar. Not the venue he was hoping for to have this conversation, but he hadn't planned on being interrupted by a malicious champagne cork. But then again, he hadn't really planned on this at all.

She returned a minute later, her face expressionless.

Adrian cocked his head. "Trouble?"

"Hmm? Oh no, not really, just... news."

"Everything okay with the gala?"

"Oh yes. My grandmother just wanted to tell me something."

"Okay, well, I guess if I'm cleared to go, there was something—"

Maggie turned. "Yes, she wants me to go back to Ireland right after the gala."

"To Ireland? Like, on a plane?"

"Of course on a plane." She stared at the floor as if she were searching for something. "There's a position in foreign relations she thinks will be just right for my next step. For my career. I'd be working in the same building as my mother."

The familiar cold sweat broke out on the back of his neck. "So, are you going to go?"

She toyed with her fingers and looked away. "Do you think I should?"

"Me? It's your decision, not mine." He knew how much her grandmother's influence meant for her career. He supposed it did sound like a good career move. It *was* what she said she wanted, after all, wasn't it?

"Well, if I go, you've been my driver, and... I wouldn't want to put you out of work."

Adrian hopped off the exam table. "I'll be fine. There's always work to be found." He'd have to give Nick Swanson a call first thing tomorrow. He found his wallet and belongings on a table and put them in his pockets, then looked for his jacket. Maggie took it from a coat rack and handed it to him.

She was biting her lip again. "I mean, you've got Charlie to think about." She wrinkled her forehead.

"Not to worry."

"Well, I just didn't want to interfere with your plans."

Adrian shook his head. "No problem. I'll be fine. We'll be fine. Charlie and I, I mean. You said it yourself, it's a good career move."

"I did?" She paused. "I suppose it will be..." She suddenly checked her watch, then backed away. "I'm sorry, I really need to get back to the venue. I'll take a taxi. So, I guess I'll see you later?"

"Sure." He put on his coat. "And good luck with the gala. I'm sure everything will go perfectly."

She seemed to remember something. "Yes, you won't be there. I forgot."

He hadn't thought of that. "Yeah, I'll be at home with Charlie."

"Well then… thank you for everything. And I'm *so* sorry again about the eye." She touched her forehead. "And… goodbye?" She turned, not waiting for a response, and quickly pushed out the curtain to the room.

"Goodbye," he said to the vacant room, putting his hands in his pockets. He felt something there and pulled it out. It was the cork from the champagne bottle. He must have put it there during the excitement. Turning it over in his fingers, he examined it as if it might somehow hold some answer he was missing. The news of her leaving now hit him full force, the empty room echoing his heart.

Interfere with my plans?

Any plans he'd made had left with the lady who just walked out the door.

Chapter Twenty-Three

THAT NIGHT, MAGGIE SAT ALONE, slumped in a mesh metal chair outside the Red Zone nursing her tea, her mind numb, her thoughts vacant. Her only friends were a pair of squirrels: the familiar, stumpy-tailed Mr. Hampton and another a friend she didn't recognize. They seemed awfully friendly, sitting side-by-side, tails brushing together as they watched her. She thought of Adrian, remembering he had wanted to ask her something before her phone call from her grandmother. Well, she guessed it didn't matter now. She tossed the waiting squirrels a few bits of biscotti, which they quickly gathered before darting up the hickory tree.

How was she going to tell Jelly she was leaving? Now that the possibility of going back to Ireland was real, she'd have to give up on the idea of being co-owner of Bella Bella. Would she care that Maggie would no longer be there? She wouldn't be surprised if Jelly might barely notice, considering how much time Maggie had spent at the embassy lately.

It wasn't until the threat of leaving that she realized she'd grown so used to calling DC her home. Was she really ready to leave? Did she even *want* to go back to Ireland, just for some vague promise of her grandmother's for career advancement?

She rubbed her temples. Why was her life always so hard? It seemed so easy for everyone else. Her grandmother. Valéry. Even Jelly, as hard as she was working, seemed to know just where she was going. But her?

She was tired of thinking. Tired of galas, tired of careers. Tired of everything.

Well, one thing she didn't have to worry about. Adrian didn't seem to care if she left. He and Charlie would be fine without her. She kept seeing his face in the ER room after she told him she was going back to Ireland, that silly red bump over his eye. That she had put there. She winced. For some reason, she had half-hoped he would beg her to stay. *Silly.* Instead, he'd seemed almost eager for her to go, hadn't he?

And that stirred up the most troubling thoughts of all. She'd realized she had become attached to him and Charlie. They'd snuck into her life and become a part of it. But until now, when she was faced with the thought of not seeming them... not seeing *him*... She'd taken it for granted.

She thought of the first time she had met him, his wide-eyed expression as her tea sloshed onto his tie, trying to keep his cool. She almost chuckled. He had almost instantly felt like a friend. All of this had started with him and that red, tea-stained tie. This job, the gala. He had been there all the time. She raised her head in realization. She had been looking at her work, at the gala, even at Valéry, at everything except what was right in front of her nose.

Silently, surely, and completely, Adrian had snuck into her heart.

* * *

"Thanks for your time, ma'am." Adrian stood. "I just wanted to let you know I really appreciated the opportunity to work for your granddaughter."

Ambassador MacCarthy also rose from behind her desk in her office on the second floor of the Irish Embassy. "Thank you. I must say, I appreciate your thoroughness, Mr. Adams. I can see why my granddaughter enjoyed her time with you. I hope you will be able to find new work quickly."

Adrian shrugged. "There are always other jobs." He knew he was being much more glib than he felt. His phone call with Nick at the company had been a dead end. All he had available was a temp job for the evening—some woman from the Slovenian embassy needed chauffeuring.

"I would appreciate it if you let me know of any other opportunities you might have in the future. Always happy to drive for the Irish Embassy again."

The ambassador came around the desk to shake his hand. "Of course. If you like, I can even put out some feelers for other driving jobs. I have a few connections with some of the other embassies."

"That would be appreciated." Shaking her hand, he turned to go, then stopped. "I would like to ask a question, though."

"Yes?"

"About Maggie's future, her job, I guess. What is your feeling about her abilities?"

"Her abilities?"

"I mean, I know she comes from a family of politicians, but—and don't take this the wrong way—are you sure she's cut out for this type of work?"

"Maggie has always seemed to struggle with her more free-spirited side, to be sure. It has taken quite some time and attention for her to find her niche. But I believe this appointment in Dublin will help provide her with an even more focused environment."

Adrian liked her free-spirited side. It was what made Maggie, *Maggie.* "Are you sure? I don't mean to interfere—"

The ambassador cut him off with a frosty smile. "I'm sure you don't. I'm sure you also know that her parents and I have known Margaret for many more years than you. I think we are aware by now what's best for her."

But were they? Adrian opened his mouth.

The ambassador cut him off. "Now, if you'll excuse me, Mr. Adams? And thank you again for your candor. Don't worry about Margaret.

She'll be in excellent hands in Ireland. Her parents and I will see to that."

"Of course." Any further argument seemed pointless.

"I believe you know the way out?" The ambassador gestured towards the door.

Adrian descended the stairs, rubbing the angry welt over his eye, which the ambassador had noticed but not asked about. Just as well. He was trying to forget last night anyway. His feelings for Maggie had surfaced at the worst possible time. What was he thinking? The night before the gala when she was already distracted, and he was going to blurt out he loved her like a dopey schoolboy.

And now that she was leaving, what was he going to do about it anyway? He had to find a new job. He had Charlie and medical expenses and house payments to think about. Feelings could change, but bills never went away.

He pulled open the heavy front door—and almost walked smack into Maggie, who was just coming in. For a second she looked like a frightened deer, her wide-eyed face inches from his.

"Sorry. Hi," Adrian managed, stepping back to make room for her. Instead, she retreated to the front steps outside.

"Oh, hi," she returned.

He joined her outside, letting the door close behind him. "I was just finishing some things up with the ambassador."

"How's your eye?" Her face looked pained.

He realized he was rubbing the spot on his temple, and shoved his hand in his pocket. "Oh, it's fine. Looks worse than it feels. Should have seen the other guy," he added weakly.

She seemed to get the joke. "And we never got to drink the champagne."

"The Jersey juice? Probably just as well."

She paused. "I need to thank you. In case I don't see you again?"

"Thank me? For what?"

"For everything. For the driving. For getting to know Charlie. For ice cream."

He fisted his hand in his pocket. He wanted to reach out and touch her face. "My pleasure. Really."

"Well, it was more than what you needed to do, I'm sure. I mean, you probably don't sing with all of your clients."

"You might be surprised. I did a round of 'Frère Jacques' with the little old lady from Montreal once."

"I'm sure you're just as charming with all the ladies."

"Some more than others," he found himself saying.

"Really?" She bit her lip. "And was I one of the more?"

"One of the more?" His neck was getting warm.

"Yes."

Adrian felt his heart spark. "Well, of course, you were one of the *more*. You were the most *more*. Wait—what do you mean by more. More what?"

Maggie threw up her hands in exasperation. "More. You know, more *more*. You and me." She pointed back and forth from her to him.

"Well, yes, you were the *most* more. Why do think I—you know." He rotated his hand on the air.

"What is *you know*?"

"*You know* is more like… *more*, I guess."

"You *guess*?"

He waved his hands. "No, I'm not guessing, I *know*." He hesitated, then said, looking in her eyes. "I wanted the *more*."

She threw her hands up. "Well, why didn't you say so before?"

"I was going to, but you seemed to be too busy chasing Valéry, and then there was the gala, and the champagne cork, and Eloise and the tennis racquet and you going back to Ireland."

"Well, all I can say is you picked a perfect time to say something about it."

"I'm going to assume you're using the word 'perfect' sarcastically?"

Maggie glowered. "What do you mean?"

"What do I mean? Just when things seem to be going more *more*, you head off to Ireland for who knows how long."

"Well, I don't have a lot of choice with that, do I?"

"Of course you do. You can stay here."

"And do what? Spend the rest of my life stamping visas and refilling the tea pot?"

"Not everything in life is always perfect."

"What is that supposed to mean?"

"All you've seemed to try to do the last couple of months is find your so-called perfect life—your perfect job, perfect career, your perfect guy with the perfect hair and the perfect accent."

"Valéry?" Maggie narrowed her eyes. "Well, at least *he* takes a chance on something every now and then. You're so brave you can't tell me how you feel until you have no choice."

"I was going to tell you until you popped me in the eye with a champagne cork. And don't tell me I'm not brave. I've single-handedly chaperoned a birthday party with twelve seven-year-old girls. *Including* a puppy."

"Right, and what about Charlie?"

"What about her?" Adrian frowned.

"You protect her like she's made of china. You're too afraid to take her to school even just because she has a sniffle."

Adrian's face darkened. "Hey, how I take care of my daughter is my business." Then he saw the hurt on her face and heaved a sigh. "Look, I appreciate how much you care about her, but I've got her to think about in all this. Especially now that I'm going to be out of work again."

"Oh, so now that's my fault too?"

"I'm just saying sometimes it's not always about what we want. We have to think about our responsibilities." His heart tightened at the thought of Charlie's face.

"I know you love Charlie, Adrian, but I think you may be selling her short."

He felt his face flush. "How do you know? How can anyone know? Maybe I had my shot. Maybe after her mother, I just can't let anything happen to her. Maybe it's for the best you're leaving. It's just too risky."

Maggie nodded at him. "There it is. Too risky. That's it isn't it? Well, do you know something, Adrian?" She reverted to her Irish roots.

"That's rubbish! You're right. You'll never find someone as perfect as Karen because there's only one of any of us. You accuse me of chasing the perfect life because I want to be successful, but you're just as bad, aren't you? You won't let go of your 'perfect' past because you don't know what's in the imperfect future. Well, nobody does. You'll never find someone as perfect as Karen, but you might not find anyone as—as *imperfect* as me."

With that, she turned and pushed through the door to the embassy.

Adrian could only stand there, rubbing the welt over his eye. A perfect reminder of how painful love can be. Was he letting something golden slip through his fingers by not chasing after her? He sighed, unmoving, eyes locked on the ground. *Now who's the crazy one?*

Chapter Twenty-Four

THE EVENING OF THE GALA came quickly. Saturday winnowed down in a flurry of last-minute details.

Maggie pushed the emotional hash of the last few days out of her mind. There was work to be done, and this was the big day.

The ice sculpture hadn't arrived yet, and her phone calls to Azad only ended in hopeless attempts at understanding Azerbaijani explanations. And she was still waiting for her string quartet, but since they weren't due to play until the dinner, she assumed they would arrive later.

Aside from those few wrinkles, the gala was all finally coming together.

Even though she was just a small part of the overall planning and preparations, she felt as if everything were riding on her shoulders. And in many ways, for her anyway, it was.

She glided as swiftly as she could through the room, repositioning centerpieces, straightening curtains, anything that needed that last final touch. A few guests were already arriving even though the official ceremonies wouldn't start for another half hour.

The full skirt of the beautiful dress Jelly had slaved to make for her swirled around her legs. She thought about the tight gown with high slit she'd turned down from Valéry. When she'd realized he intended to charge the expensive dress to the gala budget, she was even gladder she had said no.

She smoothed the sparkling pink fabric of Jelly's design and decided to do one last check on her hair and face in a small side room. When she entered, a man was already there, pulling on a tuxedo coat.

It was Adrian.

"Maggie, hi." He looked slightly embarrassed. "I was just using the mirror."

"There you are, Adri-*ahn!*" a heavily accented female voice boomed. "Why are you being so anti-social?" A busty, middle-aged woman in a skin-tight gold-lamé dress swished into the room. She noticed Maggie and frowned. "I'm Hazeltine Horvat, adjutant to the Ambassador of Slovenia."

"Very pleased to meet you." Maggie took the woman's chubby hand and hid her grimace as her fingers were fairly crushed. "I'm Maggie MacNally. With the Irish Embassy."

The woman gave a cool smile, obviously not impressed. "I see you have met my Adri-*ahn?* He has simply been a doll to accompany me tonight, haven't you, Adri-*ahn?*"

"Yes, I'm absolutely doing my best to be as doll-like as possible."

"He is my driver for this evening." Hazeltine ogled him up and down. "It has been such a *treat* having him ferry me around."

"I can imagine," Maggie said.

The older woman smiled, catlike, still gazing at Adrian. "If you'll excuse me, I must go make sure the stewards have placed me next to the Emir of Zazzau. He promised me a dance later this evening, and I am going to hold him to it." Then she chucked Adrian under his chin. "And you *too*, Adri-*ahn.*"

As she rustled out of the small room, Maggie set her purse down on a small table with a gilded mirror above it and a tufted red velvet bench beneath. Then she joined Adrian by the full-length mirror on the opposite wall. "Hello," she said quietly.

"Hi," was all he said back.

"I didn't expect to see you here." She fiddled with her pearl bracelet, a gift from her grandmother to celebrate tonight's accomplishments.

"Last-minute job." He cocked his head towards Hazeltine, who was scolding a waiter for not allowing her to take two drinks from his tray. "I didn't expect she'd want me to actually do more than drop her off, but she insisted I accompany her. I figured it'd give me a chance to see how the other half lives."

Hazeltine was now sneaking hors d'oeuvres from a side table and stuffing them in her purse. "She seems... interesting," Maggie said.

"Good news is she doesn't keep one of those little dogs in her purse. Bad news is she doesn't talk to squirrels."

Maggie smiled briefly. "Well, I have a feeling she will keep you busy."

"I figure I can handle it for just one night. Not as interesting as my last job, though."

She fidgeted with the pearl bracelet again.

Adrian held his arms out to the side, displaying his simple-but-sharp classic black tux. "What do you think?"

"Very nice." She cocked her head, noticing his open collar. "Um, is there a tie?"

He fished in his pocket and pulled out a small plastic bag. "They didn't have any clip-ons. Anyway, it's a swanky event, you know. So I have to give it my best shot trying to tie my own." He unfurled a long black bow tie and turned toward the ornate gold mirror.

She noticed him watching her in the glass, eying the sparkly pink dress.

"You look fantastic, Maggie."

She blushed, embarrassed but pleased. "Thank you. I feel kind of like a...um..."

"A princess?" he offered.

She felt even worse about yesterday. "I need to apologize, Adrian."

"You don't have to."

"No, please, let me finish." She knitted her fingers together. "I'm sorry I was so mean. I didn't mean to be so angry. It's just, there's a lot going on, and the gala..."

He struggled with his tie, looping and knotted, while he watched her in the mirror. "It's okay. Sorry if I was a jerk."

"I doubt if you've ever been a jerk."

He gave a short nod. "Tell that to my brother."

She watched him in the mirror, her reflection beside him, that image reflected back by the mirror above the table on the opposite wall—the two of them side-by-side, joined and reflected into infinity.

"I guess I'm still learning," she said, feeling she needed to say more. "About work and life and... things. I mean, how are we supposed to know?"

Adrian shrugged again, frowning into his mirror, obviously not satisfied with his tie. "There's a lot of stuff we'll never know. I don't know why a woman can't put on mascara without her mouth open. I don't know why little girls like *Frozen* so much." He paused, tugging at the corners of his tie, trying to straighten it. His voice grew quieter. "I don't know why I have a little girl who'll never know her mother. I don't know why some disease with a name I still can't pronounce kills people when they're so young for no good reason."

He jerked the bow tie from around his neck and flung it on the chair beside the mirror. "And I don't know why some moron invented the bow tie. Can you tie one of these things?"

Maggie picked up the rumpled tie. "Here." She straightened his crooked collar and looped the tie around his neck. "I learned from my grandfather when I was little. He hated these things, too." She saw him watching her face. "I think it was just a little thing he liked me to do for him." She made a last loop and pulled the knot tight. "There. All set."

"Perfect," he said, but he wasn't looking at the tie. He was looking at her. "You probably have things you need to check on."

"I do." But Maggie couldn't seem to make her feet move.

He waved his hand. "Go, go. I'll be cheering you on from my seat at the Slovenian table. We'll be the ones with all of the empty champagne glasses." He nodded at the main room where they could see Hazeltine already grabbing another glass from a passing waiter's tray. "Good luck, Maggie."

"Thanks," she said, wishing there were more to say.

She gathered her purse from the table, giving their reflections in the mirror above one last glance. Her back was now to Adrian, Adrian's back to her, their images no longer joined.

And there was nothing left to say.

* * *

Maggie concentrated on surveying the room. Everything was ready.

Almost everything. The hors d'oeuvre table was still missing its centerpiece—the swan ice sculpture.

Her stomach rumbled, not only reminding her of her frazzled nerves, but that time was running out. Guests were trickling in, and in the rush of last-minute details and seeing Adrian, she hadn't had anything to eat for hours. It would be just her luck to have her stomach growl right as she bowed for the Queen.

She grabbed a few crackers from the hors d'oeuvre table just as a flurry of foreign voices caught her attention. She turned to see Azad and another swarthy man carrying a large white Styrofoam container between them. They were making shooing motions with their heads and barking orders. The ice sculpture had arrived.

She stuffed the crackers into one of the side pockets Jelly had included in her dress and hurried to meet the two men. "Over here, please."

Azad nodded at his partner, and they followed Maggie to the head display table where black-jacketed waiters were already in place.

"Here, please." She knew Azad didn't understand English, but when she gestured to the center of the table, they carefully positioned the white box just where she wanted it. As they began undoing some wrapping, she clasped her hands, eager to see the two majestic swans, frozen and sparkling, the focal point of the decorations.

Chattering instructions at each other, the men released the top straps from the Styrofoam case and slowly lifted the protection away. Azad stepped back and beamed at her, obviously proud of his work.

Maggie's smile slowly melted as she beheld the majestic creation—two rearing roosters frantically battling each other, wings outstretched, claws raised, skillfully and exquisitely preserved in clear, shimmering ice. She looked around the room, instinctively searching for a second box. "But where are the swans?"

Azad beamed more, gesturing at the ice sculpture. The birds looked like they would be more at home at a cockfight in the backroom of a smoky bar than a gala featuring the soon-to-arrive Queen of England.

"These are roosters," she said stating the obvious. "They were supposed to be *swans*. What happened to the *swans*?"

Smile gone, Azad exchanged a disturbed look with his partner. Their ice creation was not being properly appreciated.

"They were supposed to be swans! *Swans!*" Maggie practically yelled, flapping her arms frantically.

Azad nodded vigorously in agreement. He jabbed his finger at the sculpture. "*Oldu, oldu. Coo-shay,*" he said, gesturing with both hands at the roosters.

"*Coo-shay,*" Maggie repeated. She pulled out her phone from her gown pocket and frantically looked for her translation app. Choosing Azerbaijani, she tapped in "*coo-shay.*" Why hadn't she thought to do that after she'd visited Azad at the restaurant and her cell battery was recharged?

She stared down at the screen. "*Cüce?*" she breathed, dumbfounded. "*Chicken.*" She dropped her phone on the table and stared blankly at the brawling roosters.

"*Oldu, oldu,*"Azad said, nodding in agreement. "Cheek-en." He gestured at the sculpture again as his partner began gathering the straps and Styrofoam box.

Maggie's shoulders slumped. The gala had practically started, and her glorious swan sculpture had mutated into two angry chickens locked in mortal combat. She checked her watch. Only ten minutes until the introduction of the gala committee, and the guests were already arriving. Some of them were already doing double-takes at the gleaming chickens arguing over the hors d'oeuvres.

She needed some air and a place to think. She headed to the nearest exit, a set of curtained French doors that led to a small balcony off the side of the main room.

"Excuse me, ma'am?" A vaguely familiar-looking man in scruffy denim overalls approached. "Miss MacNally?"

Maggie eyed the violin case he was carrying. "Are you helping the musicians set up? Is there a problem?" She hoped not.

"No problem, ma'am. We're all ready to play if you'd be so kind as to point us in the right direction." He motioned three other men forward from the side of the room. The trio all wore flannel shirts and overalls just as mangy, two carrying instrument cases and one lugging a huge bass fiddle.

"Play?" Maggie said, her heart beginning to sink.

"You look a mite squeasy. We don't need much space, if that's what's worrying you. Earl here can even stand."

"Happy to oblige." The man holding the bass nodded and doffed his straw hat.

Maggie could hardly speak. "*You're* the string quartet?"

"Don't you remember me, ma'am?" The leader grabbed her hand and pumped it vigorously. "I'm Smokey Hills. Well, that's my stage name. Real name's Walter, remember? The Smokey Hills Quartet, at your service."

Maggie stared at him and his friends. She opened her mouth, then closed it.

"So would that space over there in the corner be okay?"

She managed a nod. The band members gathered their cases and shambled after their leader as she forced herself through the doors leading outside.

She stepped onto the small, curved balcony and stared down at the wooded courtyard below. *Okay, think. Don't lose it. Everything will be fine.* If anyone asked, she would just tell them the chickens were a symbol of hope. No, make that a symbol of *peace*. Or better yet, a symbol of hope for *world* peace...

Oh, forget it. They were just freaking *chickens*.

Maybe she could hide the Smokey Hills Quartet's backwoods gear? She could put a curtain in front of them or something. Maybe no one would notice her elegant string quartet was dressed for a hootenanny.

Just then the first strains of music reached her ears. It could have been Mozart, Maggie supposed. It was hard to tell from the twangy sliding violin and bumping bass that bounced across the entire hall.

She leaned on the balcony railing, head down, and groaned. Who was she fooling? All her hard work and the gala was going to be a disaster. She'd made a mess of things again.

A familiar chattering interrupted her demoralized thoughts. A brown squirrel perched on the stone railing.

"Too bad you aren't Mr. Hampton." Maggie could really use a friend right now. She pulled a cracker from her pocket and dropped it near her feet. The squirrel jumped to the ground, grabbed the treat in its mouth, and scurried up a nearby tree branch. "Hope you enjoy it. At least one of us should have a good time tonight."

Maggie wished she could trade places with the squirrel. She'd love nothing better than to run up a nearby tree and hide. She could already see her grandmother's disapproving face. She groaned again. And what would Adrian think? He'd probably drive her to the airport himself tomorrow just to get rid of her.

As much as she wanted to hop off the balcony and escape, she knew she had to face the music.

The *country* music, she thought with a grimace. *Hillbilly Mozart.*

She was doomed.

Chapter Twenty-Five

VALÉRY, AS THE GALA CHAIRPERSON, was already at the front of the hall where a long red carpet led to a short set of steps and a stately dais where a gold lectern was flanked by two tall, potted shrubs. Maggie thought he seemed to be looking for her and, sure enough, he came to intercept her.

"Margaret, there you are. The guests have all arrived." He took her arm and hustled her toward the lectern. "The Queen will be making her entrance shortly. Do you have your greeting memorized?"

The question snapped Maggie out of her funk. "Yes, or at least I think so…"

Valéry frowned. "Now is not a good time for your mind to be elsewhere."

Just then, the Smokey Hills Quartet launched into a decidedly twangy version of Beethoven's Minuet in G.

Valéry rubbed his face with a hand. "We can talk about your *interesting* choice in musical groups later. Come." He pulled her along past the hors d'oeuvre table, his frown deepening when he spied the icy roosters.

Maggie wrestled herself from his arm, hurrying to get to the dais. "Those are Azerbaijani swans. Haven't you ever seen a swan before?"

He followed her to the dais, taking a place on the left side while she took her assigned spot at the right. From there, she had a supreme vantage point to observe the crowd, an array of tuxedos, slim shimmering dresses, dangling jeweled earrings and perfectly coiffed hair. The elite of Washington were arrayed before her at their tables, chatting, laughing, awaiting the penultimate moment of the evening—the arrival of the Queen of England.

Well, at least it was all for a good cause.

She searched the crowd for Adrian's face, finding him standing at a table near the front next to Hazeltine, who was busily accosting a nervous man in a tux with a red sash across the front.

Maggie caught the gaze of her grandmother, seated a short distance away. She mustered a weak smile, but the ambassador merely narrowed her eyes, then returned to chatting with her table guests.

Terrific. If nothing else went wrong, she might at least be able to keep a job cleaning toilets at the foreign relations office back in Dublin.

She tried to concentrate on her next task, rehearsing her memorized line in her mind. *Your Majesty, it is my great honor to welcome you to this, the forty-third Annual Diplomats Gala...*

Wait, it was forty-third, right? She shot a panicked look toward Valéry, whose gaze was fixed toward the entrance to the hall. There was a sudden commotion there, followed by a gradual hush of the crowd as everyone realized the same thing at once. *She's here.*

Maggie tensed and straightened a lock of hair on her forehead. From the sides of the room two men, both in full regalia and holding long, red-ribboned fanfare trumpets, solemnly stepped to either side of the dais.

"Ladies and gentlemen," a regal, British-accented voice rang out from across the banquet hall, where the red carpet began. "Her Majesty, Queen Elizabeth."

Everyone stood as one, all smiles, and applause rippled through the hall. The Smokey Mountain Quartet began playing "God Save the Queen," although with a decidedly drippy twang, as the Queen herself, in a stately black dress with a blue sash, began slowly making her way down the aisle, smiling and nodding to the guests. A set of grim-looking security men flanked her side, watching the crowd warily.

As the crowd faced the back of the hall to greet the Queen, Maggie, from her vantage point by the lectern, noticed a small and decidedly furry object scooting towards the front of the room. Her eyes widened as she recognized the uninvited guest. The squirrel had taken advantage of the balcony doors she had left open and decided to join the party.

Maggie's new friend scampered to her feet, looking up at her with pleading eyes. She recognized the look. The squirrel wanted another cracker. She tried to shoo it away with her foot, then stole a glance at each of the two trumpeters stationed on either side of the dais. Their eyes were fixed forward in attention, while the guests were focused on the Queen.

Good. No one had noticed the squirrel.

Fortunately, it had turned its attention from her toes and was searching around the lectern. Maggie almost sagged in relief when the party-crasher angled its head, its bright eyes focused in the direction of the doors that led back outside. *That's it. Go on... go on...*

The Queen was now almost to the bottom of the steps. The gaze of five hundred pairs of eyes followed her, all heads facing the dais.

The squirrel stopped, uncertain, then scampered back to the rear of the lectern.

No! Not there! Go outside, go outside! Maggie used every ounce of her will to wish her new friend out of the room and back to its tree.

The Queen arrived at the foot of the stairs and began to climb, gathering her elegant black dress in her hands, crown and jewelry sparkling in the bright lights. Maggie desperately tried to remember her greeting, which—no surprise—wasn't so easy with a wild squirrel inches from her feet.

Then the two trumpeters blasted their fanfare.

The spooked squirrel, now frightened out of its wits, darted for safety. Lacking a tree, it decided Maggie's leg was the next best thing. With a squeal, she lurched forward, arms flailing, the cold claws of the squirrel scrambling around her legs inside her full skirt. She missed a step, tripped on the next, and launched face-forward into the Queen of England's chest.

The horrified crowd gasped.

Maggie squealed more as the frightened squirrel shot out from under her dress in a furry brown streak. The two royal helpers at the Queen's side grabbed the monarch before she could tumble backwards off the steps.

Maggie, trying to recover her balance, twisted to the side, and then unceremoniously plopped down on the steps just as her skirt flew up in her face. She scrambled upright, but it was too late. The entire crowd, now silent, stared at her in open-mouthed disbelief as she smoothed her dress back into place over her legs. She smiled weakly at the guests but was met with only a sea of disapproving faces. Straight in front of her, her grandmother wore such a disappointed scowl that Maggie's heart almost stopped.

She desperately searched for Adrian's face, the one hope she had for some kind of release from this horror, but he was nowhere to be seen. She was all alone.

Chapter Twenty-Six

FROM THE SIDE DOOR LEADING OUT to the sidewalk, Adrian watched silently as Maggie leaned against a lamppost in her fancy dress, arms clutched together, staring into the street. He had tried to find her after the incident with the Queen, but she had disappeared. He knew it wasn't her fault, but he also knew how she would take it. If it had been someone else flashing their underwear at DC's finest, it would have almost been funny. But it wasn't. It was Maggie.

He pulled his tux tie loose and stuffed it into his coat pocket. He took a step toward her and then stopped, looked down, up again, and then rubbed his face with a hand. What could he say? Well, he'd come up with something. He couldn't leave her there alone.

He took another step.

"Mr. Adams," an accented voice interrupted him from the open doorway. "I thought I saw you at a table tonight."

Adrian looked away from Maggie. "Yes, I had... an assignment."

Valéry approached, hands in his pockets. "Yes, I saw your assignment. I'm surprised we didn't run out of champagne."

"You would have if I hadn't steered her towards the hors d'oeuvre table."

Valéry nodded. "Yes, of course. Well, aside from Margaret's unfortunate tumble, I believe the evening was a success."

"So I hear."

"As for Margaret, I'm sure you are aware she will be leaving soon? For Ireland?"

Adrian frowned. "I knew that was a possibility."

Valéry chuckled. "After my chat with Ambassador MacCarthy tonight, I'm sure it will be a certainty."

Adrian felt a sudden itch to punch this sanctimonious creep in his mouth. Well, maybe not that sudden. "At least she'll be away from you."

Valéry's smile froze, but he didn't take the bait. "We shall see. I myself am leaving for Paris tomorrow after another morning visit with the ambassador. Maybe my future travels will take me near Dublin, who knows?"

And without waiting for an answer, the Frenchman began walking towards Maggie just as another now-familiar voice bellowed from the doorway.

"Adri-*ahn*, there you are! Didn't I tell you that I needed to get back to the hotel? Come, come!" Hazeltine Horvat gestured with her chubby hand, wobbling slightly, as she hung onto the doorframe for support.

Adrian hesitated, watching Valéry approach Maggie, seeing her head fall forward in obvious dejection. He sighed, turned, and slowly followed his current assignment back into the building.

* * *

Maggie leaned against the lamppost outside the gala venue as far away from the scene of her crimes as she could get. Jelly's dress was torn and soiled, which fit her mood just fine. She shivered in the cool night air, but she didn't care.

Most of the guests had gone by now, and the cleaning crew was probably already at work, rolling up carpets, folding tablecloths, breaking down the sound system. The hillbilly-Mozart music had ended, the squirrel had been banished back out the balcony door, and the quarreling chickens had melted into shapeless lumps, much like her dreams. The Queen, after many, many apologies—from Maggie, from her grandmother, and from the event coordinators—had graciously waved the entire incident off as just an unfortunate accident that should best be forgotten. She had even commented on how much she appreciated the definitely *American* flavor of the music and decorations.

Fortunately, the purpose of the gala was at least fulfilled. The year's fundraising goal had been met and even exceeded. But that was little consolation at the moment to Maggie whose ambitions were disintegrating around her.

"Margaret? I hope everything is alright?"

Maggie looked around to see Valéry standing next to her, then looked down at the gutter. "Alright? How could it be?"

Valéry edged forward, seemed to consider hugging her, then put his hand on her shoulder.

"Come now, it wasn't that bad, was it? It's been a long night. I'll have my driver take you home."

Maggie looked up at the clear, starlit sky as if hoping some answer would magically be spelled out there. "Actually, if it's all he same, I'll just find my own way home."

Valéry removed his hand. "Very well, if that's what you want."

"Sure, I suppose," she said, not looking at him.

Valéry was silent, then turned and walked away to find his driver and car.

* * *

Maggie watched her grandmother, Ambassador Candace MacCarthy, apologize to one last guest, then walk briskly to where her car was parked. Desmond was waiting outside the car, stationed there for the last half hour, ready to whisk his boss away from tonight's debacle. He motioned his head in Maggie's direction.

"Margaret?" Face stony, the shamrock sprig in her hair now slightly askew, her grandmother approached.

Maggie groaned, her shoulders slumping even more. "I'm so sorry, *Mamó*. About everything. I so wanted it to be—I *needed* it to be perfect."

"Perfect? Margaret, I would have settled for just plain *adequate*." The older woman massaged the bridge of her nose with both hands as if trying to rub away the memories of the night. "Do you realize how much damage control I've had to do tonight?"

"I'm sorry," Maggie said for what she felt was about the hundredth time that night.

Her grandmother was silent for moment. "I suppose it was too much to expect for you right now. After all we did to help you." She shook her head.

"Most of those things weren't even my fault."

"Fault or not, it is your responsibility. That is one of the hard lessons you have to learn in our business."

Maggie's eyes flashed. "*Our* business? It's never been *our* business. It's always been *your* business, or Dad's business, or someone else's business. It's always been you telling me what to do."

"Child, we did that for your own good."

"For my good? How do you even know what my good is? I don't even know what my good is. I'm beginning to think I never will."

Her grandmother sighed. "Let's not talk about this right now." Maggie stepped into the street and put out her hand. "Come out of the street. You're getting your dress dirty." She helped Maggie to the sidewalk, brushing at the dusty spots on her dress. "I must admit your Mr. Adams may have been right about you."

Adrian? "What do you mean?"

"He was doing his best this morning to convince me you weren't suited for this line of work."

"Why would he do that?"

"Now, don't get defensive. I believe, in his own way, your Adrian was trying to help you."

Maggie blinked as she processed all of this.

"Oh, dearie." Her grandmother's voice softened, and she took Maggie by the shoulders. Maggie was surprised by this sudden gesture of affection. "I'm sorry this has all come crumbling down around you.

And I'm sorry I pushed you so hard." She gave her a brief hug. "Maybe this isn't the world for you after all."

"Excuse me, ma'am? Miss?" A voice interrupted them. "Will you be needing the carriage any more tonight?"

Maggie had almost forgotten about the horse and carriage she had rented for the occasion. It had been clopping in circles for some time—a big brown horse pulling a white carriage with crystal buttons studding the red velvet seats. The black-suited driver perched on his seat above the horse.

"I believe we're through for the night," Maggie said.

"Okay then, we'll just—"

He was cut off by a shriek from *Mamó*, as the horse leaned forward with its long neck and grabbed the sprig of shamrocks from her chignon.

"Ho, Jack, no!" The driver yanked back on the reins, but it was too late.

Maggie's eyes went wide in horror. The horse pulled at her grandmother's hair with its yellow teeth, happily chewing as if he'd just discovered the greatest treat in the world. *Mamó* swatted vainly, the horse oblivious, yanking and tugging until her hair, always perfect and precise, lay about her shoulders in strings and tufts. The driver hopped down, barely managing to stop Jack before he started on *Mamó*'s corsage.

Ireland's representative to the United States, queen of diplomacy, normally the epitome of perfection and poise, looked like she had just gone two rounds with the horse and lost.

Maggie had a sudden urge to laugh.

"Are you alright, Ambassador MacCarthy?" Desmond rushed forward to assist, glaring at Maggie.

"We will talk about this tomorrow," her grandmother said through clenched teeth. Chin in the air, she smoothed her hair, turned on her heel, and strode with what dignity she had left to her car, where Desmond opened the door for her.

Maggie had a sudden flash of Adrian doing the same thing for her so many times.

The carriage driver continued to apologize profusely. He was interrupted by a *plop, plop* followed by the sudden stink of fresh horse manure.

Maggie pinched her nose shut. "Party pooper." This time she did laugh, and she kept laughing until her side ached, and then her laughter dissolved into tears.

Chapter Twenty-Seven

MAGGIE PEERED OUT THE FRONT DOOR of Bella Bella, then checked her watch. The bus to the embassy wouldn't come down the block for another twenty minutes. She stared at the photo on her embassy ID card, her smiling face, full of promise. That girl felt like a stranger. That girl didn't know that she would never change, that she would always mess up every chance that came her way.

She slid the card into her wallet in her purse. *Won't be needing that any more.* She knew she had to resign. No matter what *Mamó* said last night, Maggie knew her grandmother would probably try to bail her out again. She would find her granddaughter something to do in the foreign office in Dublin, hoping it wouldn't end up involving queens or squirrels or horses or poop.

Well, Maggie was done being bailed out, and coddled, and looked after. It was time to make her own lousy way through life. *Whatever that is.*

Jelly came into the room. It had been a long night—or a short one, since there hadn't been much sleep. A night full of tears and talking and hugs, but not many answers.

"There you are. You okay? You didn't make your breakfast."

"Not hungry." Maggie didn't turn to look at her friend.

"Mmm-hmm." Jelly came over to the door where Maggie stood. "Girl, look at me." She put her hands on Maggie's shoulders until Maggie looked into her eyes. "So, I've only got a business degree and a big mouth, and I don't know if you're supposed to be the big mucky-mucky Irish dohingy lady someday, or if you're supposed to marry a Mr. Double Accent French Fry, but I do know this—you're the best natural designer I've ever seen and you're smarter than you think. You've got charm, and a crazy accent, and some weird, kooky thing for squirrels. I know not many things seem to have worked out for you the past few weeks. Except for maybe one."

"What's that?" Maggie asked, looking out the window.

"I think you know." She took her hands off Maggie's shoulders. "When were you happiest?"

Maggie sniffed. "Let's see. How about when I wasn't screwing up everything in my life? Or when a horse wasn't eating my grandmother's hair? Or how about when I wasn't planting my face in the boobs of the Queen of England?"

Jelly shook her head. "No, let's try again."

Maggie looked down at the floor, sensing what her friend was getting at. *Happy?* She thought back, before the hoopla of the gala. Laughing and working late on new designs with Jelly. Singing with Charlie at the ice cream store. Getting graham cracker-fudge ice cream with rainbow sprinkles. Being Snow White. Riding with Adrian. Dancing with Adrian. Talking to Adrian. *Anything* with Adrian.

"So I have one question," Jelly said.

Maggie sniffed, then looked up. "I suppose it's—Do you love Adrian?"

Jelly nodded, watching Maggie's eyes.

Maggie wiped an eye with the back of her hand. *Love him?* She wasn't even sure what that meant anymore. If it meant finding someone who could be a best friend, if it meant knowing that you had a family, a real family of your own, then yes. If it meant that when he held you, when he touched your cheek and he kissed you, it felt like there was no safer place in the world, then...

"Yes."

Jelly sighed in relief, her shoulders dropping. "Good, 'cause if you had said no, I was going to have to go after him." She leaned closer.

"You seen his butt? He's got a nice butt. I checked him out. Wooo, girl…" She fanned herself.

Maggie managed a laugh, hugging her. "Thanks, Jelly." She picked up her bag. "But I'm afraid it's a little late now." She winced, remembering last night's debacle. "I didn't exactly leave him with a great last impression."

Jelly shrugged. "You might be surprised. Men forget. It's what they do best."

"I'm not sure this one will. I'm not sure he can. And I think I should let him try to find someone who can make him forget better than a dense Irish twit who always makes a right bag of everything."

Jelly sighed. "There you go again, always looking for perfect."

The word reminded her of her conversation with Adrian, and stung. "What do you mean?"

"Well, so you bungled your job, and you're finding out that guys like your French stud-muffin aren't as great as you thought they were. So now you know life isn't perfect."

Maggie rolled her eyes. "I knew that before."

"Girl, if you're looking for the perfect life, if you're looking for the perfect *love*, you ain't going to find it on this planet. You know when love is perfect? If *you're* imperfect, and he's still there. That's when you know it's love."

Maggie nodded, wiped another tear, then hugged her friend again. "I have no idea what that means for me," she said into her friend's shoulder. "But you're the best friend I've ever had."

Jelly gave a muffled laughed. "Well, I gave it my best shot, anyway."

Maggie released her friend, looked at her for a moment, then turned and opened the door. Wordlessly she left, walking briskly down the sidewalk towards the bus stop, towards whatever imperfect future the world had planned for her now.

* * *

After dropping Charlie off at school in his own car, a decidedly somber Adrian made his way to Bartlett's Candy Shop. It wasn't like he had anything else to do. He'd have to stop by the Capital Transport office again just to be sure Nick hadn't missed anything. If things really got desperate he supposed he could always try taxi driving, but that was so discouraging he didn't even want to think about it right now. For some reason he thought this job driving Maggie would always be there, that it might even lead to something more.

Something more. What? More money? The thought of being financially secure used to thrill him, but now, it seemed awfully unexciting for some reason.

He wished he could have talked to Maggie last night, but it hadn't worked out. As much of a disaster as she probably felt the evening was, it wasn't that bad. Okay, tripping face-first into the Queen of England was pretty bad. But no one was hurt and no one was in jail. Besides, he'd already disrupted her life enough.

Anyway, she was leaving to go back to Ireland today.

He pulled into a thankfully empty parking space behind a familiar white and blue Diplomatic Security Service car. He knew Danny sometimes stopped in to see Beth before work, which gave each of them a few minutes to catch up. Sure enough, he could see his uniformed brother chatting with his wife outside the shop, acting as if he was just getting ready to go. Danny gave her a kiss, and she went inside.

Adrian gathered his phone, keys, and coffee mug and climbed out of his car. A nice car, but he missed the BMW he had used when driving Maggie. He missed seeing her smiling, her nose wrinkled in the rear view mirror. He missed the faint smell of perfume she left in the car when she wasn't there. He missed her.

"Leaving already?" Adrian called out as he got out, coffee in hand.

"Hey, not yet if you want to hang out." Danny came to greet his brother.

"I do have a few minutes to kill if you don't mind. You sure?"

Danny nodded. "I'm not due in for another twenty minutes."

The two brothers sat together on the iron park bench outside the front door of the store. Various shoppers came and went. It was the usual passing crowd just like any other day.

"Sorry about Maggie leaving. You have any new job leads?" Danny asked, breaking the ice.

"Maybe. I'm going to swing by the office later this morning to see if Nick has any new leads. If I really get desperate I'll have to beg for some scraps from Mr. Valéry LaBonté, primo French dillweed." He raised his coffee cup. "Yippee."

"Yeah, sounds like it's been kind of a tough week?"

"I've had worse, but yeah." Adrian took a sip from his coffee and grimaced. It was almost cold.

Danny checked his watch. "So, seeing as I only have nineteen more minutes, let's get to it."

"To what? There's really nothing much to say about it. I'll find something eventually."

"Really? Nothing? How about 'Danny, the woman I'm pretty sure I love is leaving the country to advance her career and I'm too scared to chase after her like a bad rom-com movie'?"

"You make me sound like an idiot."

"Well, you always make it sound complicated, but I have a feeling it really isn't."

"How so? Please, enlighten me, because right now I've got a little girl who's in danger of ending up on a psychiatrist's couch because she wants to drag a pink squirrel with her wherever she goes, I've got no job, and worst of all, my coffee's cold." He dumped it out on the sidewalk.

"Okay, so how about just focusing on the 'woman I'm pretty sure I love' part?"

"I tried that and almost had my eye put out by a champagne cork."

Danny waved his hand in dismissal. "You give up too easy."

"Really? And what makes you so tough?"

"Well, I've been eating Beth's chili for eight years."

Adrian wrinkled his nose. "You do have a point."

"Look, you always say you want what's best for Charlie, right?"

"Of course."

"Well, what if Maggie is the best for her?"

Adrian rubbed his eye. "Maybe, but what if she isn't? What if it doesn't work out? What if she doesn't like the Beatles or she hates barbecue or she snores? What if she... what if she gets hurt, or sick, or gets a tumor—"

"A what? A tumor?"

"Or cancer, or get's hit by a bus, or... or bit by a squirrel with rabies?" He paused. "What if Charlie falls in love with her and then gets her heart broken. Again." He shook his head. "I can't risk that."

Danny laughed, shaking his head. "What if, what if, what if. You don't get it, do you? You don't think Beth and I have to work at love? You don't think there's a risk every time I go to the grocery store and forget to get her strawberry Fig Newtons?

Adrian frowned, unamused. "That's not the same."

"You don't know how much she loves strawberry Fig Newtons. Look, the point is when you're dealing with love, you take risks every day and you just can't fill your head worrying about all the what ifs. Remember when you were dating Karen, and you took her to that—what was it? That outdoor movie place over in Silver Spring?"

"Harper's Drive-In."

"Right, Harper's Drive-In, and she said she wanted popcorn, but their machine was broken or something, so you drove Dad's old Dodge Dart eight miles to Kensington and made it back before the movie started?"

"Yeah, that was pretty dumb. That thing didn't even have safe brakes. I just about hit a cow."

"Well, I miss *that* Adrian, and I think that's the Adrian your Miss Maggie might need to see more of, too."

"Right, so I'll sabotage my brakes and drive like an idiot next time I get her in a car." He snapped his fingers. "Hey! Maybe we can hit a few mailboxes and a couple of pedestrians too. Oh, wait. I forgot. I don't have that job anymore."

"Hey, one life-altering crisis at a time. But let me ask you this. Would you have married Karen if you knew she was going to die from a brain tumor?"

Adrian paused. "That's not a fair question."

"I know."

Adrian rubbed his face. "I know what you're doing. 'Of course I would have' is what I'm supposed to say, right?"

"Like you said, it's not a fair question, so there's no fair answer. But maybe the point is you're here, Charlie's here, you're on the other side. You're not the same guy that married Karen, but maybe that's okay. Maybe that's better." He paused. "You might never find someone as perfect as Karen, but you might not find anyone as imperfect as Maggie either."

Adrian looked up. "That's exactly what she said."

"Who? Maggie? Well, then she just might be a whole lot smarter than you are."

Adrian snorted. "I wouldn't doubt that."

"So, do you love her?"

"Well, yeah, I think so."

"Are you *in* love with her?"

Adrian knew what his brother was asking, and thought of all that meant. It felt like betraying Karen, and their marriage, and even Charlie, if he said yes. But his practical side knew that even Karen wouldn't have wanted him to wallow in loneliness and fear forever. And it was undeniable that he was already missing Maggie, and that he thought about being with her every day.

"Yes," he replied.

"Great," said Danny. "Now, here's the hard one. Would you *love* her?"

Adrian was puzzled. "I just said—"

"Right, you said you'd like to be with her forever, and hold her hand, and jump in bed, and run down the beach hand in hand laughing while violins play. But that's just the beginning, believe me."

Adrian did believe him, knew what he meant, because he'd lived it already once. Even with Karen, all the good stuff, the easy infatuations, each one had a flip side. The working through a fight over spending money on a new stove he knew she wanted but didn't tell her about. Or him trying not so gracefully to get out of spending Christmas with Karen's overbearing mother. Or whether to fold the towels or roll them—all the little insignificant things that Cupid doesn't tell you about when he shoots you with his stupid arrow. The things you choose to go through for something bigger and better.

"So what am I supposed to do?" Adrian said finally.

His brother shrugged. "Go after her, talk with her, apologize for all the stuff you did wrong even if you don't know what they were. You know, the usual man stuff. Ady, I just think if you don't give this a chance, you're going to regret it."

"Maybe." Inside, he knew his brother was right. He did love Maggie, but hadn't that chance passed? "Maybe," he repeated, "but she's gone now."

Danny's forehead wrinkled. "What, did she evaporate? Did she leave the planet? Is she on Mars?"

"Worse. She's heading back to Ireland." He saw Valéry's sneering face and thought of what he had told him last night. *Maybe my future travels will take me near Dublin, who knows?* "Oh, and then there's Valerie."

"Valerie? Who's she?"

Adrian shook his head. "Sorry—*Valéry* LaBonté—the French dillweed I mentioned before."

Danny put his hand to his chin. "I see. Valéry…and this is the guy you were telling me about a few weeks ago? The one who set off your radar?"

"Yeah, it's like, I know he's just a jerk who wears too much pomade, but I can't shake the feeling there's something more going on there. I heard a conversation a few weeks ago. It was in French, but there was a lot about paper trails and shredding documents."

"And he works for the French Embassy?"

"Yeah… What's up?"

Danny snapped his fingers. "Now I remember. Hang on, I need to make a call."

Adrian checked his watch. "Um...aren't you going to be late for work?"

"That's who I'm calling. You said LaBonté, right?"

"Yeah?" Adrian stared at his brother quizzically but knew enough not to ask him questions at the moment. Danny already had his phone out and was waiting for an answer from the other end. After a minute or so of conversation and note taking, he touched the screen, put the phone back on his belt and sat back.

"Well, you were right to have me check on him. This guy is probably greasier than his hair."

"Really? I knew it!" Adrian touched his fingertips together and leaned forward. "What is it? He murder someone? He's actually a weasel wearing a man suit?"

Danny shook his head. "Sorry, not quite so fancy, but still pretty serious. So, I'm not in on the investigation, right? But I asked around and I was able to get the gist. Apparently Diplomatic Security has received and cross-matched records from a bunch of embassies—Irish, British, even Luxembourg. They found out this guy's been siphoning money from a bunch of accounts for a few years, including this annual gala, using a false name and routing it through a couple of banks until it ends up in the Cayman Islands under another account for someone named Carlos Galyaga."

"Who's that?"

"Him. Apparently, as soon as we get confirmation from the French Embassy and the go-ahead from the locals, he's going to find out what the inside of a Diplomatic Security holding cell looks like." He chuckled. "Actually, your Maggie may have been the one that tipped them off."

"Maggie? How?"

"Not sure exactly, but she filed a report about some strange ledger balances at her embassy a few weeks ago." Danny looked at his notes. "Some guy at her embassy named Desmond? That connection led right to your Valerie."

"Wait a minute. That's probably why he's leaving. He told me last night he's flying to Paris today."

"Might be skipping town."

Then it hit Adrian. "Is there a Metro police station near Sheridan Circle? On Embassy Row?"

"Why do you ask?"

Adrian frowned, remembering his conversation with Valéry last night. "I think I know where the greaseball might be. And we'd better move quick." He pulled his phone from his belt, activated it, and touched the "call" icon under Maggie's name.

Chapter Twenty-Eight

MAGGIE PAUSED AT THE ENTRANCE to the Irish Embassy, looking up at the green, white, and red flag drifting in the breeze. She was trying to muster the courage to talk to her grandmother, but the thought of facing her made her just want to run. The thought of facing just about *anything* from the last few weeks made her want to run. Right back to Dublin, if that was what they wanted.

"Well, here goes," she whispered as she grabbed the weathered bronze door handle.

A waft of familiar cologne greeted her as a well-groomed figure almost bumped into her.

Valéry stepped back, then smiled broadly. "*Ma chère!* I was just going to call you. I was hoping you were inside. I was just finishing up some final business here. I wanted to see you before you left for Dublin."

Dublin? How did he know already? "Yes, I'm running a little late." She stepped into the small marble-floor entryway as the heavy door closed behind her. He must have talked with *Mamó.*

Valéry stepped back, making way for her. "Well, this is better. I can talk to you more privately." He took her hand.

"Certainly, yes," she said, following him. She wasn't really in the mood for this, but she didn't want to be rude.

Once inside the small room where they had practiced dancing, Valéry turned. "Good news, *ma chère.* I have it on good authority that

I will be taking a junior minister position in Paris." He drew closer, taking her hand. "Which means it will be a shorter trip to come see you in Ireland."

"That's... great."

"Or, if you like, you can always come to visit me in France." Valéry suddenly kissed her hand. "We could visit my family's villa at the vineyard. All the wine you can drink!"

Her face involuntarily squinched at the thought of his family's wine. "Sounds lovely," she lied.

"It would be, I assure you. I will say, I have thoroughly enjoyed our time together, especially these past few weeks. I hope that we can continue our relationship abroad, no?"

"I suppose." Maggie wasn't sure what to say. He sure seemed to be in a hurry. Why hadn't he mentioned anything like this before?

Valéry checked his watch. "Now, I would love to stay and talk, but I must be at the airport soon. *Au revoir.*" Valéry's phone began to ring. He pulled it out, checking the screen. "I must take this." He squeezed her hand, then headed for the embassy entrance, speaking into his phone in low tones in French.

Maggie just stared, still puzzled by the exchange. Then her phone began ringing as well. She checked it, nibbling her lip as she saw who the caller was. Terrific. "Adrian, this is really not a good time."

"Maggie, I'm sorry, I didn't call to talk—"

"You called me on the phone to not talk?

"No, I mean...we tried contacting the ambassador, but she was in a meeting or something. Look, is Valéry with you?"

"Valéry?" He was still at the front entrance talking on his phone. "What do you want with him?"

"Okay, I know this is going to sound crazy, but he's wanted for questioning by Diplomatic Security."

Maggie eyebrows arched. "Questioning?"

"Yes. Wait, my brother will explain."

There was the slight commotion of a phone being passed to someone else.

"Maggie? Hi, this is Danny Adams."

"Adrian's brother?"

"I'm with the Diplomatic Security Service, and we have solid information that Mr. LaBonté has been misappropriating funds from his embassy, and possibly yours, over the past few years. Adrian said he might be with you?"

"Misappropriating? What do you mean? He's been *stealing*?"

"We think so, yes. If he's with you, you need to let us know so we can send some officers to quietly pick him up. We don't want to spook him. If he knows we're looking for him, he might try to dispose of the stolen funds."

"Stolen from where?" she asked, though a niggling suspicion was already taking root.

"Well, for one, the fund for the gala you were working on, I'm afraid."

Maggie grabbed the edge of a nearby chair and slumped into it, still holding the phone to her ear. "But how could he have…" She trailed off, trying to sort through a jumble of thoughts now cascading through her mind.

She raised her head, eyes closed. It was all coming too fast, but it was also all becoming too clear, too real, and too much. Of course. *Valéry.* She closed her eyes, seeing it all now. It was no coincidence that he just happened to meet her at the Red Zone. Her grandmother must have already told him her flighty granddaughter would need his help with the gala, and Valéry had used that to his advantage. Different goals, but with the same purpose. It was all just a plan by everyone around her to control her—the simpleton, the waif from Ireland in the big city. Her face burned.

"Maggie? Miss MacNally?" Danny prodded on the phone. "Are you okay?"

Her back stiffened. "Yes, I'm fine." Then she remembered something. "Did you say from our embassy as well?" she asked.

"I'm sorry?"

"You said he might have possibly stolen from our embassy as well, the Embassy of Ireland."

"Yes, we think he may have, as well as others in the past. We think he's been using his position as chairman for these galas to inflate budgets, change line items. We're not totally sure of all of the details yet, but the evidence is pretty overwhelming. We've contacted his embassy, but he wasn't there. They did tell us he has booked a flight to Paris for later today."

"Yes, he said he taking a new ministry position there." Maggie was thinking, her eyes narrowing.

Just then Desmond strode past the doorway of the room carrying a folder and some papers. He slowed, gave her a nod and then hurried on, glancing back at her twice. He stopped at the front door where Valéry still stood and greeted him. The two men then began talking in hushed tones, occasionally shooting furtive glances her way.

She turned and spoke into her phone in a hushed voice.

"And these other embassies, how did they lose their money… their funds?"

"I'm not at liberty to share all the details," Danny responded carefully, "but I can tell you that Mr. LaBonté may have had inside help. Someone on staff at a few of the embassies."

Maggie began sorting memories. Supposedly lost paperwork… extra bills that she needed to sign off on… work orders for jobs she wasn't sure had ever even been completed. She had mentioned all that in her report a few weeks back. And all of it had one factor in common. One *man. Desmond.*

"Miss MacNally? Maggie? Are you still there?"

"Yes," she said finally. "Mr. LaBonté is definitely here." She could hear the Frenchman's oily laughter bouncing off the walls of the embassy's entryway as he continued his conversation with Desmond. "And you can add someone else to your list. Desmond Cooney."

"Desmond Cooney? He's the one you mentioned in your report a few weeks ago?"

"He's the assistant to the ambassador here. I'm almost positive he's in on it as well."

"As a matter of fact, your report is what broke the investigation."

Maggie felt some sense of satisfaction, although now there was a growing sense of urgency as well. "They're both still here. Together."

"Good," Danny said in a relieved voice. "Great. I'll let my superiors know where they can pick both of them up."

"But I think they're about to leave. Do you want me to stop them?"

"What? No! Maggie, just stay put," Danny instructed.

There was the sound of scuffling.

"Just let them be," Adrian said, his voice back on the phone. "The police will take care of everything. There's a Metro Police station about ten minutes from you. They can be there in just a few minutes, and they'll take care of everything."

She could hear Valéry and Desmond's echoing voices and the creaking of the front door as it opened. They were getting ready to leave.

"They won't get here in time," she said.

"What? No, Maggie, just let them be."

Adrian's pleading voice was still talking as she lowered the phone and ended the call. She thought for a moment, then raised it again, punched some buttons on the screen, and hunted for and found the map application. After a few moments of searching, she pressed another button and shoved the phone in her skirt pocket.

She jogged after the pair, just catching the door before it closed. Desmond was making a beeline for the ambassador's car, obviously heading somewhere in a hurry. Valéry was already halfway to his car in the entryway, its motor running, no doubt to make sure the interior was kept cool for him at all times. His driver was missing, however. She searched and found him, on his phone and finishing a smoke by the side of the building.

Desmond had started the black BMW and was already pulling into traffic, but he could wait. Maggie glanced from Valéry's driver to the car where Valéry was now waiting in the back seat. Through the window, she saw him leaning forward, using the rear view mirror as he primped his hair.

Her eyes narrowed and the corners of her mouth slowly curled into an impish smile. *Well, Mr. LaBonté, you've taken me for quite a ride.* Maybe it was time to return the favor.

Chapter Twenty-Nine

MAGGIE WAS ABLE TO REACH the driver's side door before the driver, who was stamping out his cigarette, knew she was there. She opened the door and, without a word, got in and locked it behind her. Digging her phone out of her pocket, she pressed the icon she'd pre-set on the screen and tossed the phone on the seat beside her.

"Margaret!" In the back, Valéry jerked his head away from his preening in the mirror and flashed her a surprised smile. "What are you doing here?"

Maggie turned in her seat. "If I were you, *Valerie*, I'd buckle up."

She wrestled the gearshift into drive, sat back, and pressed hard on the gas pedal. The black sedan roared, lurched, then bumped up on and then back down off the curb. She wove down the road, tires screeching as they grabbed at the pavement.

"Margaret!" was all Valéry got out before he careened into the side of the door. "What are you doing?"

"Just trying to get you to your next appointment."

Valéry tried to regain his composure, obviously confused. "But the embassy is the other direction."

"Oh, I meant your appointment at the police station." She slammed a little too hard on the brakes to avoid a car backing out of a parking place, then swerved around it.

"Police station?" She could see the sweat on his forehead in the rear view mirror.

"Yes, that's where they put people who embezzle money, isn't it?"

"Please, *chérie*, stop the car." His tone had grown darker.

"Not quite yet. We still have quite a few blocks to go." She swerved to miss a particularly deep pothole.

Valéry slid sideways across the backseat. "Have you lost your mind?" He cursed—something in French that Maggie suspected had something to do with an impossible anatomical function—and then slammed back in the other direction against the door.

The GPS app on her phone gave her a friendly instruction to turn right in five hundred feet.

"Maybe." She swerved to avoid a parked car's door that just opened ahead on her right. Her gaze darted from the dashboard to the road, trying to get the feel for the wheel as the car careened down Massachusetts Avenue. "I guess we'll see if I get you there alive."

"I don't know what you think you're doing." Valéry intoned as he scrambled to find his seat belt. "But you have just lost any hope for a future in diplomatic circles. I will make sure of it."

Ignoring him, Maggie whipped the steering wheel to make a sharp right onto Decatur, sending him scooting across the seat again. This time he nose-dived into the opposite door.

"Oops," she said with a glance in the mirror. "Sorry about your *nez*."

Eyes back on the road, she let out a yelp. The car rebounded over a pothole she couldn't miss. She realized she was in the left lane just as an oncoming car swerved to her right, whizzing past her on the wrong side of the road, horn blaring. She was trying hard not to wander into the other lanes, but she wasn't that accustomed to driving, much less on the right side of the road. Both hands with a death grip on the wheel, she checked the GPS on the seat then glanced in the rear view mirror. Valéry had his cell phone to his ear.

"While you're at it," she offered, "maybe you should call your embassy to let them know you're going to be a little late to whatever important meeting you might have planned." Cars honked wildly as she drifted left into oncoming traffic. "I think they're going to have a lot of questions for you."

Valéry sneered. "I doubt that. I'm afraid it is *you* who will have the questions."

She swerved right, speeding up to pass a lumbering FedEx truck.

"Where is Leclerc? Get me LeClerc," he barked into his phone between jostles. "What? Where? No, I am being driven by a maniac woman and I need Leclerc." He looked out the window. "Questioning? What questioning? No, I am on some road somewhere in this filthy town."

"Tell them I'm taking you to the Metropolitan Police station on V Street," Maggie said helpfully.

"In five hundred feet, make a right turn," soothed the GPS voice.

She looked for the turn signal—she knew it had to be somewhere. Instead, the windshield wipers whumped maniacally across the glass.

Valéry was speaking into his phone. "She says we are going to some police station. I don't know! She's crazy!" The swerving car bounced him into the door again. "*Awf!* Have Bernard meet us there so they can arrest this fool before she kills me."

Maggie looked in the mirror, shaking her head. "Oh, Valéry, you're not thinking. You'd be dead way before I'd get arrested."

Valéry's eyes grew wide. He stared past her. "Watch the road!"

Maggie had drifted to the left side of the road again, and an oncoming car screeched to a halt in front of them as she whipped the car back into the right lane.

"Sorry, forgot to mention I haven't driven in years," she said sweetly. She fumbled for the brake pedal, pushed too hard, squealing the tires, then made a hard right. "You can't tell, can you?"

The GPS calmly directed her to take the next right onto Sixteenth Street.

Caught off guard, Maggie whipped the wheel, and they sped into an alley, tires squealing. Valéry went head over heels, his two well-polished shoes waving in the air like three-hundred-dollar antenna. In a muffled voice he shouted something unintelligible but definitely angry.

She grinned. "Guess I took that turn too soon. So sorry. I warned you to buckle up."

She rumbled down the alley and out the other side onto the adjoining street where the recalculating GPS directed her to take a left. She could now see the blue signs marking the way to the police station up ahead. She wasn't exactly sure what she was going to do once she got there, but at this point she didn't really care.

Moments later she lurched to a stop in front of the brick building and hopped out of the car. As she approached the two officers standing out front, Valéry's window glided down.

"Officers, thank goodness! This madwoman has kidnapped me! Call the French embassy at once," he demanded.

Maggie handed the closest officer her embassy ID card. "I have to apologize for my passenger, sir." She lowered her voice to a whisper. "I think he's been drinking again."

The officer eyed her and her card. After returning it, he said something to his colleague, who checked his clipboard, then stepped to the back window.

"And your card, sir?"

Valéry looked like he was fuming. He fumbled for his identification card and jammed it out the window. "I am Valéry LaBonté, assistant to the Ambassador of France," he announced as heroically as possible.

The officer didn't look up from the card. "So you are," he said, unimpressed.

The other officer approached, hand on his sidearm. "Mr. LaBonté, please step out of the vehicle, sir."

"What? Why? I have done nothing. This...this maniac almost killed me. You should arrest *her*," he fairly spat.

Maggie spoke up. "Actually, I'm a little embarrassed, sir. He asked to stop off at the Go-Go Rama. It's this—well, it's not really a *bar*. It's more of what they used to call a 'gentlemen's club.'" She made air quotes with her fingers and managed a shrug. "He insisted, and you know, the boss is the boss, right?"

"Right," the second officer said while he continued to look at his clipboard. "Well, regardless of that, your passenger is wanted for questioning by the Diplomatic Security Service. I'm afraid he's going to have to accompany us." He gave Valéry a stern look. "Sir? I repeat, please step out of your vehicle." He motioned with his hand.

"This is outrageous! I have diplomatic immunity." Exiting with his nose in the air, Valéry tried to act as if he were still in charge. He smoothed his rumpled Armani suit and was straightening his bent sunglasses when the first officer brought his hand around his back and handcuffed him in one smooth motion.

"Sir, you are being placed under restraint by order of the Diplomatic Security Service."

Valéry's eyes went wide, then fiery. "Outrageous! Call the ambassador! Call the French consulate!"

The officers gently but firmly led him along the walkway to a side door as Valéry continued his protests.

"Say hi to Desmond for me," Maggie called out. "Oh, and your wine is *atrocious!*"

She watched as a sputtering Valéry was dragged into the door of the building, the two officers flanking each of his arms. He yelled what was certainly something unrepeatable in French and disappeared.

Then she was alone, the street empty, the air quiet. Smile disintegrating, she crumbled down, exhausted, onto the dusty curb. Long-fallen cherry blossoms from a nearby tree were gathered in the gutter at her feet, dead and decaying. Then she thought of Adrian and sadness and loss descended on her like a cold, heavy blanket.

Knees together, courage gone, Maggie wrapped her hands around her head and sobbed.

Chapter Thirty

THE INSTANT DANNY STOPPED HIS CAR, Adrian exited the passenger side and dashed toward the police station. He spied a black car, parked at an angle in the vehicle entrance. He glanced at the diplomatic plates, recognizing its number as French embassy staff, then walked quickly toward an officer who was just exiting the building. Of all the crazy—he didn't care about Valéry, but she could've hurt herself. He shook his head. He had to admit he was impressed by her hutzpah.

"Can you tell me if the woman—the lady who was driving that car—is she still here? Is she inside?" He pulled out his security card and handed it to the man.

The officer took it, examined it and returned it. "No, sir, not inside. The car was abandoned when we came back out."

Adrian frowned, then looked around to see if he could spot her. No one up the street looked familiar, then he looked the other direction—*there*! He saw a flash of dark hair and a pink hair ribbon as the back of a woman disappeared through the doorway that led down to the Metro tunnel. He took off, running down the sidewalk, dodging pedestrians, hoping to reach her before she got too far.

At the entrance of the station, he paused and looked at the escalator, hoping to catch another glimpse of her. *Nothing.* Pushing left past the slow-moving commuters on the right, he rushed down the escalator with frequent excuse me's, then did another search for her at the bottom of the stairs. Still no Maggie.

He eyed the two entrances that led down to the train platform, one on the left that went uptown and one on the right that ran the opposite direction. He took a guess and chose the right, pulling his Metro card out of his wallet as he ran, flashing the entrance checkpoint, and pushing through the gate. The steps were empty, only a few passengers on his side waiting for the next train.

Then he spotted her. Maggie was on the opposite side, the pairs of tracks between them. She was walking slowly, alone, head down, hands drooping beside her, the picture of defeat.

"Hi," he called out, not sure what else to say.

She turned her head suddenly, saw him and kept walking. "Hello," she said quietly.

"Uh, I'm sorry you had to deal with Valéry," he called across, keeping pace with her.

"It's fine," she called back. "It's done. Don't worry about it." She kept walking, not looking at him.

"Are you okay?" No response.

A few commuters were starting to pass on either side carrying backpacks and briefcases, most staring at their phones, lost in their own worlds.

He tried again. "Charlie misses you, but she won't say it. She sleeps with that squirrel every night, the one you gave her."

Maggie turned her head and scowled at him. "That's a dirty trick."

Adrian shook his head. "No, Maggie, it's not a trick. It's just the truth. We need you. And I realized I need you." It felt good, after all this time, to just say it.

Maggie stopped, an exasperated look on her face. "You can't just come here and get all concerned and think it's just going to make everything okay. It's not okay." She started walking again, this time more determined.

Adrian moved along with her, wishing he could reach across the tracks separating them. He knew he had to come up with something quick. "Look, everyone has bad days. Sometimes, you just have to look at the bright side."

"Really?" she called back. "And what would be your bright side to me mashing my face into the Queen of England because a squirrel ran up my leg?"

"Um... lucky squirrel?"

"Very funny—that's very funny." She stopped again and turned to face him. "You don't understand, do you? I messed it all up. I messed up my career, if you could call it that, and, oh—I picked another real winner of a man to get involved with."

"Thank you."

Maggie scowled. "I meant Valéry."

"Maggie, I—"

She cut him off. "No, Adrian, this was my last chance, and I muddled it up, and I don't want to drag anyone else down with me." She returned to walking, now more briskly.

"That's what you're worried about, dragging me down? Or dragging Charlie down? Maggie, we've been down." He was struggling to keep up with her now. "Down as in raising a little girl who'll never know her mother. Down as in trying to understand why some people have to die so young."

Maggie was silent but slowed her walk.

"So... where are you going?" Adrian asked.

She looked up the tracks and into the dank darkness of the tunnel. Adrian followed her gaze, wondering if she were somehow trying to search the future. Maybe it was time to face his own. Trains had lights for their path, didn't they? Maybe he had already found one for his own.

"I don't know," she said finally.

"Will I see you again?"

Another pause. She said something he couldn't hear.

"What?"

"I don't know!"

A few people were beginning to line up at the sides of the tracks, knowing the next trains were due in a few minutes. Adrian knew didn't have much time before she would have to decide to stay or go. He looked back at Maggie across the tracks, her shoulders slumped, her face confused. Everything felt like now or never.

"I don't like that!" he called over.

"Like what?"

"Not seeing you again."

"I don't either."

"What?"

"I said I don't either! But I can't—"

"Ma'am, is that guy bothering you?" A large man in a red Washington Nationals cap gestured to Adrian across the tracks.

Maggie shook her head. "He's fine…it's fine. We're just—"

"So, why can't you?" Adrian called over, interrupting.

"Why can't I what?" she called back.

"Why can't you stay?" a short, rotund woman yelled out helpfully. She'd wandered over next to Adrian, holding a pair of shopping bags.

"Maybe she doesn't love you," a short man in glasses yelled back. He was standing on Maggie's left.

"Why not?" This time it was a white-bearded senior in suspenders and jeans on Adrian's side.

"Have you ever told her?" Maggie's short man in glasses called back.

The shopping-bag lady touched Adrian's arm. "Have you?" she asked.

Adrian looked at her curious expression and the small but equally curious crowd that was beginning to grow around both his and Maggie's sides of the track. Men in suits, students with backpacks and wearing earbuds, a woman in a hijab carrying a baby, all waiting for the train.

And his answer.

A distant rumble accompanied by a slight breeze moving out of the tunnel indicated a train was getting closer.

"Well…no…" Adrian finally responded, now embarrassed by all of the unwanted attention.

"What'd he say?" Maggie's short guy called over.

"He said no!" Adrian's rotund woman answered.

"Why not?" demanded a gray-haired man in a black leather jacket. He edged forward next to Maggie, joining the fray. "You love her, right?"

Adrian, not sure who he was talking to anymore, raked a hand through his hair.

"What'd he say?" the first man by Maggie shouted.

"Hang on, he's thinking about it!" Adrian's suspender man yelled back.

"Well, if he has to think about it, maybe he doesn't love her!" Leather jacket man called.

Adrian's rotund woman spoke up. "Well, you want him to just say it if he doesn't mean it?"

"I suppose not," said the first man. A few of the people around Maggie nodded in agreement.

Adrian felt the ground shaking beneath his feet. He couldn't think straight. The air howled, pushed down the tunnel as the train approached, now only seconds away. "Maggie?" he called out suddenly.

"What?" she called back.

"I love you!"

Maggie just stood and stared at him.

"How do we know you mean it?" the short man on Maggie's left yelled.

Adrian had to yell louder to be heard over the noise of the imminent train. "Because I'm standing in a giant freaking subway yelling I love you across the stupid tracks in front of a crowd of strangers! Maggie, I love you!"

Then the train on Maggie's side whooshed into the space between them.

* * *

"I think he means it," the short man told Maggie, then shuffled through the open doors of the train. In a few seconds a recorded voice announced the doors were closing. They did, air hissed, and the train slowly picked up speed, moving down the tracks. She could see Adrian still there with his crowd. What was she supposed to say? After today, the gala, all of it. Yet there he was, still with her, waiting.

A tall man behind him yelled, "So, does *she* love *him*?"

"He's asking if you love him," an Asian woman in a gray business dress told Maggie.

"I..." Maggie started to say, then looked down.

"What did she say?" Adrian's man yelled.

"Hang on. We don't know yet," Maggie's woman yelled back.

Maggie looked down, thoughts jumbled. Finally, she looked up across the tracks, her crowd also watching her, waiting for an answer. He was there, smiling. She remembered the first time she had met him, standing there with his stupid tea-stained tie and his crooked smile.

"Yes. I love him," Maggie said too softly to hear, drowned out by the grumble of a new train whose light could now be seen shining out of the dim tunnel.

A large man with a huge beard and flannel shirt standing behind her heard her and raised his hands. "Yes! I love you!" he repeated exuberantly. Then noticing the confused faces around him, he said, "I mean, *she* loves you!"

Maggie called louder. "Yes, I love you, but I can't—" Her voice was drowned by the rumble of wheels and squeal of brakes as the train on his side rushed in and slowed, separating the two again with a hiss and a blast of damp air.

* * *

Adrian tried to see through the train windows to the other side of the tracks, but the crowd of people both getting on and off was too thick. No pink ribbon, no familiar face. No Maggie. The exiting crowd packed the platform as well.

After a few moments, the pre-recorded voice called, "Step back. Doors closing." The doors did just that, and the train began moving slowly forward, picking up speed until it had completely disappeared. Adrian's smile slowly faded. The exiting passengers were now a mass of people of every style and age, moving towards the stairs that would take them up and out into the street. He spotted a flash of bobbing pink ribbon on black hair, moving against the crowd, farther down the walkway into the tunnel. Maggie looked like she was crying, her hand swiping her cheeks, trying to keep up with the flow of tears.

She was going, and he couldn't stop her. The strangers who had crowded around him a minute ago as unknown allies were now gone, into the train, on with their lives.

He was alone in the sudden, booming silence.

Chapter Thirty-One

MAGGIE FOUND A BENCH near a kiosk directory, and collapsed like a broken doll, tears flowing, back heaving, the emotions of failure, deceit, and now love rolling out in a confused flood. She had wanted to reach out to Adrian, somehow, across the tracks, but they might as well have been the expanse of the Atlantic. Even if they were together, she'd just end up messing that up too.

Like everything else.

And Charlie! How she loved her. She found a tissue in her bag and began to dab at her blotched face. She didn't care now—not what job she had, not being a success like her grandmother, not even what train she took next. She just needed to get away, to somewhere.

She started checking the arrival times of the next trains on the red LED signs overhead as an overhead speaker clicked and an announcement about a Mr. Hampton echoed down the cavernous tunnel.

Mr. Hampton...

Her brain lit in recognition.

The voice continued, "Will Miss Mistletoe, Miss Maggie Mistletoe please report to the Red Line station you just left, crying. Mr. Hampton would like a nut, or a cracker, or probably pretty much whatever you have."

Maggie's eyes flew open. She felt a rush of shock, surprise, and hope. *No. He wouldn't be that crazy.* She quickly gathered her things and began moving back down the walkway.

"Miss Maggie Mistletoe, please, I'm begging you. If you don't get here soon I'm going to have to start singing or something."

Maggie was smiling, laughing almost, now moving as fast as she could. The few new commuters moving along both sides of the tracks were starting to smile and point to the speakers overhead.

The now-familiar voice echoed down the tunnel again. "Miss Mistletoe, I'm afraid you're leaving me no choice. If you don't arrive in five seconds, it's all on you." There was a pause. "Okay, never mind the five seconds, here we go." The voice cleared its throat, then began singing in a wavering but sincere voice. *"You are my sunshine, my only sunshine, you make me happy, when skies are gray..."*

Maggie could now see back up to the top of the stairs to the main ticket booth where a silhouetted figure, still singing, waved when he saw her. She wiped her tears as she ran down the walkway.

* * *

The booth attendant Adrian had tricked into letting him into the ticket booth by pretending he had just been robbed was pounding on the door. "Sir! You can't be in there, sir. I'm going to be calling the police. Sir!" The man leaned his head to his shoulder and began talking into the microphone attached there.

Adrian kept singing, arms crossed, impressed with the acoustics of the huge subway as his voice bounced down the tunnel. *"The other night, dear, as I lay sleeping*—Maggie, I could really use you for the harmony part here—*I dreamt I held you in my arms..."*

Then he saw her through the glass attendant's booth. Racing toward him, pushing past the startled commuters. Adrian stopped singing, put down the PA microphone and came to the door, smiling at her though the glass.

"I'm sorry, ma'am—I mean, miss—this area is for authorized personnel only."

Maggie was bouncing on her toes, hands pressed against the glass. "Are you crazy? You're going to get arrested!"

Adrian nodded. "Pretty, sure, yeah. The police should be here any minute." A flurry of movement caught his eye up at the entryway to the gates. "Yup, I expect this is them now." He turned back to Maggie. "Do me a favor, huh? Come see me in prison?"

Maggie's eyes were wide. "*Prison?* Come out of there, Adrian, please!"

"I will for a kiss."

Maggie was almost beside herself. "Okay! Okay! Just come out before—"

Adrian opened the door, grabbed her in his arms, one hand behind her head, and kissed her.

Two uniformed officers rushed up with the flustered attendant in tow, wondering exactly what this was all about. The attendant pointed at Adrian. "That's the guy there."

One of the officers grabbed Adrian by the arm. "Sir? Please, sir…"

Adrian and Maggie were still kissing, oblivious to the rest of the world.

Adrian felt his arm being pulled slowly back, followed by the feel of cold metal handcuffs on his wrist. Maggie's hands around his neck still held him close, as his second arm was pulled back and calmly cuffed to the first. She was gazing at his face, smiling, her face still wet from tears, but now shining in joy.

"I'm glad you came," he said.

Now she beamed, still cradling his neck. "Me too," she said, nodding. "'Cause I really couldn't remember the words to the next verse."

She laughed.

"Sir," the first officer said. "I'll need to see some identification. You know this is a restricted area?"

"I do. You can find my license in my right back pocket there."

The officer found the wallet, pulled out his driver's license, and called in Adrian's information over his radio.

Maggie grew concerned again. "What are they going to do to you?"

Adrian shrugged. "They'll process me down at the nearest station." He saw the worried look in her eyes. "Don't worry. I called Danny before I started my, uh, *concert.* He should be here any second. I'm just hoping he'll vouch for me. If he doesn't kill me first." Just then he heard Danny's familiar voice echoing down the entryway. He turned to look. "Uh-oh… and there he is." Adrian grimaced, then turned back to Maggie. "He looks mad. Listen, put in a good word for me, will you? Tell him about how I was crazed with love or something."

"Adrian, you didn't need to do"—she waved her hand—"all *this* just to impress me." She took his arms, then looked down. "I do love you. And everything else… I guess I was just trying so hard to get someplace else I didn't know where I was. How *good* I was. When I was with you and Charlie."

Adrian returned her smile. "Well, I love you, too, Miss Maggie. And I know Charlie does." He sighed. "I guess I was trying to get somewhere too. A better job, something that I thought would make Charlie and me safer. But I don't know, maybe I just needed to learn to let loose a little more."

She shook his handcuffed hands. "Yes, and look where that got you."

"True." He smiled. "So I guess neither of us knows where we're going now, huh?"

Maggie tilted her head. "Mmm, maybe." She got a sudden, impish grin. "But I have an idea."

"What's that?" Adrian asked, smiling.

"Why don't we go there together?"

* * *

After twenty-some minutes of explanation and unconvinced looks from the authorities, the officer in charge removed the handcuffs, although he still eyed Adrian closely. Danny, even though he wasn't directly involved with the case, was able to convince the officer that Adrian posed no real threat. And since Adrian had passed a sobriety test they seemed to be accepting his explanation, although not with any amusement.

After finishing his conversation with the officer in charge, Danny came and put his arm on his older brother's shoulder. "You sure you still want to get mixed up with this knucklehead, Maggie?"

Maggie cocked her head. "Pretty sure."

"Hmm. Well, sorry, Ady. Looks like you might have to spend the night in the tank."

Adrian nodded. "Right, for trespassing."

Danny shook his head, grimacing. "Actually, it's for your atrocious *singing*."

Maggie suppressed a laugh with her fist, while Adrian resisted an urge to punch his brother in the arm, realizing that someone seeing him strike a police officer might get him in even more trouble.

"But really," his brother continued, "you're probably just looking at some probation."

Adrian nodded, rubbing his wrists where the handcuffs had been. "So, how long do you think they'll give me?"

Danny considered it. "For federal trespassing? Thirty, maybe sixty days."

Chapter Thirty-Two

~ *Thirty, Maybe Sixty Days Later* ~

THE WEDDING was a simple summer affair. Maggie and Adrian both felt that the gala had been more than enough pageantry for one year. Plus, there really hadn't been much time to plan anything else.

However, after a little cajoling (and calling in a few favors) Maggie's grandmother had convinced them to hold the ceremony in the Washington National Cathedral. A majestic structure of arching stone and brilliant stained glass, the cathedral was about as elegant and romantic a place as could be found in Washington, DC, to hold a wedding. Even though they were only using just a tiny section of the huge nave, it still held all of the solemnity and grace that Maggie said she had always dreamed of. Family and friends gathered near the front platform where the couple, bathed in multicolored sunlight filtering through the immense, circular rose windows, said their vows.

Charlie, of course, was overjoyed, not only because she got to be the flower girl but that she also got to give a short speech during the ceremony. Most of all, she said she was gaining both a mom *and* the most fun friend in the world. And Adrian's smile never seemed to leave his face, nor his eyes Maggie's, as the sweet and simple ceremony culminated with the presentation of the new bride and groom, marching down the aisle to Mendelssohn's Wedding March, as interpreted, of course, by the fiddle-playing Walter and his overall-clad Smokey Hills Quartet.

A small reception kicked off in the nave entryway, where Gerard had set up a mobile coffee bar on an elegantly trimmed table along with an assortment of candies from Bartlett's Candy Shop. Danny and Beth were trying to keep their kids from stealing too many chocolate caramels before the other guests got to them, as Adrian and Maggie entered, arm in arm.

"There you are," Danny said, releasing his wife's arm as the couple approached. "We're ready for the toast." He looked around at the tables. "Is there any champagne?"

"No champagne!" Adrian and Maggie shouted together, horrified.

Danny stepped back in surprise. "Okay, well..." He looked around, then retrieved his coffee cup from the table and raised it. "Let's all raise our, uh, cups together," he called out.

The happy crowd obeyed, lifting a wide variety of mugs, glasses and cups into the air.

Danny took his wife Beth's hand and squeezed it. "To my brother and his new wife, Maggie, an old Irish proverb if I may."

"You may," shouted Maggie from the side of the room.

"Very well then." He cleared his throat. "Walls for the wind, and a roof for the rain, and drinks beside the fire. Laughter to cheer you, and those you love near you, and all that your heart may desire." He turned to the new couple. "May your roads be smooth, may your children behave"—he flashed a knowing look at Charlie, who playfully stuck out her tongue—"and may all your squirrels be without rabies."

The laughing crowd cheered, "Hear, Hear!" and plunked their cups together.

"Now, if you'll all head outside where we will see the happy couple off," Danny announced.

The crowd began filtering down the stone steps that led to the bright outdoors.

Maggie turned to her new husband. "Well, mister, you look as handsome as ever in a tuxedo."

"Thank you, and thanks for your help with the tie again."

She tugged at it playfully. "You're welcome."

"I really thought about wearing the red tie, but they're still trying to get the tea stains out at the cleaners."

Maggie slapped him on the arm playfully. "None of that."

Ambassador MacCarthy approached the couple, smiling, wearing a cream-colored dress that complemented her small corsage of cherry blossoms perfectly. "Maggie, dear, I must say, that was the loveliest ceremony I can remember." She gave her granddaughter a squeeze on her arm. "Your mother and father would be so proud."

Maggie smiled. "I wish they could have been here."

The ambassador nodded knowingly. "We'll just have to have another celebration, only this time in *Dublin*." She gave Maggie a smile, then turned to Adrian. "And have you yet told my granddaughter about my proposition?"

"Proposition?" Maggie's eyebrows arched.

Adrian nodded. "Yes, your grandmother has been quite gracious in offering me a job at the Irish Embassy. As a full-time driver, I believe. And if the incentives are right, I may be just inclined to take the position."

Maggie couldn't resist giving her a hug. "*Mamó!* Thank you!" She released her surprised grandmother, then cocked her head at Adrian. "Wait, what incentives?"

"Well, that you agree to become partners with Jelly at the dress shop, of course."

"I hear my name. What's going on?" Jelly asked as she bustled forward. She was wearing one of her own flower-print dresses and carrying a coffee mug.

"I was just telling your new partner she can start right after we get home from the honeymoon."

Jelly flashed a huge smile. "Well, it's about time." She turned to Maggie. "That deal with the buyer at the national chain came through. They want to sell a line of Bella Bella scarves, starting in the Midwest."

Maggie's eyes were as wide as her smile. "Jelly, that's fantastic!" She gave her friend an enthusiastic hug. "I always knew you'd make it."

Jelly laughed. "Well, it's not just me, you know. I'll need you there by my side. You think you'll be ready?"

Maggie laughed. "I guess I'd better be." She took her friend's hands. "Sorry you're losing a roommate."

Jelly shrugged. "I figure I'm gaining a partner. Besides…" She turned to Adrian and poked him in the chest. "Now it's *your* turn to put up with all that snoring."

Adrian raised an eyebrow at Maggie.

But before he could say anything, his new bride was pulling him by the hand down the steps to the open door.

"Ready?" Adrian asked as he and Maggie stood hand in hand at the exit of the church. Sunlight spilled into the arch of the door. Squinting, they could see all of their friends and family arrayed outside, eagerly waiting for them to emerge.

Maggie nodded, beaming.

"Here we go, then." And with that, the couple ran down the front steps of the cathedral as the gauntlet of friends and family let out a cheer, throwing handfuls of sunflower seeds at the newly married couple.

"Really? Sunflower seeds?" Adrian said as he ran towards the car, brushing some from his hair.

"For the *squirrels*," Maggie said, as if he should have understood.

Adrian could only shake his head and smile, wondering if that would be just one of the many tiny, happy, crazy moments that lay ahead for him. As if on cue, a gaggle of brown squirrels hustled out of the nearby trees and chased after them, jostling each other for the seeds. One of them who sported a stumpy tail blazed past Maggie, leading the pack. The couple only had time to exchange a quizzical glance as they had just reached the car, the last of the sunflower seeds raining down around them.

Adrian checked the back of the Irish Embassy's BMW where Charlie was already buckled and waiting in her booster seat. "All secure? Do you need me to go through the checklist?"

Charlie rolled her eyes. "No, Dad, c'mon." Then she waved through the open window. "Hi, Maggie!"

Adrian turned to see his new bride, glowing almost as bright as the mottled sunlight drifting through the trees behind her, the corners of her eyes crinkled in laughter. He grinned as well, not just a smile of happiness but of joy, knowing that whatever was to come he would face it with her and with Charlie, together, no matter what might happen.

He opened the passenger door for his new wife as friends and family continued cheering and clapping, a few errant sunflower seeds raining around them. Running around the front of the car to the driver's side, he got in, shut the door and sighed. Then his eye caught the cork from their champagne bottle swinging on a tiny chain from the rear view mirror. He looked at Maggie, smiling, neither saying a word, enjoying the moment.

Charlie beamed from the back seat, smiling as she kicked her feet back and forth, watching one parent and then the other.

Neither spoke for a moment, until Maggie cleared her throat. "Driver?" she said.

Adrian smiled. "Yes, miss?"

"Take me home."

THE END

About the Author

D. J. Van Oss writes sweet and sunny romantic comedies with an emphasis on second chances; kind of like the book version of finding an extra pack of icing for your cinnamon roll.

When not writing you can find him working in the yard, walking the dog, or staying up too late watching BBC mysteries while eating honey peanut butter straight out of the jar.

He lives in the country suburbs of Iowa with his wife and three stepdaughters. His writing partner is Jack, a pretty-boy golden retriever who grunts when you rub his ears.

Books by the Author

Golden Grove Series
Call It Chemistry
Write By Your Side
D.C. Diplomats Series
Driving Miss Crazy

Made in the USA
Monee, IL
07 July 2026

56550062R00142